Dear Jane

RACHEL WARD

BONNEVILLE
BOOKS
An imprint of Cedar Fort, Inc.
Springville, Utah

ISBN 13: 978-1-4621-1893-9

Published by Bonneville Books, an imprint of Cedar Fort, Inc.
2373 W. 700 S., Springville, UT 84663
Distributed by Cedar Fort, Inc., www.cedarfort.com

LIBRARY OF CONGRESS CATALOGING-IN-PUBLICATION DATA

Names: Ward, Rachel, 1982-
Title: Dear Jane / Rachel Ward.
Description: Springville, Utah : Bonneville Books, an imprint of Cedar Fort, Inc., 2016.
Identifiers: LCCN 2016012505 | ISBN 9781462118939 (paper back)
Subjects: LCSH: Mormon women--Fiction. | Self-actualization (Psychology) in women--Fiction. | Mormons--Fiction. | GSAFD: Love stories. | Christian fiction.
Classification: LCC PS3623.A7344 D43 2016 | DDC 813/.6--dc23
LC record available at https://lccn.loc.gov/2016012505

Cover design by Rebecca J. Greenwood
Photography by Sergey Zolkin via unsplash.com
Cover design © 2016 by Cedar Fort, Inc.
Edited and typeset by Justin Greer

Printed in the United States of America

10 9 8 7 6 5 4 3 2 1

Printed on acid-free paper

Prologue

Email was the undeniable highlight of my weekly P-Day. During the bad weeks, after record numbers of doors slamming and unending phone tag, it was all that kept me going from one day to the next. The few minutes reading the letters from my family every week kept my homesickness at bay just long enough to make it to the next P-Day. Plus, the library's air conditioner worked so much better than the one in our cockroach-infested apartment. And so, every Monday afternoon we reserved an hour to hit the local library. It was a charming old library, tucked away in an Orlando neighborhood—its rundown and old-fashioned façade blending in with the row homes, all built in the fifties. The white wooden siding was chipped in places, but the huge oaks out front, draped with Spanish moss, went a long way to enhance its appeal.

"Sister Petersen! Sister Matthews! How are you this week?" A tall librarian with huge, bright-red curls and a wrist full of bangles stopped unloading books from the return cart to smile and say hello.

Sister Petersen, my companion, returned her huge smile and added a wave.

"We're doing really well! How are you, Jeanette?"

Jeanette had noticed our clockwork arrivals every Monday during her shift, and after she read our name tags, we quickly struck up a friendship a couple of weeks into our area. She wasn't interested in the discussions—"a Baptist from birth, honey"—but we fascinated her, both our purpose and how normal we were. While she had heard that Mormons had horns—"never did hold with that nonsense"—she was surprised at our up-to-date, albeit modest, fashion sense. That, and the fact that two "beauties like yourselves would give up two years in the prime of your life to come all the way out here and not even bring a bathing suit!" We tried to explain as best as we could. It was difficult, though, to explain why I had wanted to do this since I was a little girl.

You know that Primary song? *I hope they call me on a mission.* When I was about seven I learned that one for the first time, and I took it literally. When my mom wanted my brother Nathan to do something, like try a new food or meet new people, she would always say, "When you're on your mission you'll have to eat crazy stuff . . ." or "When you're on your mission you'll have to talk to all kinds of people." But she never said it to me. And then we learned that song. *I hope they call me on a mission.* I remember asking my Primary teacher if girls could go on missions too, or if boys should just sing it.

"No!" she replied emphatically. "You sing that song, sweetie. And you go on a mission. Can't let those boys have all the fun." And since that day, I was going on a mission and nothing was going to stop me. Especially not falling in love six months before my nineteenth birthday. No man would keep me off a mission. Even if he was the perfect man—my best friend's big brother.

Olivia and I had spent every waking moment together through elementary school and junior high, most of the time at her house. Josh was there for much of that time and was as gorgeous then as he is now. He shared Olivia's blonde hair, but where her eyes were a deep shade of amber, his were startlingly blue. He was tall and athletic, an Adonis so far out of my league that it was laughable to even hope. Those hours spent in his presence were during an unfortunate ugly duckling phase. My transformation didn't happen until I was in high school and he was on his mission. The braces came off, the glasses were replaced with contacts, and the final say on my haircut was reluctantly signed over to me by my mother.

When he got home from his mission, about halfway through my senior year of high school, I was old enough to be more than just his little sister's annoying friend. My dark hair was long and sleek, and my own bright blue eyes were no longer hidden behind a pair of cat-eye glasses.

Things began gradually. Josh and I were both runners, something that Olivia had never shared with me, and Josh would call me when he discovered some great new trail. After a while, we decided to run a marathon together. And then I graduated from high school and all of a sudden had so much more free time. Both of us were working days, granted, but most nights I hung out at Olivia's house and that just happened to be where Josh was. By the end of the summer, things were pretty serious. I turned nineteen in January after a single semester at the local community college. Josh and I agreed that he wouldn't wait for me. But he did say that he would write and that he figured that since it had taken him this long to fall in love with me, he didn't expect it would happen with anyone else in the eighteen short months that I would be gone.

"You're in love with me?" I asked, a smile on my face. He leaned over to kiss me lightly.

"That shouldn't be too surprising," he replied softly as he pulled away.

"No," I murmured. "It's just nice to hear it." I leaned back in for another kiss and he wrapped his arms around me, pulling me closer.

"Are you sure you need to go?" he murmured, nuzzling his face into my neck.

Honestly, at that moment, I wanted to forget all about going on a mission. I had dreamed about this, being Joshua Adams's girlfriend, literally for years. The unattainable little girl crush had miraculously come true. Could I really be so crazy to turn my back on him to go on a mission? The voice of my Primary teacher echoed through my mind: "Can't let the boys have all the fun."

"We've got two computers reserved just for you gals, right over in the corner." Jeanette's voice pulled me back to the present.

I glanced across the library. "Thanks, Jeanette! That is so nice of you!"

Jeanette beamed. "Now, go catch up with your families—and Sister Matthews," she called after me, "be sure to give me an update on that young man of yours!"

I couldn't help the grin that spread across my face. "I will!" I turned back to Sister Petersen next to me. Her grin matched my own. My explanation of why I was serving a mission wouldn't be complete without Joshua, and I couldn't pass up the opportunity to talk about him for a good twenty minutes to someone who wasn't sick of the sound of his name.

"I think she gets more excited to hear from him than you do," my companion commented.

I laughed. "That might actually be true." Jeanette had insisted that I bring in a photo of "my young man," as she called him, to which I happily obliged.

The musty book smell, only found in old libraries, rose from the carpet as we walked. I preferred it to the sterile scent of new ones. The computers, an obviously recent addition, were tucked away in a corner, with wires taped to the carpet and the walls. We sat down at our respective computers, and I logged into my email account and gave a little sigh of contentment. I loved weeks when the inbox was full. There were emails from my parents, my sister, my grandpa, and Josh. I saved Josh's email for last, and began with my sister Annie's. Annie had just turned sixteen. She told me all about her ridiculous trip to the DMV and her first time driving completely solo.

"You know how Mom never lets us turn up the music loud enough? I had it up so loud that people in the other cars could hear it. I think I burst my eardrum. But it was totally worth it. I can't wait for you to get home. Then I can drive you anywhere! You'll have your own personal chauffeur." I smiled as I finished her email and, in my reply, promised to take her up on her offer as soon as I got home.

I read the message from my parents, which updated me on everything happening at home: Ezra had a soccer game, my cousin left for his mission, Annie got her license. Then a quick one from my little brother Oliver, mostly about the gross science project he had done at school, and one from my grandpa, and one from my best friend, Olivia. After replying to all of them, I eagerly clicked open Josh's email and leaned forward to read.

> *Dear Quinn,*
>
> *This is a hard letter to write. I have been thinking a lot about us for the past few weeks, and I can't shake the feeling that we just aren't meant to be. I think that we are both different people than the ones that said goodbye at the MTC, and we would only be kidding ourselves to pretend that this will work out once you are home.*
>
> *Quinn, I met someone. Her name is Jenny. She just moved out here from Texas. I met her at institute one night, and we kind of hit it off. We've been dating for a few months. Jenny understands me in a way that I didn't think was possible. She is really different from you and it makes me realize that what you and I had was fun, but it was never the real thing.*
>
> *I want you to know how sorry I am for the pain that this will cause you. I asked her to marry me, and she said yes. I hope that you and I can still be*

friends, but if you feel like that will be impossible, I understand. I won't write again, unless I hear from you first.

I wish you the very best of everything, Quinn.

Sincerely,

Joshua

I sat back in my chair, stunned. Last week's email—the last month's worth of letters—hadn't given any indication that Josh was having second thoughts or even an inkling that he was seeing anyone else. I've heard other missionaries say that they saw their Dear Johns coming, that the letters got shorter, less personal, and further apart for weeks and sometimes months. But this, this was out of the blue.

"Hey, are you about ready?" Sister Petersen glanced over from her screen and paused. "Sister Matthews? Are you okay?"

I nodded numbly and pointed at the screen. She leaned over the armrest of her chair to read the message I had ignorantly saved for last.

"Oh," she muttered softly, glancing back at me in concern. She reached across me and closed the window on my screen.

"C'mon. Let's go," she murmured pulling me to my feet. As we walked past the front desk, Jeanette looked up expectantly.

"So?" Jeanette asked. "That young man still as gorgeous as ever?" Sister Petersen just shook her head and a concerned look crossed Jeanette's face. "Will we see you next week?" she asked.

"We'll be here," confirmed Sister Petersen as she pushed open the front door of the library and led us into the bright day. There were heavy clouds looming on the edge of the horizon. The afternoon storm was rolling in. *How appropriate*, I thought.

"Wait, we have a dinner in half an hour," I commented as I realized that she was guiding me in the direction of our apartment. She shrugged.

"I'll call and reschedule. You're not feeling well. Can't go to dinner if you're sick." She unlocked the door and pushed it open. It was a tiny apartment, with windows to match and so dark after the bright sun of the afternoon that I felt as if I was walking into a cave. "Go lie down," she advised. "We'll pick things up tonight."

I nodded, grateful not to have to face anyone just yet. I kicked off my shoes and climbed into my bed. It was over. Josh and I were done. I stared numbly at the dirty ceiling of our apartment. Time passed quickly and my eyes flew open at the sound of Sister Petersen calling me. I hadn't even realized I'd fallen asleep. I stood in front of my mirror, studying the circles under my eyes, and decided then and there that I would not let this destroy the last three months of my mission. I took a deep breath, choking back a sob, squared my shoulders, and headed back to work.

1

6 MONTHS LATER

"Quinn! Get up! I'm going to be late!" The pounding on my bedroom door grew louder and even more irritating. I rolled over groaning, grabbed a shoe, and chucked it at the closed door. The resulting crash, however, had the opposite effect that I was hoping for. Annie just screamed louder.

"I'm coming!" I yelled, pushing myself up to sit on the edge of the bed. I looked at my alarm clock. 7:30 a.m. There is no way that school started this early when I was still going. I rubbed my eyes, trying to shake the sleep out of them. I sighed as I pulled on a nearby pair of questionable socks and shoes, dreading the trek out into the cold, and let out a whimper at the thought.

It was only October, and already I was struggling to stay warm. It had been a shock walking off the plane from Florida into the dry heat of July in Utah, and when the dry cold arrived, that had been even worse. Running in the mornings was becoming almost unbearable for several reasons: the weather was at the top of my list, followed closely by the conspicuous absence of a former running partner. After acclimating to Florida, I longed to go back to the constant warmth and sunshine. I would even take the roaches, lizards, and alligators to avoid the bone-chilling cold.

"QUINN!"

I jumped at Annie's renewed effort to get me out of my room. "COMING!" I screamed, trying to top her volume and pulling on a trashed BYU hoodie and a baseball cap.

Annie had her license, but we shared the car, at least until I could somehow save up enough to buy my own. On the days that I needed the car for a job interview, I had to drive Annie to school. The school bus was out of the question ("I spent two years on that nasty excuse for a bus; never again!"), but why she couldn't get one of her friends to pick her up and take her was beyond me. I yanked my bedroom door open to find her still standing there, livid.

"I—am—going—to—be—late!" she yelled in my face. I took a deep breath, using up every bit of my willpower not to slap her across the face.

"Keys," I demanded sternly, holding my hand out to her. She threw them at me and twirled on her heel, her mousey brown braid whipping me in the face. She stomped to the garage as I pulled my coat on and counted to ten. Eighteen months of living with companions had done a world of good in the patience department. Annie's temper was nothing compared to Sister Gale's. And it was a breath of fresh air compared to my mother's.

"Are you coming or not?"

I gritted my teeth and followed her to the garage.

If I hadn't been so broke and desperate, I would have seriously considered throwing the keys back in her face, climbing back in bed for the rest of the day, and canceling the three job interviews that I had miraculously managed to secure for the day. Since I returned home from Florida three months ago, I had been taking online classes and doing everything in my power to find a job, which turned out to be almost an impossible feat. I was reduced to babysitting and taking odd jobs doing yard work and cleaning houses. My parents were kind enough to put a roof over my head and food in my mouth, but beyond that, I was on my own. I could use the car as long as I put gas in it. I could go to school as long as I paid tuition.

My dad had taken pity on me a few times, either hooking me up with someone who needed some serious house cleaning done or paying me to do some project around our house. In the last month, I had cleaned out the garage, painted the house, and totally relandscaped the backyard. I was still sporting blisters from that last one. I was desperate to find a job that didn't require hauling manure, or really anything that kept my hands clean, as soon as possible. I was a pencil-skirt-and-heels kind of girl, not so much an overalls one.

The atmosphere in the car was chilly the entire way to school, even though the heater was working great. I finally pulled into the high school parking lot and had barely rolled to a stop before Annie was out of the car, slamming the door shut without a word. She didn't look back once as I drove away.

"Good-bye to you too," I muttered as I pulled back out into traffic. I drove home, belting off-key to "Make You Feel My Love" the whole way, and pulled into the driveway in a much better mood. It's amazing what some good love songs can do for the soul that early in the morning. After a long shower with only three interruptions by my eleven- and thirteen-year-old brothers, I was ready to take on the world, or at least Springville.

My first interview of the morning was with a local realtor's office, Jonas Realty. I was interviewing for the secretary position. I had literally no experience as a secretary or in real estate, but I was a big believer in the whole "fake it till you make it" mentality. I pulled into the tiny parking lot and realized that this office used to be a house, and I was currently parked in what had once been the front yard. I took a deep breath and attempted to squash the butterflies that had been plaguing me the whole way here. I was terrified I was going to walk in there and sound like an idiot. My heels echoed across the parking lot, and I fought off a chill. *I should have worn a heavier jacket*, I thought as I pushed the front door open, plastering on my largest smile.

The waiting room of the office was warm and inviting. It was small, but not cramped, a desk situated to the right of the doorway and chairs lining the opposite wall. I could see a couple of doors down a narrow hallway. Though the décor had obviously been updated, the house still held much of its vintage charm. At the front desk sat a frazzled-looking woman, almost dwarfed by the stacks and stacks of paper surrounding her. Her short red hair was curled in all directions and her glasses sat low on her nose as she studied a file lying open in front of her.

"Hello?" I said hesitantly.

She looked up, arranging her features into a tired, but cheerful smile. "How can I help you?"

I smiled back and took a tentative step forward. "I'm here for the job interview? For the office assistant? I'm Quinn Matthews."

A look of relief spread across her face as she stood. "Thank goodness!" she exclaimed. She studied me silently for a brief moment. I bit my lip self-consciously under her scrutiny. It was an odd feeling, like she could see right through me. "When can you start?"

"What?" I asked in confusion, my eyes widening. "I'm just here to interview!"

She raised her eyebrows at me. "You don't want the job?" she asked primly, cocking her head to one side.

"No, no it's not that," I stuttered. "You just caught me off guard. I was just expecting the interview today." I mentally kicked myself for sounding like an idiot. "But, I mean, if you want to hire me, I guess I can start whenever you want."

"Great," she said decisively. "How about now? All of these need to be filed alphabetically." She waved her hand over the towering piles of paper on the desk, and then pointed to a row of filing cabinets against the wall behind the desk. "Then I need these appointments entered into the computer and confirmed." She held up an appointment book and looked at me expectantly. "Phone numbers are in the book."

"Oh, well . . . um, right now?" I asked, sounding even more like an idiot.

"You have somewhere else to be?" Her glasses slid even further down her nose as she looked at me.

Well, considering the fact that you just gave me a job . . . "No, I, um, just need to make a couple of phone calls and then I'm all yours," I hoped she wouldn't fire me for my complete lack of composure as I rifled through my bag, groping for my phone. I briefly considered running to the other two interviews in case this was some kind of a joke. Who hires someone without an interview?

"Fantastic." She shut the file she had been reading and stacked it on top of an overflowing binder. "We've been without a secretary for over a week now and there will be a lot of catching up to do. I'll get the employment paperwork printed out and to you by the end of the day. Phone is there, bathroom is there," she pointed to the back of the office. "Lunch is at 1:00. You'll have forty-five minutes. I have an appointment in . . ." she glanced down at her watch, "Twenty minutes. I have appointments and showings lined up and I will be out until at least 4:00. My associate should be back by 12:00. If you need to get ahold of me, my phone number is on the card in the top drawer. I do not text; if you need me, call. If a client calls or comes in, you take their name and number, set up an appointment, and enter it on the computer. Got it?"

I nodded slowly. *Heaven help me*, I thought.

"Great. Quinn, is it? I'll see you this afternoon," she reached down, grabbed a designer purse, and headed out the door.

"Wait," I called after her awkwardly. "I didn't catch your name."

She glanced over her shoulder. "Marie Jonas. Jonas Realty?" she added impatiently.

"Thank you, Ms. Jonas. Nice to meet you. I'll get to work right now."

"Marie," she called over her shoulder, the door banging shut loudly behind her. I took a deep breath and looked around the empty office. *All right, Quinn*, I thought to myself, *you got this.* I pulled out my cell phone to cancel the other interviews, texted Annie to get a ride home from school, and got to work.

I spent the next hour and a half filing. It didn't take too long to figure out the system, but the jam-packed drawers made getting in those additional papers almost impossible. It also created a perfect storm of paper cuts. I had made my way through about a third of the massive pile when the door opened. I glanced down at my watch. 11:45. There was no way it was Marie back already. *Please don't let it be a client*, I begged silently, my heart pounding.

I turned around to greet the newcomer, but in my flustered state, I dropped the stack of papers I was holding and immediately dropped to my knees, frantically picking them up. *What a great first impression*, I chided myself silently. *The boss thinks I'm an idiot, and now her client will think I'm a klutz. Fantastic.* I gathered the rest of the papers and rose to my feet, straightening them in my hands as I looked up. I almost dropped them again when I saw who stood there, his expression as surprised as mine.

"You were not the person I was expecting to see here," I was still too shocked to respond. "Sister Matthews."

"Elder Ryan," I replied shortly, completely flabbergasted. "How can I help you?"

Elder Nicholas Ryan: the bane of my missionary existence. I bit my cheeks to hold back the sigh of exasperation and the snarky comment dying to get out.

"So, you work here?" he asked. I nodded.

"What can I do for you?" I repeated, hoping beyond hope that he would leave once he found out Marie was not here and I could get him in and out of my life for the last time.

"Well, I suppose you can enter these contacts into the computer, and then email them all our monthly newsletter," he began, handing me a stack of papers. "And if you could order some lunch from Beto's, that would be fantastic. Two beef enchiladas and a Coke."

My eyes widened and my stomach plummeted as he spoke. I swallowed the dismay that had been building through his list of instructions.

"You?" I began slowly, "You're Marie's associate?"

"Guilty as charged," he joked, a smug smile across his face. "I assume she hired you this morning?"

I nodded mutely.

"On the spot?" he asked.

I nodded again.

Elder Ryan shrugged with a smile. "That's just the way she does things. She can look at a person and decide right away if she likes them or not. And she's always right. It's a little unnerving. She must have liked you."

"I guess so," I replied weakly, sitting down in the desk chair.

"Let me know when lunch is here," Elder Ryan said, moving toward the hallway where, I assumed, his office was. "Oh," he said, stopping next to my desk, "and call me Nick." I just nodded again and stared down at my desk.

Deep breaths. Deep breaths. I should have known that this was too good to be true. *The pay had better be good*, I thought as I picked up another stack to be filed. *Really, really good.*

Elder Nicholas Ryan was possibly the most arrogant, obnoxiously conceited man that I had ever come in contact with. We met about halfway through my mission, although I already knew who he was. He sang at all of the zone conferences, and while he had an incredible voice, the appeal was dampened by his cavalier attitude about it. The first time we met, he had been transferred into our district with his companion, Elder Torres. One Sunday after church, we got together to do a quick needs assessment of the area, and I introduced myself.

"Hi! I'm Sister Matthews and this is Sister Birch. You guys new in the district?" I held out my hand to shake his, and he reluctantly took it and nodded. I continued awkwardly, "I've heard you sing at mission conferences. You have an amazing voice."

He studied me for a moment and nodded curtly again, pulling his hand out of mine and turning back to his companion without a word. I glanced at Sister Birch next to me, eyebrows raised. She had an awkward smile on her face and a little giggle escaped her lips.

"All right then," I muttered softly and she giggled again, sliding her arm through mine and leading me to an empty chair.

He hadn't improved with time. For a while, I tried to give him the benefit of the doubt, thinking that maybe he was shy, and sometimes shy can be interpreted as conceited. But the more I came in contact with him, the more that I realized that this wasn't the case. He was friendly and outgoing with investigators and ward members, talking to everyone, smiling at everyone. But any time Sister Birch or I tried to have any conversation with him, it was like we were speaking in a foreign language. I gave up on him before long, passing any pertinent messages through his companion, who was, happily, the exact opposite of Elder Ryan.

Later on in my mission, we served together in a tiny district, Okeechobee, which was about as far away from the mission home as we possibly could be. There were six of us in that district, four elders and my companion, Sister Giles, and I. It was a hard area, with few members in the branch and fewer investigators. For the short time we were there, the six of us became close, relying on each other after painfully long days of tracting and disappointment. And still, my relationship with Elder Ryan was unchanged. Our conversations got slightly longer, mostly out of necessity, but his attitude remained as aloof and standoffish as ever.

Sister Giles was treated to many long-winded rants about his attitude and arrogance. I even overheard Elder Ryan's companion Elder Trevan rebuke him for it one day. It was after a quick prayer meeting we had with them before heading out for several appointments without much potential. I was waiting for Sister Giles just beyond the drinking fountain, when Elder Ryan and Elder Trevan walked past me without realizing I was there.

"Seriously, man," I heard Elder Trevan say. "You need to lighten up a bit. She's actually really nice, if you gave her a chance. I respect that you want to keep your distance from the ladies, but you don't have to treat Matthews like she's a leper. It's not Christlike no matter how you look at it."

"That's great. She's nice. Keep her away from me, Trevan. Do what you've been doing." Elder Ryan glanced at his companion and caught sight of me, standing awkwardly against the wall, pretending that I hadn't heard a thing, and wishing that I could fall through the floor. "Just drop it, okay?" he muttered. Elder Trevan swiveled his head in my direction and offered a slightly awkward smile and then dropped his eyes to the ground as he left the building.

Elder Ryan got transferred from Okeechobee more quickly than the rest of us and went home shortly after. I knew he was from Utah, but I had never bothered to find out exactly where. Apparently, closer to me than was comfortable.

I completed a successful first day of work and arrived home that night just as the rest of my family was sitting down to dinner.

"Just in time," Dad announced, as I walked through the garage door. After shedding my jacket and purse, I collapsed into my seat.

"How did it go?" Mom asked as she passed the salad around, almost knocking over Ezra's drink.

"Mom!" he protested loudly. She shrugged it off and dished up Oliver. "Um, good?" I replied, taking a long drink of water.

"So, she hired you just like that, huh?" Dad asked, trying unsuccessfully to cover the concern in his voice. "You're sure it's a legit business?"

"I sincerely hope so," I replied with a laugh. "Because I filled out all the tax forms this afternoon and she's got all kinds of personal information." I laughed harder at the worried look on my father's face and decided to let him off the hook. "I'm sure, Dad. I like her."

"And your coworkers? You like them as well?" Mom asked.

Oliver burped noisily, resulting in giggles from Ezra and Dad and a glare from Mom.

"There's only one." I grabbed the salad tongs and piled the lettuce high on my plate. I glanced at Annie. "Remember Elder Ryan that I told you about?" She nodded. Many a late night had been spent regaling Annie with stories from the mission. And none were more loved than Elder Ryan horror stories. "He works there."

Her eyebrows shot up. "That jerk?" she asked, her mouth still half full of potatoes.

"Yep," I replied, stabbing a tomato. "He's basically my boss. If I don't kill him or quit, there is a car with my name on it, just waiting for me."

"And hopefully soon after that, an apartment," Dad added, stabbing his salad with his fork and shooting a wink in my direction.

2

I dropped Annie off at school the next morning and headed straight to the office, still slightly in shock that I finally had a job. Until I did manage to make enough money to buy myself a car, I would still have to drop her off at school in the morning before work, and she had reluctantly agreed to get a ride home from a friend in the afternoon. Although the realtor's office didn't officially open until 9:00, Marie told me that she would be there by 8:00 if I wanted to get a head start. I didn't get the feeling that she meant it as a suggestion. I pulled into the tiny parking lot, bracing myself for another day spent with Elder Ryan. I sighed. Nick. I tried to conjure images of the car that I would buy, the apartment that I would move into, maybe even a few new outfits, anything to make the impending sacrifice worth it, and hoped for a busy schedule of showings to keep him out of my way.

"You need this job. You need this job. You need this job," I chanted as I pushed myself out of the car and stood a moment in the frosty October morning, watching my breath curl up in front of me, a novelty that never happened in Florida. I can't say that I had missed it much. Nor did I miss the irony: this was the coldest October on record. It *would* have to happen after I got home.

"You haven't readjusted to the cold yet, have you?" I whirled in surprise to find Elder Ryan—Nick—on the porch, leaning against the house and watching me.

"No," I replied shortly. "Not yet." I readjusted the shoulder strap on my bag and walked toward him, head held high. My heels clicked in the parking lot, echoing through the quiet morning. I nodded toward the door. "You waiting for something?" I asked, reaching for the handle.

"Yeah," he replied as I tried, unsuccessfully, to turn it. "Marie."

I glanced at him and then down at my phone. 8:00 a.m. I turned my back to Nick and stared longingly at the parking lot, wondering how rude it would be to leave him alone on the porch and escape to my car until Marie showed up. I could always use the cold as an excuse. I had almost decided to make my move, let him think I'm a brat, when he spoke to me again.

"How long have you been home, Matthews?" he asked.

"Quinn," I corrected, shooting him a look. "Three months. You?" I asked reflexively. The sun was just beginning to send its rays over the tips of the mountain peaks, outlining them in a brilliant gold. I kept my eyes determinedly on the scenery.

"Six. Came home in the dead of winter. Thought I was going to freeze to death."

I turned back to look at him after doing the math, one eyebrow raised. "April isn't the dead of winter," I pointed out.

He shrugged. "In Utah, it might as well be. When I got on the plane in Florida, it was eighty-five wonderful degrees. The day I got home, it snowed six inches. I was on the verge of hypothermia by the time we got to the car." He smiled at his exaggeration.

I turned back around just in time to see a bright red Lexus pull into the parking lot, Marie at the wheel. Her heels echoed loudly as she strode through the parking lot and up the front steps.

"Morning, Quinn, Nick." She unlocked the door with a click and Nick and I filed in behind her silently. I set my purse down next to my desk and surveyed the remaining pile of papers. I had made a major dent yesterday, but I still had a long way to go. I took a deep breath, wincing at the thought of all the inevitable paper cuts, and dove in. An hour later, Marie clicked back to the front of the office again, flipped on the "Open" sign, and unlocked the door. She turned around and watched as I attempted to shove a sheet of paper into one of the jam-packed cabinet drawers.

"As soon as you get the filing and newsletters all caught up, I'm going to have you go through those cabinets, scan the files into the computer and clean out those blasted drawers." She offered me a wry smile. "I have told my last two secretaries the same thing, but they never managed to get around to it. When it gets busy in here, there is really no time for side projects." Marie slowly approached me, scanning the amount of papers still on my desk. "That stack looks quite a bit smaller. Are you settling in okay?" I slid the drawer shut and nodded.

"If filing and making phone calls are all that's involved, I'm going to be great at this job," I quipped with a smile. She flashed one back. Her bright red hair was a little less chaotic today and went well with her plum-colored suit. She was shorter than I was, but only a little, although it was hard to tell with her heels. Her face was kind, especially when she smiled. I didn't notice a ring on her finger, and I admired her for running her business solo.

"I realize I didn't give you much, well, really any training yesterday. Do you have any questions?" she asked kindly.

"The appointment book? I think I've got the hang of it, but I would hate to get it wrong and have you show up where you're not supposed to." I felt a little stupid, but it was the truth. "If you could check on that and show me where the newsletter file is, I think I'll be set."

Marie walked around the desk and double-checked the appointments that I had entered yesterday. They were all correct, thank goodness. As she clicked out of it she looked up at me again.

"Looks like I have showings again today, beginning at 10:00, and I'll probably be out of the office until at least 2:00 this afternoon. I'm not sure what Nick's schedule looks like for the day, but chances are he'll be in and out as well. We're beginning to move into the slow season, so you'll most likely see much more of us by the end of next month. And then maybe you'll have time to clean out those files."

Before I could respond, the front door banged open loudly, rattling the tiny bells attached to the door almost beyond capacity. A tall, middle-aged man came barging in. He was casually dressed, with streaks of silver through his dark hair. He glanced at Marie and me before speaking.

"I'm looking for Nick Ryan," he said gruffly, shoving his hands nervously into his jacket pockets. I nodded.

"If you'll just have a seat, I'll let him know you're here," I said, gesturing to the padded chairs against the wall. "Can I give him your name?"

"Jim Richardson," he replied as he sat down. I gave him a nod of acknowledgment before heading down the hall. I caught an approving smile and nod from Marie as I turned back to Nick's office. I hadn't gone inside the day before, just peeked through the open door, and I realized that his office had, at one time, been a bedroom. The closet had been converted to built-in shelving, which was now overflowing with reference books, piles of office supplies, and brochures, but it somehow still felt like a bedroom. Nick's desk took up most of the room, leaving only space enough for a couple of chairs for clients. Nick was so focused on his computer screen that he didn't notice me stick my head in until I spoke.

"You've got a client," I said softly. He glanced up at me and nodded. "Jim Richardson." His eyes widened and a strange expression crossed his face. He sat back in his chair and pushed back his dark curls with one hand. "Should I send him back?"

Nick shook his head quickly. "I'll be—I'll be right out."

"He'll be right with you," I informed Mr. Richardson, who was flipping absently through a magazine as I reentered the waiting room. He nodded briskly and turned back to his magazine. I picked up yet another client form to file and was jamming it into its proper location when Nick appeared.

"Jim?" Nick asked, his voice guarded. "What are you doing here?" The man stood up cautiously.

"We need to talk, Nick. I don't think you gave me the whole story—" Nick held up his hand, cutting Mr. Richardson off. He glanced at me and back at Mr. Richardson, then motioned Mr. Richardson to follow him into his office. I went back to filing, my mind drifting to more interesting things, almost completely forgetting about the man, until I was stopped short by the sound of yelling coming from the back of the building. At first the words were too muffled to understand, but the sound seemed to be moving in my direction and I turned back to the filing cabinet, surreptitiously making room for yet another piece of paper.

"I will do what I have to do," Jim yelled as he approached. I could feel the muscles in my back tense, and I began to file even more strenuously, keeping my eyes locked on the open drawer in front of me.

"Jim," Nick protested loudly, close behind him, "wait, please—"

"No. And don't think that I don't know that you've been dodging my calls. I'm not stupid, kid. You got a week to get this taken care of. I've given you as much latitude as possible. Don't blow me off again!" he continued, pulling the door open. "I tracked you down once, Ryan, I will do it again!" he bellowed, slamming the door behind him. I jumped at the crash. I turned slowly to look at Nick, my eyes wide. He stood in the entryway limply, staring at the closed door. When he realized I was watching him, he turned on his heel and disappeared back into his office, slamming the door behind him.

"And he didn't tell you who the guy was? Or anything?" Annie asked curiously. We were sprawled on the living room floor, a mostly empty bowl of popcorn between us. My long, dark hair was pulled in a high ponytail and out of my face, my legs propped up on the couch. I shook my head.

"Marie came running out after he left, wondering what was going on. I didn't know, so I sent her in to see Nick. Apparently he had a good explanation, because the next time I saw her, it was like nothing had happened. And then Nick stayed in his office for an hour and when he came out, he told me he would be showing houses for the rest of the day and I didn't see him again." I threw a handful of popcorn into my mouth. I could almost see Annie's brain whirring, coming up with her usual overdramatic explanations. I pulled a blanket off the couch to cover me. Even with the sweatpants I had donned after work, I was still freezing. I wanted to move back to Florida.

"And you didn't ask Marie about it after she talked to Nick?" Annie asked anxiously.

I shot her a look. "It was my second day of work. I barely know these people. It's absolutely none of my business."

"Still," she scoffed. "Maybe he has a gambling problem, and he's late paying his bookie!" Annie exclaimed, her eyes widening in excitement. "Or he could be a loan shark! Wait, is that that same thing?"

I looked at her with raised eyebrows. "You watch too much TV." I washed down the popcorn with a swig of Diet Coke.

"Or maybe he has some deep, dark secret and that guy is blackmailing him! Or he got a girl pregnant while he was in Florida, and her father is coming to make him pay for everything! Or . . . or . . . or . . ." Annie trailed off, out of ideas.

"Or it's none of our business and we should just forget about it," I offered. Annie just rolled her eyes at me.

"If you honestly wanted to do that, you wouldn't have told me about it in the first place. You want to know as much as I do," she accused, reaching for a handful of popcorn.

"Okay, all right, you got me," I admitted. I had been running through possible scenarios all afternoon. Mine were, for the most part, less exciting and a little more realistic than Annie's, but I couldn't deny that I was curious. "But can you blame me?" I smiled mischievously and rolled onto my stomach.

"Nah," her eyes widened. "Maybe he's secretly gay, and Jim is a spurned lover!" Both of us burst out laughing.

I had spent a lot of time with Annie since I got home from my mission. More, I think, than I had in my entire life. She was only fourteen when I left, and more awkward and moody than fun. That, and I spent most of my free time with either Josh or Olivia. Now, at sixteen, the worst of the hormonal fluctuations had passed and she was surprisingly delightful. And oftentimes, even more unexpectedly wise.

Coming home had actually been more difficult than I would have imagined. When I left for my mission, I had this idea in my head of what life would be like after I got home. It was all planned out before I even left. Olivia and Josh would be waiting for me at the airport with my family for a glorious homecoming. A reasonable amount of time later, Josh would propose and we would get married in the Manti Temple and live in a little apartment in Orem while we both attended Utah Valley University. I know life rarely turns out the way we plan, but this was the only future that made sense.

I had heard about the culture shock of returned missionaries, but this was more than that. After receiving Josh's letter, I had been heartbroken, but I was kept so busy with missionary work that I had been able to throw myself into the service of others, teaching and serving, and it hadn't weighed me down. Until I got home. There was no job for me, only online school, and no driving purpose in my life. I mourned the loss of my perfectly laid out life almost as much as I mourned the loss of Joshua.

Then, losing Olivia on top of all of that had been almost more than I could bear. Olivia knew that Josh had been dating Jenny, but never said anything to me, as per his request. In the weeks following Josh's email, Olivia's story came trickling out in her emails. She hadn't known that Josh was going to propose to Jenny. In fact, she had no idea how serious their relationship had become. And, according to one of her emails, she refused to speak to Josh for a month and wouldn't even look at Jenny. She had been just as excited as I was at the prospect of becoming sisters-in-law and she was almost as devastated as I was when it became apparent that it was not to be.

When I got off the plane in July, she had been waiting at the airport with my family, and she had come to the homecoming and all the festivities following. But the elephant in the room made our relationship awkward. So much so, in fact, that both of us had stopped trying to see the other altogether. The last time I had talked to Olivia, she said that Josh and Jenny had finally set a date: a Christmas wedding. Liv had relented, with much convincing from her mother, and had even agreed to be a bridesmaid. One night, while we were hanging out in my room, she had begun to describe the bridesmaid dresses for the wedding.

"You should see it, Quinn. It's terrible." Her nose wrinkled as if she could smell the unattractiveness. "The color's not too bad," she continued, not noticing my tight expression. "It's kind of coral, but it's tea length and it's poofy. I look like a broken umbrella."

I held up my hands, my face drawn. "Olivia, please. I really don't want to know," I begged.

She closed her mouth immediately. "I'm sorry, Quinn, I wasn't thinking," she bit her lower lip, apparently nervous that I might break down sobbing or lose my temper or something.

I tried to get things back to normal, change the subject, but failed miserably, and she headed home soon after. That happened a month ago, and I hadn't seen her since, except for brief, slightly awkward sightings at church.

I sighed, pulling myself back to the present. "Hey," I announced, glancing at the clock. "It's almost midnight. We should go to bed." I wrapped the blanket around me as I stood up and grabbed the bowl of popcorn and my Coke. Annie stretched out on the floor like a cat.

"You do know that I'm going to wait impatiently until you find out what that was about today," she mumbled, accidentally pulling her blanket up over her face as she stretched. "You kind of need to make it your job to find out."

I dumped the bowl in the sink. "Don't get your hopes up," I called and closed my bedroom door behind me.

3

Despite ardent protests to the contrary, I was fairly convinced that my father was secretly disappointed when I finally obtained full-time employment. Don't get me wrong, he was happy for me and believed that I should, in fact, be a fully contributing member of society, but I'm pretty sure he missed having his own personal day laborer. He had made a long list of jobs for me to do after he had given up hope that I would ever find outside employment, and now that I had, it seemed he was determined that his list would get completed one way or another. This became glaringly apparent about 8:00 a.m. my first Saturday morning after starting work at Jonas Realty.

I rolled over and pulled my pillow over my head to drown out the pounding on my door. *Why can't Annie just drive herself to school? I have to get a car*, I thought to myself, annoyed and frustrated at being woken like this again. The thought registered and I sat up abruptly, suddenly frantic that I was late for work. And then it hit me: It was Saturday. I collapsed back onto my pillow in relief, but the incessant pounding didn't stop.

"What?!" I wailed.

"Time to get up!" Dad called through the door cheerfully. I moaned and pulled the covers back up around my neck.

"It's Saturday," I protested, nestling myself back into my bed with every intention of going right back to sleep.

"Right," called my dad again. "Time to paint the garage!"

"I got a job, Dad," I whined. "I don't need any chores to earn extra cash. But thanks for thinking of me," I threw in, hoping desperately that it would get me off the hook.

"You do if you still want to live here," he called back, his voice as chipper as ever. "I'll see you in the garage in twenty or I'm sending the boys in!" I listened to his footsteps retreating from the door and groaned. He had pulled out the ultimate threat. I loved my brothers, but Ezra and Oliver's idea of serving as an alarm clock included way too many bodily noises for my liking.

I groaned, threw the covers off of me, and pulled on my painting sweats. I looked at myself in the mirror before venturing out. This shade of gray did nothing to alleviate the dark circles under my eyes. I took a closer look, hoping that they were at least partially due to day-old mascara, decided to burn these sweats the first chance I got, and pulled the bedroom door open. Ezra and Oliver were sitting impatiently outside my door with a timer.

"Awww," they moaned in disappointment when they saw me.

"You enjoy that just way too much," I chided, snatching the timer out of Ezra's hands and heading to the kitchen. Annie sat at the counter with a bowl of cereal in front of her, wearing clothes that were much too nice to be painting in. I cocked my head at her.

"You're going to ruin *those* jeans?" I asked, pouring myself a bowl of cereal. She shook her head, her mouth full of Cap'n Crunch.

"Have a hair appointment," she mumbled around the cereal.

"Not this early?" I asked dubiously. She shook her head. "Why are you up already then?" I asked, sliding into the chair next to her.

"The threat of those two," she pointed to the boys. "Apparently it doesn't matter that I can't help. Dad has suddenly become morally opposed to sleeping in." She turned back to her cereal as I poured milk on mine.

Dad came marching into the kitchen a few moments later, gleefully announcing that everything was ready. This early in the morning, his enthusiasm was beginning to get on my nerves. Annie and I threw our bowls in the sink, and when she retreated to her room to finish getting ready, the boys and I reluctantly followed Dad out to the garage. He had pulled both of the cars out into the driveway, and a huge five-gallon bucket of paint sat on the ground in the middle of the empty garage.

"Okay," Dad began. "First we need to clear off the shelves and take them down, then we can start painting!"

"Dad," I protested, "I just cleaned out the garage a couple of weeks ago. It's all organized."

"Exactly," he said, pointing to me. "It will just make it that much easier to put it all back when we're done!"

"Why didn't we paint it before? When everything was off the shelves the first time?" This was the very last thing I wanted to spend my Saturday on.

"Didn't have the paint!" Dad shot me a warning smile and began to unload the shelves. I sighed and resigned myself to a day of manual labor. After hours of moving boxes, he pulled out the paint rollers and handed one to each of us, with an emphatic warning to the boys about what would happen if they chose to use their paint rollers for evil. Once the actual painting had begun, I didn't mind so much. It was one of those jobs that required a minimal level of attention and allowed my mind to wander freely. I had just begun to ruminate on all the possibilities that my paycheck would bring, after the car of course, when Dad became my painting buddy.

"How's the new job?" he asked, following me with his paint roller, catching the spots that I had missed.

I shrugged. "It's all right, I guess. Mostly I'm excited about the regular paycheck."

He nodded in agreement. "It's quite a deal. More than I made after I got home from my mission, that's for sure."

I laughed. "I hope so. How long ago was that? The Dark Ages?" I teased. Dad just shook his head good-naturedly. I noticed little flecks of white paint dotting his rapidly graying hair. It was one of the first things that I had noticed coming down the escalator at the airport. My family had stood in a semi-circle, smiling up at me, and all I could think was how gray my dad's hair was. When I left for Florida his hair was still as dark as mine, with only a few distinguished streaks of gray around the edges. By the time I got home, I was a little sad to see that the gray had almost overtaken the brown.

"Have you thought more about school?" he asked.

I nodded, keeping my eyes on the roller. "Yeah, I figured I can keep taking generals online while I'm working."

"You can't take everything online, though, can you?" He bent down to run his roller through the paint again.

I shrugged. "Probably not. But I don't really want to, anyway. It just works out best for now." I glanced at him. "Honestly, Dad, I don't know what I want to do."

"You like to read," he suggested.

I laughed. "There's hardly a major for that."

"English," he argued.

I shook my head. "I don't think I could survive that many papers." I paused, considering. "I like working with people," I offered.

"Medicine? Nursing?"

I wrinkled my nose. "I can't handle the blood."

"What about Family Science? Counseling?"

"I don't know," I mused. "It just doesn't feel like a good fit." I turned back to the garage wall, the uncertainty that I had been fighting off for the past couple of months threatening to close in. I had been over this list in my head before. Nothing seemed to fit just right. I kept hoping that one of my online classes would spark something, but so far, no such luck.

"Well," said Dad, patting my back with reassurance. "You'll find something, and you'll love it."

"I hope so," I replied, with much less confidence than he had.

Dad finally announced that we could take a break for lunch, and I was incredibly grateful. My arms were already aching. Oliver and Ezra took the opportunity to play football in the backyard and I watched them from the window as I scrubbed the paint from my hands before examining the contents of the fridge. I heard the kitchen door slam behind me and turned, expecting to see Dad coming in from the garage. Instead, I found Annie, her hair shorter than it had been that morning, and slightly darker chestnut with streaks of purple running through it. My jaw dropped.

"What do you think?" she asked spinning around, a huge smile on her face.

"I think you're crazy," I said slowly, "and I love it."

"Really?!" she exclaimed with a smile.

I nodded and twirled a lock of purple hair through my fingers. "Mom's going to kill you," I teased in a singsong voice.

Annie's smile grew. "Worth it."

I laughed. "Did Dad see you?"

"Not yet. He wasn't in the garage."

I shook my head again, just waiting for this show to get started. Sure enough, within the next half hour the kitchen was a full-blown war zone. Mom chewed Annie out for looking like a punk, a miscreant, a drug addict, and when her initial insults didn't yield satisfactory remorse, a prostitute. At which point Dad jumped in, making it a family affair.

"Melanie!" he barked, "don't you think that's a little extreme?"

She looked at him incredulously. "I'm the one who is extreme? Your daughter just came home with purple hair, and I'm the one who is extreme?"

"Melanie—" he tried again, but she cut him off.

"You can't tell me you approve."

"Of course I don't approve, I don't like it any more than you do, but calling your daughter a prostitute seems just a little uncalled for."

"A little?" I muttered under my breath. Dad, the only one close enough to hear me, shot me a warning look.

"She cannot go to church tomorrow with that in her hair. I refuse to take her with us." Mom's face had gone her customary shade of red.

"Seriously, Mom?" Annie appealed. "Jesus said love everyone."

"Annika Matthews!" I put my hand over my mouth, fighting back the hysterical giggle threatening to erupt, and I caught Dad biting back a smile. Mom sent Annie a look that would wither lesser human beings, but all of the Matthews children had developed an immunity long ago. Mom stomped out of the kitchen and down the hall, Dad following her quietly. He stopped next to Annie.

"It wasn't your best plan, sweetie," he said quietly. Her eyes dropped and for the first time, true remorse crossed her face.

"Sorry, Dad," she muttered contritely as he continued after Mom. We were all aware how this would play out. Mom would rant to him alone in their bedroom, he would calm her like no one else could, and tomorrow Annie would be at church with us, but Mom would not be speaking to her, likely for the next few days.

"You got guts, chick, I'll give you that," I commented, pulling open the fridge door to replace the meat and cheese. Annie slid onto one of the counter stools and snagged a chip out of the bag and popped it in her mouth.

"There is a horrible sort of satisfaction after doing something like this," Annie tugged absently at her hair. "She didn't even ask if it was permanent. It'll wash out after a couple of weeks. She's totally unreasonable."

"I know," I said simply, finishing off the last of my sandwich. "Trust me. I know."

The next day played out as expected, with Mom sitting as far away from Annie as possible, while the rest of us tried to ignore the uncomfortable silence. Much to Mom's dismay and Annie's delight, the purple hair got loads of compliments and despite Mom's dire warnings, Annie was not excommunicated on sight. The end of sacrament meeting was a relief, and we all went our separate ways to Sunday School. I caught sight of Olivia's parents at the back of the chapel. Josh had been going to church with Jenny since I had come home, so I hadn't had the misfortune of running into him, or worse, the two of them together. And Olivia's and my interaction had been reduced to a generic greeting. Sister Adams waved in my direction and I waved back halfheartedly.

With Annie in her own Sunday School class, Mom suddenly became unbearably loquacious, particularly on the subject of the boys in the ward who had returned home from their missions over the past year.

"That Jeff Atkinson got home a couple of months before you did," she whispered in my ear as he sat down a few rows in front of us, his sandy hair meticulously rumpled. "And you remember Travis Holt? He decided to live at home this year while he's going to school." She raised her eyebrows pointedly at that juicy tidbit of information. I learned long ago that it was just easiest to nod and smile at my mother, rather than try to convince her that there was very, very little chance of anything happening with any of these guys. This was the same ward in which I had attended Primary, Young Women, and Relief Society right up until my mission. I had grown up with these boys, seen them all the way through adolescence. And that was enough for me.

After the opening prayer, she decided to try another tack. "You know Quinn, if you don't put yourself out there, no one is going to know you're available. I really think that you should start going to the singles ward!" This suggestion had been met with derision numerous times before, but today for some reason, possibly the incessant hiss in my left ear, it had more appeal to me than ever before. I sighed and nodded.

"Maybe I will, Mom," I whispered back, and turned pointedly to the front of the classroom to at least pretend to listen to the lesson.

4

Without even opening my eyes, I could tell that it had snowed. A lot. The pale light shining through my curtains was much too bright for 6:30 a.m. on a November morning. I closed my eyes again and settled more deeply into my bed, reveling in the warmth and the light before I had to face the reality of the cold. It was early November, almost too early for a storm like this, but I reminded myself that I lived in Utah, and anything could happen.

I took a deep breath, pushed the pile of blankets off of my legs, and padded to the window to peer out. An odd orange glow filled the air, only present after a heavy night snow, while the clouds are still hanging low. It was my favorite part of a snowstorm. It only happened once or twice a winter at most and I reveled in it every time. It had been two years since I had seen it last, and I stood at my window until my breath fogged up the glass and my toes felt like they might fall off. It was beautiful, but I couldn't help thinking that I should make Annie drive this morning. It had also been two years since I had driven in the snow, and I was never very good at it in the first place.

I traced my initials in the fog on the window and contemplated the day ahead of me. I had been at Jonas Realty for almost a month now. It had gotten better. A lot better, actually. I really liked Marie, but I still felt like I didn't know her much better today than the day that I started. She was guarded about everything but work. I didn't even know if she was married, or had ever been. As for Nick, he and I had developed a working relationship. He still wasn't my favorite person, but he was surprisingly more talkative and light-years more friendly than he had been in Florida. He was out of the office a lot, doing showings and meeting with clients, but when he was around, he had developed a habit of stopping by my desk to chat on his way in and out. And I was surprised to find myself enjoying the conversations.

After a hot shower and about four layers of clothing, I was ready for the day. Annie laughed when she saw me.

"You know, just because it snowed, it doesn't mean it's *that* cold outside," she quipped as we backed out of the driveway.

I glanced down at my overcoat, scarf, and knee-high boots and shrugged. "It's cold enough," I snapped, rubbing my gloved hands together for warmth.

Annie laughed again. "You look like you're going on a trek to the Arctic, not a day at a realtor's office."

"Ha, ha. Just keep your eyes on the road."

It took twice as long as usual to make it to the school that morning. I glanced at the clock. 7:38. That left me twenty minutes to get to work. Usually that would be plenty, but today I wasn't so sure. I slid into the driver's seat and said a little prayer before pulling back into traffic. The roads were a mess. Most of them hadn't been plowed yet, and it was a miracle I didn't get stuck anywhere.

By the time I pulled into the tiny parking lot, my knuckles ached from gripping the steering wheel so tightly. I breathed a sigh of relief that I had made it alive and glanced out at the tiny parking lot. It had been plowed, or shoveled, from the looks of things, as had the front walk and steps. I whispered a quick prayer of gratitude as I pulled my bag out of the car with me and made my way carefully up the front steps. Marie and

Nick were already both there. I pushed the front door open and found both of them standing next to my filing cabinets.

"Good morning," I called out, the question in my voice obvious. Both of them glanced up at me. Nick nodded his hello and Marie held up her hand in a motionless wave. I put my things on my desk, keeping my eyes on them. This was my territory and it was unusual for them to invade. When either needed a file, they gave me a name and I pulled it for them. They apparently didn't care that I was there, because they continued their argument as if nothing had happened.

"Marie, that is not part of my job description," Nick argued.

Marie pursed her lips. "How many appointments have you had in the last couple of weeks, Nick? How many showings?" Nick didn't answer and I knew that the numbers had decreased drastically over the last month; I was the one who kept track of them.

"I am not a secretary," he protested. "No offense, Quinn," he called in my direction.

Marie continued as if he had never spoken. "And how many new clients do you think you're going to get after a day like today?"

Nick grimaced as he glanced toward the front window. "If I'm spending all of my time doing clerical work, that's time I can't spend drumming up business, isn't it?"

Marie let out a sigh of exasperation. "Nicholas Ryan, I hired you on the promise that you would work hard and you have not failed me. But don't think for one second that any disrespect you feel you might be able to show me because I am your aunt will not get you fired just as quickly as it would anywhere else."

My eyes widened a bit at this revelation. Nick opened his mouth to protest but Marie held up her hand.

"This discussion is over." She looked over at me. "Quinn, I need you in here all day tomorrow. The snow will slow business down enough for the next week or so to get all of these files digitized. You and Nick can get a head start on that tomorrow." She turned on her heel without waiting for a response, marched into her office, and closed the door with a bang. I turned to Nick, my mouth slightly agape. I was surprised to see that his irritation of moments ago had diminished; he looked oddly pleased.

"All day tomorrow?" I asked dejectedly.

He nodded briefly. "Looks like it. But it'll be a little bit faster with both of us working on it." He shot me a reassuring smile. "I have to make some phone calls. I'll be in my office." And then he was gone too.

I sat down at my desk with a sigh. All day tomorrow. An entire Saturday of sleeping in and shopping, gone. And I wasn't quite sure how I felt about spending an entire day alone with Nick either. Sure, things were great when we chatted for ten minutes here and there, but an entire day?

It was a long day, between dreading a wasted Saturday, dealing with several disgruntled clients on the phone, and anticipating an evening I had been looking forward to for a while. My older brother Nathan and his wife Sasha were coming down to visit tonight from Salt Lake. They were both going to school up there, and even though it was only a 45-minute drive, we almost never saw them.

I had met Sasha once before I left on my mission, and then they had gotten married before I got home. I was furious when I got the news, I so wanted to be at the wedding, but someone had been pretty insistent. My guess was Mom, but I wouldn't be surprised if it had been Sasha either. Nate and Sasha had been there to greet me at the airport, and then for my homecoming, but I think that I had maybe seen them only two or three times since then. And I missed Nate like crazy.

Nathan was almost exactly two years older than me, our birthdays only a few weeks apart. We were inseparable growing up. Annie was almost five years younger than I was, so for a long time, there was only Nate and I. We fought like any brother and sister would, but I loved that kid and looked up to him. For a long time, he was my hero. It may have been the Batman cape that he wore around constantly when he was six, but whatever it was, he was my idol.

As we got older, the fighting gradually stopped and we started talking. He gave me reluctant permission to date a few of his friends—only the ones he approved of, of course—and he never put on the annoying big brother act at school when he would see me walking down the halls. He left for his mission to Spain when he was just shy of his nineteenth birthday and came home in time for us to spend exactly one month together before I left for my mission. So, really, I felt like I hadn't seen him in four years.

When I pulled the car into the driveway after work, I was excited to see Nate and Sasha's car already there. I hadn't expected them for at least another hour. I jumped out of the car and ran into the house.

"Nate!" I yelled, coming into the kitchen. Mom was stomping around the kitchen, slamming cupboards and throwing things, and generally making me nervous. I wondered if she and Annie had a fight. I glanced into the living room and saw Nathan's sandy head just peeping over the back of the couch. I walked up behind him and ruffled his hair. He shifted in his seat to smile at me.

"Hey Q, it's about time," he greeted me. I glanced around the room looking for Sasha, but he was alone. His hair was shorter than he normally wore it, disguising the curls that had kept him from ever being lonely a single day of high school.

"Where's Sasha?" I asked, hopping over the back of the couch to sit next to him.

"She couldn't make it," he mumbled, keeping his green eyes on his hands. "But hey," he glanced back up at me, "let's hear about the job with the jerk missionary."

I told Nate all about Jonas Realty, about Marie's quirkiness and about Nick's attitude adjustment. "Honestly, it's not as bad as I thought it would be. He's a lot different than he was in Florida. I mean, he's still not my favorite person, but I don't know. He's a decent human being." I shrugged. "Maybe the Florida heat just went to his head." I paused and considered the coming day's task. "Although, I have to go in to work all day tomorrow and start on a project with him. So, ask me again tomorrow night."

Nate smiled and opened his mouth to respond, but we were interrupted by Mom's announcement that dinner was ready. Chicken enchiladas, Nate's favorite. Mom was oddly quiet all throughout dinner and would hardly even glance at Nate. She definitely wasn't talking to him. Every once in a while, I would shoot him a questioning look, but he seemed to be carefully avoiding my gaze as well. Annie shot looks between the two of us, but it appeared she was in the dark as well. Luckily, Ezra and Oliver kept us entertained with stories of junior high exploits.

By the time Mom brought out the dessert, Dad had caught on that something was up and was shooting concerned glances between Mom and Nate almost constantly. After we were finished eating, Nate took the boys to the playroom for some video games and I helped Mom clear up dinner. She was in a quiet mood and any time that I did try to talk to her, she snapped at me. I gave up on conversation pretty quickly. As soon as the dishes were done, she announced that it was time for prayers and that she was going to bed.

When Nate finally resurfaced from the playroom, I was reading on the couch. Annie had gone out with her friends and my parents were in bed. He wandered into the kitchen, obviously looking for something to eat.

"There are some chips in the pantry," I called over to him. "And I think there might be some ice cream in the freezer."

Sure enough, he pulled out some Rocky Road and dished up before coming to sit next to me on the couch. I peered at him over the top of my book.

"What is up with you and Mom tonight?" I asked. He shrugged slightly and focused on his ice cream. "Mom is weird," I continued, "we all know this, but something was up tonight, Nathan. What is going on?"

He glanced at me out of the corner of his eye, debating. After a few more mouthfuls of ice cream, he turned to face me.

"Sasha and I are going through some stuff," he said carefully. "That's why she didn't come tonight."

"What kind of stuff?" I asked hesitantly. He paused again, refocusing on his ice cream.

"I think she may be, um, seeing someone else," he began hoarsely.

"Seeing someone else?" I repeated numbly, sincerely hoping that I severely misunderstood what I just heard.

Nate sighed and pressed his fingers against his eyes. "I'm pretty sure she's cheating on me." He spoke so softly I could barely hear him.

"What?!" I asked, sitting up straight, my book falling soundlessly to the carpeted floor. "Nathan! Are you serious? Are you sure?"

Nate opened and closed his mouth several times, trying to find the right words. I tried to wait patiently, but found myself more and more irritated as the seconds passed.

"She's been staying late at work for the last few months, and a couple of weeks ago, she locked her phone and she won't tell me the pass code." He stopped and looked at me, almost defensively. "I know that doesn't sound like a lot, but she has the pass code to my phone, and we know"—he paused again—"knew each other's email passwords. But she changed that too. It's just a bunch of little things and I'm not sure what to think."

"Nate," I began softly, but his words went on top of mine, almost as if he had been waiting to pour it all out.

"I tried to ask her about it. She has excuses for all of it, or she calls me paranoid. She showers when she gets home from work now. She'll barely look at me. And we haven't—"

I saw where he was going and held my hands up in defense. "Too much!"

He nodded and noticed that he was still holding his ice cream bowl. He almost looked surprised to see it there. "We never should have gotten married in the first place."

"Nathan!" I yelped, shocked. You hear all the time how marriage isn't easy, how the first year is the hardest, and true, I wasn't married so I could hardly judge, but I thought that was going a bit too far. "How can you say that? You love her!"

He looked at me with wide, sad eyes and shook his head slowly. "Nate," I whispered again. "What?"

"You were gone. Mom never told you, did she?"

"What, that you don't love Sasha? Nope," I replied sarcastically. "She must have left that out of the weekly emails. Seriously, Nate."

He shook his head again. "Not that. About the wedding."

"Nobody told me about the wedding, Nate. I figured everyone was too busy, because you guys got married spur of the moment, right?"

Nate laughed ironically. "Right." He leaned forward to set the bowl on the coffee table and then shifted on the couch so he was fully facing me. "We got married spur of the moment because we had to."

"You had to?" I asked, not fully grasping the implications. He raised his eyebrows and all of a sudden it hit me. "You had to?" I whispered again in disbelief. "But—"

"She found out she was pregnant. We told our parents. They had a wedding set up within a week and a month later we were married. Three weeks after that, Sasha miscarried.

But we were still married." His voice was full of annoyance and regret.

"So," I said stupidly, "you didn't get married in the temple?"

Nate chuckled ironically again. "I hear they frown on pregnant brides there."

"Why didn't anyone tell me?" I asked furiously, punching the back of the couch. "I was on a mission, not dying!" I paused as more and more questions popped up in my head. "Annie? How in the world did you get Annie to keep that secret?"

Nate shook his head. "Annie doesn't know. Never did. I think Mom told her that we wanted to get married so quickly that there wasn't time for Sasha to get ready to go through the temple. It was a stupid excuse, but Annie didn't seem to care. She got to walk down the aisle in a bridesmaid dress. That was good enough for her."

"Annie is not stupid, Nate."

He shrugged. "She probably figured it out. She just never said anything."

"I can't believe no one told me," I said again. "I can't believe you didn't tell me, Nate."

Nate raked his hand through his hair. "I wanted to, Quinn, I did. I could have used a little Quinn wisdom, but Mom thought it would be best not to. Honestly, no one but our parents knows exactly what happened. I think Mom was so humiliated to have to throw together a shotgun wedding that she didn't admit to anyone what was going on. I'm pretty sure everyone guessed pretty accurately, but she never told them. And when Sasha miscarried? I could actually hear Mom's sigh of relief over the phone."

"No!" I said, praying that wasn't true, but knowing my mother, it probably was. Nate shot me a look to confirm. Another thing occurred to me, and as much as I hated to ask it, I had to know. "But you, I mean, you already went through the temple, Nathan. What . . . what happened? Did you—"

I found that I couldn't say the word out loud. Nate could see where I was going and shook his head briefly.

"Disfellowshipped," he replied.

He began to talk and the whole story spilled out of him. What it had been like when they had told Mom. How Sasha's mom had reacted. About the miscarriage, and Sasha's subsequent depression. He talked and he talked and he talked, and I heard most of what he was saying, but all the while my mind was screaming. Nothing like this had ever happened before. I had known people in high school who got pregnant, who had to get married, and then got divorced within a year. I had known girls who had gotten pregnant and then been disowned by their parents. I had a friend whose father had taken off after he had an affair and then had been excommunicated. But they were nothing more than stories. They were removed. None of them had touched me. Until this.

Nathan had been my hero, my big brother, my protector. I don't know if all little sisters felt this way, but in my eyes, Nate could do no wrong. And he hadn't. He graduated from seminary. He was an Eagle Scout. The deacons and teachers quorum president. He went on a mission. He was an assistant to the mission president. But this. I didn't know how to react. Part of me wanted to hit him for being an idiot, and part of me wanted to cry for the loss of my hero, but mostly, I just felt like throwing up. And now Sasha was cheating on him? That, more than anything, was causing my nausea. It was too much all at once for my brain and my heart to handle. Nathan kept talking long after I couldn't stomach it anymore. It was almost one o'clock when he finally stopped. I stared at him blankly for a moment, wondering what to do next, his anticipatory silence filling the room.

"I have to go to work tomorrow," I muttered slowly, getting to my feet. "I really should go to bed." I hoped he wouldn't press for a response, because at the moment, I just wasn't capable of giving one.

"You okay?" he asked as I walked around the couch.

"I'm fine," I lied, waving him off. "Night." I went into my room, shut the door, and lay in bed staring at the blank ceiling until sleep finally overpowered me.

5

Despite the near arctic temperatures the next morning (well, to me anyway) I got up early to run. I needed to process everything, and nothing helped me think more clearly than a long run, even if I did die of hypothermia in the process. As I got up to speed, I realized how lazy I had been over the past few weeks since the cold had really set in. The frigid air made it hard to breathe and I had to navigate carefully around ice patches in the road. The rhythmic pounding of my feet against the asphalt was soothing, and for a few minutes, I managed to shake off the gut-wrenching uncertainty and disappointment of the night before and think through the situation with less emotion clouding my reaction.

As soon as I got home though, my ears burning with cold, everything came rushing back, and I was grateful that Nate was sleeping in and I didn't have to face him just yet. I spent a long time under the hot shower, trying to revive the feeling in my limbs, something I was sure Annie wouldn't appreciate later when the hot water was gone. I pulled on jeans and a sweater, wishing that I could get away with sweats. It was Saturday after all.

Rather than run the risk that I might bump into Nate in the kitchen, I quietly slipped out the door and stopped at McDonald's for hot chocolate and hash browns on the way to work, effectively negating my run. I ate in the parking lot of Jonas Realty, with the heater blasting. I watched the snowdrift in front of me brighten from a dull gray to a sparkling white as the sun's edges rose over the nearby peaks. I tried to focus on the scenery, the task ahead of me, anything, but no matter where I tried to redirect my mind, it just kept coming back to Nate and Sasha. I flipped on the radio to drown out my thoughts and I had just polished off the hash browns when Nick pulled up in his silver Mazda next to me. I acknowledged him with a nod, grabbed my hot chocolate, and followed him silently into the office. The snow from the day before had solidified and the parking lot was littered with frozen puddles, just waiting to take me down. Nick watched me leap lightly over the last one, trying not to spill the last of my hot chocolate.

"What?" I demanded as I made it up the steps, interpreting his seemingly smug smile as amusement at my expense.

"Nothing," he replied, his smile widening. I scowled and followed him through the open door. Marie had obviously given him her key for the weekend.

"Well," he said slowly, after flipping on the lights and opening the blinds. He scanned the row of filing cabinets. "Which end should we start with?" I pointed to the far end wordlessly, and he opened the first drawer and pulled out a stack of files. The office was still dim—the sun hadn't quite hit the windows yet—and it did nothing to improve my mood.

"Here we go," he announced sarcastically. Within no time papers were spread across my desk and on the floor, organized into piles and waiting in line to be scanned. The trash can was full of shredded, outdated documents, and the floor was scattered with bits and pieces. My fingers were beginning to turn black from old ink on the long-forgotten info sheets, and my scanner was whirring constantly after being used more than it ever had been before.

Nick sat sprawled on the floor, flipping through the files and organizing them into categories, while I sat at the desk, scanning. Nick spent most of the morning gallantly trying to make conversation, but I wasn't exactly in a chatty mood. After yet another failed attempt, he studied me, his head cocked in concern.

"Are you all right? You seem a little off today."

I glared at him. "I'm fine," I snapped impatiently. "Working on a Saturday morning is not exactly what I wanted to be doing." Nick held up his hands apologetically and silently went back to the stack in front of him. Within a few minutes, guilt had gotten the better of me. "I was up too late last night, that's all," I muttered, a hint of remorse in my voice. Nick glanced up at me.

"Doing anything fun?" he asked with a forgiving smile. I pulled a page out of the scanner and slid in a new one.

I shook my head quickly. "My brother came over last night."

"And you don't like your brother?" he asked slowly, obviously confused. I shook my head again.

"No, it's not that. I, just, never mind." I flipped open the scanner to slide in another paper. "He doesn't love his wife." I blurted out randomly.

"And that was why he was at your house?" Nick asked, trying to decipher my terrible explanation.

"No," I sighed and shook my head, and suddenly the details began to spill out, unchecked and unorganized. I found myself telling Nick the entire story. I began with the shotgun wedding that I didn't even know about, all the way to last night. Everything that Nathan had told me, even things that I didn't remember hearing. The details seemed to have lodged themselves permanently in my brain. "And now he thinks that she's cheating on him. She locks her phone and works overtime constantly," I finished, the stacks of files long forgotten.

Nick had stretched out on the floor, listening intently, his legs long and his hands behind his back, propping him up. He was as casual as I was in a T-shirt and jeans today. I studied him for a moment. Between the mission and his daily uniform of a shirt and tie, I had never seen him so dressed down. Jeans worked for him.

I realized Nick was staring at me and I glanced away, suddenly embarrassed by the sudden confidence I had given him. "I'm sorry," I said, fumbling to grab a paper out of the scanner and shove it clumsily through the shredder. "You didn't need to hear about all of my family drama."

Nick laughed shortly. "Maybe," he replied, "but if you're looking for someone who's used to dealing with family drama, I'm your guy."

"I feel so stupid," I blundered on. "This shouldn't be that big of a deal, right? I mean, I served in Orlando. In the ghetto. There are a million worse things that could be happening to him right now, but this just seems almost like a tragedy. I don't know. Maybe I'm just stupid and naive." My voice cracked with emotion and I choked back the sob that threatened to erupt. "I feel so lost. You know, when you're out there," I gestured vaguely in the direction of Florida, "the Spirit just carries you. You know?" Nick nodded his agreement. "It always made it so easy to know the right thing to do or the right thing to say. But now," I wrung my hands helplessly, "it's not like it's gone, but—" My voice was too thick to speak and I turned back to the computer, focusing on the meaningless names and numbers until I had calmed down. I felt a hand on my shoulder.

"Let's go get lunch," Nick said, standing over me. I glanced at the clock.

"It's only 11:30," I said, glancing up at him.

"And it will be just about noon by the time we get to Orem," he replied, pulling me up out of my chair.

"All the way to Orem, huh?" I asked, swinging my purse over my shoulder.

Nick pushed the door open for me. "Hey, if we have to spend our entire Saturday doing this," he waved his arm at the unfinished piles we were abandoning, "the least we get is a decent lunch. I'll drive." Nick walked me to the passenger side of the car and unlocked the door. I slid into the seat and watched as Nick got in and started the car.

We were almost to the freeway before either of us spoke. "So, you know all about my family drama now; let's hear about yours." It was an attempt to take some of the embarrassment off of me, but as soon as it was out of my mouth, I wondered if it was totally inappropriate.

Nick glanced at me out of the corner of his eye. "What do you want to know?"

"So," I began slowly. "Marie is your aunt? Let's start with that."' I watched as a grin flashed across his face.

"Yes," he agreed. "Marie is my aunt. That was easy."

"On your mom's side or your dad's?"

"Dad's," he replied shortly.

"And now we all know how you got the job," I teased.

"Hey," he yelped defensively. "I passed the test. I did the training. There was absolutely no nepotism involved!"

I smiled at his reaction. "Of all the people in this world, I think that Marie would be the last one to give someone a break because they're blood."

We pulled up in front of California Pizza Kitchen shortly. The day was cold and the parking lot was full, forcing us to walk a little farther than desired. Despite the fact that it was a busy Saturday afternoon at the mall, there was no wait at the restaurant, which was fantastic because I was starving. I ordered a huge plate of pasta, the ultimate comfort food, and Nick ordered a pizza. We were just taking our first bites when I heard my name from across the room.

"Sister Matthews!" I looked up from my plate to see one of my favorite companions, Sister Giles, walking toward us. I put down my fork and jumped up quickly to hug her.

"How are you?" I asked as I pulled away. She looked different without the mandated skirt and tag, but it was so refreshing to see her.

"I'm great," she smiled, "I'm sorry to interrupt your lunch, though . . ." she trailed off as she glanced down at Nick and realized who he was. "Elder Ryan?!" she asked, her eyes wide and her voice incredulous.

"Sister Giles," he acknowledged with a nod of his head.

She glanced back at me, her mouth wide and her eyebrows asking the silent question. I hurried to explain. "Nick, Elder Ryan, and I ended up working in the same office. Isn't that crazy? We're just here on our lunch break."

"Oh," she replied, with obvious disbelief. "So, um, what kind of office is it?"

"Um, Nick's a realtor," I answered, gesturing towards him, "and I'm the secretary."

Sister Giles looked back at me. "Do you like it?" she asked significantly.

"Yeah, it's a good job," I emphasized. "What are you up to?" I asked, desperate to change the subject.

"I'm just back at the Y this semester," she replied distractedly, her eyes still darting between Nick and me. "Um, hey, listen, I've got to run, but it was good to see you." She pulled out her phone. "Give me your number and I'll give you a call. We'll hang out." I gave it to her and offered one last quick hug before she left to catch up with the rest of her group.

I slid back into my chair, my eyes focused on the plate of pasta in front of me. "Well," Nick spoke up. "That was awkward."

I started giggling and couldn't stop. The irony of it all was too much. The one person who knew just how intensely Elder Ryan drove me crazy would be the one I bumped into while having lunch with him. It took some deep, cleansing breaths to finally calm down enough to eat again.

"So, why was she so shocked to see us together?" Nick ventured, once I had finally conquered the giggles.

I shrugged quickly and shoved another bite of pasta into my mouth. "Dunno," I mumbled.

"Seriously, Quinn, she looked at you like you were having lunch with a serial killer or something."

"She did not," I retorted loudly, still not meeting his eyes. I took another bite and glanced up at him hesitantly. He was staring at me, face full of disbelief, obviously waiting for an answer. I took my time chewing and tried to figure out how to respond. "Okay, so, it might possibly be because when she and I were companions, and you were in our district, I may have said some things that could possibly have led her to believe that I might not have liked you very much."

"You don't like me?" he asked. It was difficult to decipher his tone.

"No! Well, I mean . . . I just . . . no," I said, embarrassed. "Maybe just a little while we were in Florida. But in my defense, you were pretty, you know, reserved while we were there."

"Reserved?"

"Withdrawn."

"Withdrawn?"

"Conceited," I muttered, keeping my eyes down.

"Anything else?" I shook my head a little too quickly. "Quinn," he pressed.

"Well, you were just kind of a jerk." I felt a little bit terrible admitting it out loud.

"Oh," he replied.

"I just . . . you were just so . . . I mean, sorry," I finished lamely.

"I guess I was a little less than friendly. So, do you still not like me?" he asked hesitantly.

"No!" I yelped, a little too loudly. "You're like a real person now."

"Because I wasn't one in Florida?" he asked wryly.

"No, I mean, you're like a friend now and just—different than you were there. I don't know, Nick. I'm sorry."

He studied me for a moment before replying. I sincerely hoped that I hadn't said too much. I was a little worried that Elder Ryan would suddenly return with a vengeance and go storming out of the restaurant.

"I'll take it," he said with a small shrug.

We finished our lunches and headed back to the office. In the car, Nick cranked up the radio and sang along most of the drive back. When a commercial came on, I couldn't help asking him. "You really like performing?"

"What? Oh, um, I guess. I really like singing, and it seems like as soon as anyone finds out, they insist that I perform, so I guess it comes with the territory." He shrugged and glanced at me. "You sing?"

"No," I shook my head vigorously. "And even if I did, no one would ever know. I hate being in the spotlight."

"I remember," he said softly.

The first time I had to give a talk on my mission, I hadn't prepared a word. It was totally spur of the moment. The assigned speakers ended too early and the bishop used us as a way to fill the last ten minutes so he didn't have to. I knew every time we attended sacrament meeting that this was a possibility. I couldn't count the number of stories Josh and my brother Nathan had told me in which this happened to them. That didn't make me any more prepared, however. The thing is, I hate having the spotlight on me. The first time I was asked to be a youth speaker, I was so terrified I cried all morning before church. My dad gave me a blessing, and I managed a one-minute sped read talk. Over the past seven years I had improved to about three minutes, and for my farewell I had even managed to slow down a little and eke out seven. But all of that was with copious amounts of preparation. This was on the fly, and I felt like that terrified twelve-year-old again, on the verge of tears and absolutely unable to speak that five minutes. I prayed frantically as I followed my companion to the stand. She spoke first and, as a direct answer to my prayers, she spoke for eight minutes, leaving me only two.

So, when the missionaries were officially asked to speak in sacrament meeting a few weeks later, both the sisters and the elders, and I had a whole week to prepare, it suddenly didn't seem quite as daunting. I woke up Sunday morning totally nauseated, but I could handle it. I had a whole talk written down, no improvising necessary. Sister Birch and I spoke first; I managed to get through my talk without tears or vomit and sat down, thanking the Lord for tender mercies. After the interim hymn, Elder Ryan got up to speak. Near the end of his talk, he spoke about the big part that music had played in helping him get through hard times and gain a testimony. And then, out of the blue, he volunteered the four of us to sing for the congregation. Sister Birch, knowing my predisposition to stage fright, gripped my hand reassuringly. My nausea tripled, and I began to hyperventilate. Elder Ryan turned around to gesture us to the microphone. Sister Birch shook her head frantically, while trying to discreetly indicate my pale face.

"What?" Elder Ryan mouthed, clearly not getting the message.

"Just you," Sister Birch whispered. "You and Torres." Elder Ryan finally took a good look at me and realized how terrified I looked. He shrugged and turned back to the microphone.

"It seems I volunteered the sisters prematurely. Elder Torres and I will sing 'I Stand All Amazed.' " And they did, and it was beautiful, but it took a good half hour to get my heart to beat normally again.

After sacrament, Sister Birch took up my cause without provocation and confronted Elder Ryan. "You can't just get up there and volunteer other people to do things like that without asking them first! You made us both look like idiots!"

"Then you should have just gotten up to sing! Would have solved the entire problem," Elder Ryan retorted.

I jumped in. "Not everyone feels perfectly at home as the center of attention."

"I really didn't think it was that big of a deal! You just gave a talk in front of the ward. Why is that so different from singing a hymn?" His eyes were narrowed and his shoulders were tensed.

"You just dropped it in my lap! No warning, no permission! The very least you could do was ask before you stood up. It would have saved us all a lot of embarrassment." I took a step closer to him in emphasis, and somewhere in the back of my mind, I registered how loud my voice was.

Elder Ryan took a responsive step back and held up his hands in surrender. "I'm sorry, okay? Won't happen again." He turned on his heel and stalked off angrily, Elder Torres in his wake.

I turned to look at Sister Birch. Her eyes were wide. "Whoa," she muttered. "We need to take a little time out, okay?"

"What?" I snapped, still irritated. "I'm fine."

"Ooooh-keee," she drawled, unconvinced. I strode briskly down the hall toward Sunday School and away from the scene that I had to reluctantly admit I had created.

Once we arrived back in Springville, Nick and I spent the rest of the afternoon shredding, scanning, and swapping mission stories, all punctuated with curious texts from Sister Giles.

—Are you dating Elder Ryan?

—No

—You need to explain right now.

—Explain what?

"Who keeps texting you?" Nick asked over the pile of garbage bags on the floor. We were on our fourth one.

"Sister Giles," I laughed awkwardly. "She's still a little in shock." Nick laughed good-naturedly.

—You hate that guy. You don't just go to lunch with him.

—It's really not a big deal.

—Matthews. It's a huge deal.

"She really is, isn't she?" Nick commented after the fourth or fifth text. "I'm getting the feeling that you may have understated the extent of your dislike for me."

"I don't know what you're talking about," I replied uncomfortably, running yet another document through the shredder and furtively silencing my phone.

We were so caught up in our stories that we didn't notice when 5:00 rolled around. I finally glanced up from my pile of papers and realized that the windows were dark.

"What time is it?" I asked Nick. We had traded spots and now I was the one on the floor, with him at the desk.

He glanced at the computer screen. "5:30. Huh. I guess we're done." He looked back at me but didn't move. I was surprised by the minor pang of disappointment that shot through me.

"We probably shouldn't leave it looking like this." I advised, looking around at the paper-strewn office. "But yeah, as soon as we get it cleaned up, we're done." I reluctantly pulled myself to my feet, and Nick slowly began to clean up my desk. It didn't take us too long to get the office put back together. Nick walked me out to my car and then unlocked his.

"See you Monday," he called as he slid inside. He waved through the closed window as he turned the key.

"Monday," I repeated, pulling my own door closed. For possibly the first time, the prospect of Monday didn't seem quite so bleak.

6

We got the phone call on a Tuesday night, one week before Thanksgiving. I sat in the living room, just off the kitchen, with my computer on my lap. I was researching the process of becoming a realtor myself. I couldn't deny the hands-on experience I gained daily by working so closely with Marie and Nick. It wasn't exactly a degree, but it was definitely a means to one.

The house was already quiet, the boys were in bed, and everyone else was doing their own thing. Nate had moved back home last week after a final blowout with Sasha, ending in their mutual agreement to divorce, but none of us saw him very often. He spent most of his time commuting to Salt Lake for school or in his room, mourning the end of his marriage. The kitchen was dim, with only a reflection of the light from the living room spilling across the tabletop.

It wasn't too late, a little after nine, but the sudden ringing in the kitchen jarred me a little. My dad must have been close by. He answered the phone before I could get up, and I could hear his end of the conversation from the living room.

"Hello . . . Anna?" My grandmother. It was unlike her to call so late. ". . . I can't understand you . . . Oh," the drastic change in his voice made me shift in my seat to look at him. "When?" he asked softly. "And Steven? And the kids? . . .

We'll head up first thing. I'm so sorry, Anna . . . Yeah, I'll tell her. Good night." He hung up the phone gently and leaned his forehead against the wall.

"Dad?" I called with concern and curiosity. "What is it?" He pulled himself away from the wall and glanced at me. I couldn't see him very well in the dimly lit kitchen, but the way the shadows fell across his face made him look suddenly older.

"Where is your mother?" he asked, his voice choked with emotion. I set the computer on the couch and stood up.

"Downstairs, I think." I watched as he took a deep breath and squared his shoulders. "Dad, what is going on? You're scaring me."

He shook his head and started slowly down the stairs. I trailed quietly behind him.

"Melanie," he called softly as he reached the bottom step. She was in the corner of the family room, preoccupied at her sewing table. Scraps of fabric were strewn all around her, and her machine whirred noisily. "Mel," he said again a bit louder, laying his hand on her shoulder. She jumped slightly at his touch and took her foot off the pedal. I sat down on the steps, anxious to know what was going on, but not wanting to interfere. Dad took her hands in his own and knelt before her, making their eyes level. She looked at him oddly, her shoulders tense.

"Dan?" she asked slowly, obviously concerned and confused. "What is going on?" He held both her hands in his.

"Mel, that was your mom on the phone just now," he began slowly, locking his eyes on her. He struggled to keep his voice steady. I tried to remember the last time I saw my father cry. "It's Lydia, Mel." He was fighting back tears now. "She's gone."

"Gone where?" Mom asked slowly.

Dad paused and attempted to regain his composure. He managed to steady his voice before speaking again. "She took her own life," he said softly.

I gasped and covered my mouth with my hand to muffle the sound. Mom's eyes widened in shock and I could see her shoulders tense further.

"What," she gasped, "what happened?" She stood abruptly and jerked her hands out of his grasp. "No, no, I just talked to her yesterday, she was fine, Daniel, you're wrong. No." Dad stood and looked at her solemnly, and Mom took a great choking breath and sobs began to wrack her body violently. Dad wrapped his arms around her and held her tightly to him. I could feel a painful pressure in my own chest as I fought back panic and sorrow. My breath came rapidly and I pressed my hands against my chest, struggling against the weight of the grief and a feeling of suffocation. I barely heard Mom ask through her sobs, "How?"

"Steven found her in the garage," choked Dad. "She blocked the tailpipe of her car." A fresh wave of sobs overcame Mom and tears began to fall silently from my eyes, the pressure on my chest still making it hard to breathe.

I leaned my head against the wall and thoughts of what it would be like to lose Annie floated unbidden through my mind. The image didn't help my mental state and the pressure became even more painful. I began to breathe harder and faster, sucking in air frantically. Lydia had kids. Aaron was on a mission, Lizzie was a senior, and Jace was only fifteen. I couldn't sit here and listen to my mother sob for a moment longer. I couldn't breathe. I ran up the stairs and out the front door. The biting wind felt good on my hot face, the searing cold waking me up, bringing my jumbled, grief-stricken thoughts into painfully sharp focus.

Lydia was the oldest. She was the sister that my mom had looked up to. They were inseparable growing up, according to Grandma. Mom had gotten married first and had actually introduced Lydia to one of Dad's friends, Steven. Our families had been especially close since I was a little girl. When we spent time with family, it was generally with Lydia and Steven. My Aunt Katherine lived in Vegas and Uncle David was in Idaho. But Lydia and Steven were just in Salt Lake, closest in every sense of the word.

I stared sightless into the clear night sky, trying to conjure an image of Lydia the last time I saw her. It must have been at my homecoming. That was almost five months ago. Had she seemed despondent? Or . . . or . . . or . . . I didn't even know what qualities to look for in a suicidal person. She was lovely. She had a beautiful smile. She was happy and friendly and outgoing. She would always compliment me, always tell me how beautiful I was or how smart I was or something; she always made me feel amazing. I couldn't quite comprehend how this could be happening.

All of a sudden my happy little world seemed so deceptive. I grew up believing heart and soul that if a person went to church every Sunday and looked nice and said the right things, it meant they were, well, perfect. Okay, so maybe not perfect, but happy, unburdened. But the bangled wrists, the white teeth, the perfectly coordinated outfits were suddenly a disguise. There were always stories, yes, and the horrible warnings. Things that happened to people who didn't come to church, who didn't read their scriptures, whose lives were obviously out of line with the standards of the gospel. But the bad things never happened to the good examples. Nothing could touch you if you held a temple recommend. Well, I had mine in my purse and in the last month, my brother had been disfellowshipped and my aunt had committed suicide. The protective walls were shattered and I felt vulnerable and cold.

The tears began again, and as I glanced around, I realized how far from home I had walked. The stinging cold had sunk into my bones, my fingertips numb. As I walked back up the street toward home, shivering and crying, Nate came out to meet me.

"Dad sent me after you. You okay?" He wrapped a coat around me and studied me with concern.

"Did he tell you?" I whispered. Nate nodded solemnly.

"It's horrible," he replied softly. He beckoned toward the house with a nod. "But let's go back inside before you freeze to death," he advised, putting his arm around my shoulders and pulling me along with him.

"How's Mom?" I choked, glancing up at him.

"In bed," he replied shortly.

"I think that sounds good to me too," I said, pulling away from Nathan. "See you in the morning."

I went straight to the bathroom and rifled through the medicine cabinet until I found a bottle of Tylenol PM. I popped a couple and went to bed, wishing and hoping for oblivion. I wasn't that lucky, despite the medication. I spent the night tossing and turning, chased by dreams of loss and fear. One in particular disturbed me. I couldn't remember the details after waking up. All that was left was a horrible feeling of abandonment.

The unease of the night followed me to work the next morning, along with a slight hangover from the pill. The thing about taking Tylenol PM is that you have to take it early enough that it wears off before morning. Since it had been almost 11:00 when I finally took it, I was a zombie Wednesday morning. I managed to make the confirmation calls for upcoming appointments, but beyond that it was almost impossible to do more than just stare blankly at my computer screen.

"Quinn!"

I jumped at the sound of my name and whirled around to find Marie, looking impatient. She had obviously called my name more than once. She studied my face a moment. "Are you all right this morning?" she asked with concern. I nodded briefly.

"Fine, I'm sorry. What do you need?" I asked, unwilling to discuss anything other than work.

"There is a new housing development going up in Price and the builders have asked us to do some consulting work for them. Nick will be going down there on Friday and I'm going to send you with him. There will be a lot of paperwork, possibly future appointments to set up, and honestly, I want a woman's opinion of the operation."

I nodded briefly again. "I only have one small concern," I replied. "I am going to need to attend a funeral in the next week or so, but we haven't heard yet what day it will be held. So, if it is on Friday, I won't be able to go."

Marie's brow furrowed with further concern. "Not family, I hope?"

I nodded. "My aunt."

"I'm sorry to hear that." She reached out and squeezed my arm sympathetically.

"Thank you." I was surprised by how stoic and removed my voice sounded. It didn't waver once.

"Well, barring funeral arrangements, we will plan on having you and Nick leave for Price early Friday morning. Do you think you could be here by 7:30?" I nodded, realizing that Annie would have to drop me off that morning.

"And you'll want to dress warm," Marie added as she headed back to her office. "It's cold out there."

The rest of the week was a painful blur. Mom and Dad spent all day Wednesday in Salt Lake with Steven and Grandma making funeral arrangements. The funeral, it was decided, would be held the following Monday in Salt Lake at Lydia and Steven's ward building, which would allow travel time for the out-of-state family. Nate made himself available to drop off and pick up the boys from school while my parents were gone. Ezra and Oliver didn't even seem to notice a difference in the house, other than that everyone was quieter than normal, but they didn't know the circumstances either. Mom decided that it would be best if they were simply told that Aunt Lydia had died. Annie handled it better than I did, but Nate was a bit of a mess. I think that Aunt Lydia's death just compounded his emotions from dealing with Sasha.

Thursday night, after another long day in Salt Lake, Dad headed out to pick up some pizza. The Relief Society brought dinner by the night before, but there was no chance anyone was cooking tonight. At the last second, I decided to go with him, desperate to escape the somber house. I leaned my head against the cold window and let my breath fog it up. I was tempted to write my name in it, wishing all of a sudden to be a little girl again, in a world that wasn't full of scary things like divorce and suicide. I watched the town fly past as we drove, unable to wrench my mind away from Lydia.

"Dad?" I asked slowly, "Did she leave a note? Does anyone know why—" I broke off, unable to finish the thought.

Dad glanced at me briefly. He sighed in resignation. "Lydia had bipolar disorder." His voice was soft. I raised my eyebrows in surprise but kept quiet, waiting for more details. "For the most part," Dad continued, "she kept it fairly well under control. She was on several kinds of medication and saw a psychotherapist regularly. Steven told us that the doctors changed her medication regimen recently. There was a new drug available and it was supposed to be more effective, but one of the possible side effects was a suicidal tendency. They didn't catch it quickly enough."

"Oh," I said slowly, processing this information. "So it was the medication? That made her do it?"

Dad shook his head slowly. "Not entirely. She was going through a depressive episode and that, coupled with this new medicine, exacerbated it all."

We pulled into Papa John's parking lot. Rather than getting out of the car, I turned to Dad. "Why didn't I know this already? Why didn't anyone say anything? Why didn't you ever tell me?"

Dad gazed out the windshield. "Well, it's not really something that you tell little kids," he began.

"I'm twenty-one, Dad, not exactly a little kid," I scoffed.

"True," he agreed reluctantly. He pulled the keys out of the ignition and turned them over in his hands. "It's mostly that your mother doesn't like to talk about it."

"Wow," I replied sarcastically. "Mom doesn't like to talk about anything, does she? First Nathan and now this? Is there anything else I need to know?"

Dad offered an apologetic shrug. "Not stuff like this, no." He pushed his door open. "C'mon. The boys will be starving by now."

"Yeah," I agreed, pulling myself out of the car and shaking off the feeling of vague distaste for my mother.

7

When Annie dropped me off in front of the office, Nick's car was already parked, but he wasn't in it. I grabbed my purse and pushed open the car door, glancing back at Annie as I swung my legs out. "I'll text you when we're on our way back. It'll probably be around five," she nodded as I stood and slammed the door.

She had been less than thrilled about getting up early to drop me off. I just considered it payback for the months of crawling out of bed to drive her to school. She sped off with a little wave and I headed inside. I had taken Marie's advice and worn long underwear beneath my slacks, plus my heaviest coat. I pushed the door open and stepped inside.

"Nick?" Most of the lights were still off, but I could see a sliver of light streaming under the door of Nick's office. I knocked softly on his door, and pushed it a little further open. He glanced up from his desk with a smile.

"Hey, just finishing up some stuff. I've just got to send this email and then we'll go." He pointed to a chair. "Sit for a minute." I dropped my purse next to the chair and leaned back, stretching out my legs in front of me.

"I realize that I'm only thirty minutes earlier than usual, but it feels more like an hour or two," I commented, watching him type. "It was very difficult to get out of bed this morning." A quick smile crossed his face.

"I know how you feel," he replied. "Done." He stood up and flipped off the monitor. "Let's go."

Both of us were quiet as we drove out of Springville. I gazed out the window, studying the landscape. There was hardly any snow left from the storm a few weeks ago, just dirty patches here and there. It was cold, but it hadn't snowed since then. As we pulled into the canyon, Nick made a couple of unsuccessful conversation attempts: the weather, "coldest November in a long time"; the business, "interest rates keep going up and it's going to kill us"; and then fell back into silence. We had been on the road at least half an hour when he tried again.

"Hey, are you okay?" he asked. I glanced over at him. His focus was on the road, but he kept shooting concerned looks my way. I nodded.

"I'm fine," I replied quickly. "Just tired." I shifted my focus back out of the window again. I still felt a little detached from the rest of the world. It seemed like somehow my family's tragedy had separated us from everyone else. The shock and the grief were still too raw to feel much of anything else.

"You sure?" he asked again. I turned back toward him, and for a moment I was struck with how strange it was to be alone in a car with Elder Nicholas Ryan. If you had told me a year ago that I would get a job that required me to spend copious amounts of time alone with him, I would have laughed in your face. And to look at him, he really hadn't changed since the first time I saw him in Florida. His chestnut hair was a little bit longer, his face not quite as meticulously shaven, but he hadn't changed at all. Except for the fact that he had become an entirely different person. He glanced away from the road again and his deep brown eyes found mine. I relented.

"My aunt died this week." I felt like I had been talking about it all week, but somehow, I hadn't really said anything. It had all been about the funeral, the viewing, my cousins, Steven, the details. But never really about what had actually happened.

"I'm sorry," he replied sincerely, obviously waiting for me to continue.

"The funeral will be Monday. In Salt Lake, where she lived."

"You were close?"

I nodded and began telling him everything. About Lydia, how beautiful and wonderful she was. I told him how she could light up a room with her smile. I told him about the time we went waterskiing and she fell off the boat. And then I told him about the night that we got the phone call. About the last horrible week. About her family. "She has kids!" I exclaimed, my voice rising in anger. "How selfish of her to just leave them like that! How could she just leave them like that?" I clapped my hand over my mouth, and I realized for the first time that I was angry with her. "I can't even imagine what they must be feeling, how horrible it must be." The thought closed my throat and I fell silent.

"It is," Nick offered quietly a few moments later. I turned to look at him, confused. And then it dawned on me.

"Did you, I mean your mom, she . . . ?" I trailed off, unable to finish the sentence, suddenly incredibly embarrassed. Nick shook his head almost imperceptibly.

"She didn't kill herself. She just left." His voice was tight.

"Oh," I breathed. "I'm sorry, I didn't mean—"

"You didn't know," he cut me off. We were both silent for a few minutes. "I was ten," he offered, startling me. "She was gone when I got home from school that day. It was the worst day of my life. To be abandoned," he shook his head, "I can't imagine anything worse." His voice was hoarse.

"What did you do?" I whispered, almost not wanting to know.

"My dad was devastated, but he wasn't that surprised. They always fought, but her just disappearing like that," he shook his head, "It was awful. I have a brother and a sister.

Blake was eight and Hannah was six when she left. Hannah hardly remembers her at all."

"Nick, I'm so sorry," I offered. He shrugged.

"It was a long time ago. Hannah's eighteen now. She'll graduate in the spring. She's a dancer," he smiled softly at the thought. "She's incredible."

"And Blake?" I prodded gently.

The smile immediately fell off of Nick's face. "Blake's twenty. He never handled it well." Nick paused briefly. "I shouldn't say that. None of us handled it well. But he never got over it. My dad had to kick him out of the house. It was while I was gone." Nick's sentences were short and choppy.

I almost didn't dare ask, but I couldn't help myself. "Why?"

"Drugs," Nick replied shortly. "He came home completely trashed almost daily and when he ran out of money, he started stealing stuff from my dad to sell. So my dad kicked him out. That was after I left. Nobody saw or heard from him for six months. I was in Winter Park when I got a letter from Hannah. He turned up outside of her school and told her he was starving. He was living on the street. She said he looked awful. She gave him all the cash she had on her, and then went home and begged my dad to take him back. He refused. So then I wrote to my dad and asked him to let Blake come home. Dad was furious. And obviously he said no. So I started sending money to Hannah in case she saw him again. She did. As soon as he realized that he could get money off her that easily, she saw him all the time." I could hear the bitterness lacing his words. He continued. "I sent him money every month for close to a year."

I interrupted. "Wait, where did you get the money to send him?" I asked. "We could barely live on our mission budget."

Nick shrugged. "I ate peanut butter sandwiches for almost a year."

"That's it?" I asked, shocked. I remembered how starving I had been every day after walking all over Orlando. "That's really all you ate?"

"Unless a member fed us." He glanced at me with a wry smile. "But hey, I lost like thirty pounds. So, you know. There's a diet for you."

I just shook my head in disbelief. "So, what happened? To Blake?"

Nick's hands tightened on the steering wheel. "My dad found out that I was sending all of my money to Blake. He wrote me a horrible letter and told me that if I sent Blake another dollar, that he would stop paying for my mission altogether. So, I stopped. I hated it, but I didn't have much of a choice. When Blake realized the handouts were gone, he disappeared again. Hannah waited for him to show up for weeks and he never did. We didn't hear from him again until after I was home. And that was only because I went out looking for him."

"You found him?"

Nick nodded. "Under a bridge," He replied in disgust. "It took a couple of months. After I got the job working for Marie, I found a cheap studio apartment for him. I pay the rent, so it's always on time and everything, but the landlord realized that Blake was using, and possibly dealing, and he wants him out. Jim's been pretty lenient with me, but Blake's gotten worse in the last few months." Nick sighed angrily. "He doesn't need another apartment though. He needs rehab."

"Jim?" I asked. "Did he—"

"Come into the office a couple of months ago? Yeah. I had been dodging his calls for a while."

I stared out the front window. The car was silent for a long time. I played with my CTR ring, twisting it around and around my finger, a nervous habit I had developed in Florida. I could feel Nick's eyes on me periodically.

"I'm sorry, I shouldn't have told you all that. You didn't need to listen to me whine."

I turned my gaze on him. "That wasn't whining, Nick. And I don't mind. I'm . . ." I paused looking for the right word. "I'm processing. Honestly, I feel like I have aged about twenty years in the last month and it's catching up to me."

His face betrayed his confusion.

"You know," I continued, "you would think that the mission would have opened my eyes. Really. I saw so many things, poverty and abuse and crime, but it always seemed like once an investigator accepted the gospel, the darkness would recede. It didn't make their lives easier necessarily, but they changed. And I always thought that's kind of how it worked. We have the gospel, we have testimonies, we go to church. So nothing like this should touch us."

I laughed mirthlessly at myself and stared out the window. "I grew up with that. Every Sunday in Primary they tell you that if you do what you're supposed to, Heavenly Father will protect you. Keep you safe as long as you follow the commandments. I held on pretty tightly to that. I mean, you know, stuff would happen, but stupid stuff. Boyfriends broke up with me, I fought with my mom, it's just—" I shrugged. "It happens all the time here, and to people who are totally faithful. Look at Lydia. She was always faithful and strong and she had this disease that would make her do such a terrible thing. Why do they make you think that everything is going to be okay, when obviously, everything is not okay?" My voice caught in my throat and I shook my head quickly trying to shake off the emotion.

"I feel so stupid," I muttered, mostly to myself, a little embarrassed about my outburst.

"Quinn," Nick protested, "don't feel stupid. It's a lot to deal with. Have—" he paused and glanced at me. "Have you ever lost anyone close to you like this before?"

I shook my head. "My dad's parents both died when I was really young. Too young to totally understand what was going on."

"My grandpa died right before my mission," Nick explained. "I mean, it was different, because he was older and sick. At the very least, we had time to prepare, but it was still hard."

I took a deep breath. "It's awful. And for me, it's just death. For her kids, it's death and abandonment."

"I can relate."

I turned to him thoughtfully. I had not expected this when I got up this morning. I would have never guessed Nick's history. But then, I never would have given Elder Nick Ryan a second thought if not for this job. "How does a ten-year-old survive that?" I asked softly.

Nick was quiet for a few minutes. "Luck. Good timing." He shrugged. "Miracles."

I smiled hopefully. "Miracles?"

His brow furrowed. "Angels." He laughed awkwardly. "I know. As cheesy as it gets." My smile grew as I waited for him to elaborate. He didn't disappoint. "First, it was my Cub Scout leader, and then my deacons adviser. I'd probably be huddled under that bridge with Blake without them."

"What did they do?"

"They were always checking up on me, on my case. Didn't let me miss a Sunday or an activity. Blake and Hannah too. Dad stopped going to church after Mom left. Someone came to get us every Sunday until I could drive. We all went to church every week, until Blake was about fourteen and then he decided he didn't need it anymore and he stayed home. I kept taking Hannah, though."

We pulled off the freeway and I realized that we had arrived in Price. I gazed out the window, watching what could barely be called a town fly by. I was a little disappointed at how quickly the drive had gone as we pulled into a muddy parking lot. Nick turned off the engine and turned to me.

"Too much?" he asked, an anticipatory grimace on his face.

"Too much what?" I asked as I reached for the handle.

"Information." Nick clicked open his seatbelt and it slid noisily back into place.

"No, not at all," I offered a reassuring smile before climbing out of the car. For the first time all week I had been able to take my mind off of Lydia.

I was surprised to find that Nick and I spent the rest of the day together. I thought I would be stuck in an office organizing paperwork all day while he was off with the builders and the contractors, but everywhere he went, he insisted that I come with him. I learned more about foundations and contracts than I ever wanted to know, but I was so grateful that I wasn't condemned to a drafty trailer office all day long.

At lunchtime, we found an old-fashioned diner on Main Street with greasy hamburgers and spectacular fries. Nick's burger was almost twice as large as mine, so he didn't seem to mind when I finished my fries and began stealing his.

"You know the only thing that can make fries this good even better?" I asked, snatching another fry that was hanging off the edge of his plate.

"Fry sauce?" he ventured, checking his tie for spots of ketchup.

"Fry sauce," I agreed vehemently. "Why are there no fries like this in Springville?"

"You been to Art City Trolley?" Nick asked, sampling a fry of his own.

"Yeah, but these are definitely better. Although," I added, glancing around the diner, "I do have to give Art City the nod for better décor."

The walls were lined with black-and-white photographs, chronicling the history of Price. Most were so old that the subjects were obscured almost to the point of abstraction. It wasn't the photographs that had captured my attention, however. It was the wallpaper behind them. I had never seen wallpaper quite like it. It had to be as old as the café itself, featuring cowboys and Indians. I thought it was odd but quaint at first, until closer inspection revealed that the scenes portrayed were not innocent interactions, but rather graphically violent images of cowboys being scalped and Indians being shot down. As I realized what I was seeing, my eyes widened in disbelief.

"Have you really looked at the walls?" I asked, fighting off the laughter rising in my throat. Nick shook his head.

"Most places like this, I find it better to focus on the food rather than wonder how long it's been since those walls were wiped down."

I giggled. "I really think it's worth a look."

Nick glanced over at the wall briefly and then back to me without full comprehension. "What—" he paused. "Wait." He looked back over and studied the wallpaper more intently. I laughed as his eyes got bigger. He turned back to me. "How old do you think that stuff is?"

"No idea," I laughed, "but I think the walls are rated R."

Nick laughed aloud and looked back. "Nah, I'm pretty sure they're only PG-13. But they are the very definition of politically incorrect."

The remainder of lunch hour was spent analyzing the scenes portrayed and laughing hysterically. After the bill was paid, we gathered our things and left. As we walked to the car, Nick told me about Hannah's last dance performance and I told him about Annie's last embarrassing date, when she had accidentally punched an old lady in the face.

"How do you accidentally punch anyone, let alone an old lady, in the face?" Nick asked laughing.

"Leave it to Annie, she'll find a way," I joked. I shivered as we neared the car, grateful for Marie's warning about the extra layers. Nick noticed and put his arm around me, rubbing my arm briskly, trying to warm me up.

"I'm glad I don't live here," I murmured as Nick unlocked the car door. Nick just smiled as I sat down, and he closed the door behind me.

We left Price a little before 5:00 that evening. "I hope that we got everything done that Marie wanted us to do," Nick muttered to himself as we drove out of town.

I laughed softly and shivered obviously again. "If we didn't, I vote that we don't come back at least until spring."

A smile spread across Nick's face. "You really haven't gotten used to the cold yet, have you?"

"I don't know that I ever will," I laughed ironically. "Going to Florida was like going home. I would be perfectly happy to come visit Utah for a week every winter, get my white Christmas, and then go back to where the lows are only ever in the 50s. And honestly, I think I was just made for the beach."

Nick agreed. "Although, I think I would miss the snow."

"Maybe," I sighed, turning my attention out the window. "But only at Christmas." Nick asked about one of the areas on my mission, sparking a long conversation about Florida that lasted the entire way home. By the time that Spanish Fork came into view, I had learned more about him than ever.

Nick glanced at me as he changed lanes. "Hey, so you want to get dinner before we head home?"

I turned my attention outside the car and realized that we were quickly coming up on the Springville exit. I glanced at the clock. 5:45 and I didn't have anywhere to be tonight.

"Yeah. I'd like that," I replied with a smile.

"Great." Nick pulled up to a little Mexican restaurant known for its amazing salsa. The tiny lobby was painted in bright colors and smelled of chilies and fresh tortillas. We were seated right away at a little table next to one of the few windows. The moon, beginning to rise above the mountains, was brilliant in the cold, clear night sky. Once seated, we continued our conversation, which winded its way from the mission all the way back to our childhoods. Nick told me about taking over the household responsibilities after his mom left, about the relationship that he had developed with his siblings, and about his disastrous first attempts at making dinner.

"It was so disgusting. I didn't know what I was doing. The spaghetti came out in one giant lump and I totally burned the sauce."

"Did they eat it?" I asked with a laugh.

"Nope," Nick laughed at the memory. "We had cereal that night." I smiled and watched as he stirred his drink with a straw. He glanced up at me and smiled back, catching me stare. "I got better. I make a killer spaghetti now."

"And a mean peanut butter sandwich," I joked.

"Absolutely," he agreed.

"So, why were you the one cooking?" I asked slowly.

Nick paused a moment, his eyes focused out the window as he considered what to say. "Dad kind of shut down after she left," he explained as he selected a chip from the basket on the table. He concentrated on heaping a generous amount of salsa onto it. "He went to work, he paid the bills, but otherwise it was all on the three of us, really. He was at work all day and when he came home the TV went on and that was it. I helped Hannah with her homework; we cleaned the house and did the laundry. I read to her every night." A nostalgic smile flitted across his face. "She wanted all princess books, but I hated them, so she was introduced to Harry Potter and Percy Jackson at an early age." He popped the chip into his mouth.

I played with my straw and studied him. "How did you end up on a mission?" I asked, hoping I wasn't overstepping my bounds.

"My Young Men president." Nick paused thoughtfully. "He made me part of his family," he said simply. "I spent more time at his house my senior year of high school than I did at home. He was—he is a great guy." A smile spread across Nick's face. "Week after I got home? He asked me to stand in the circle while he blessed his new baby. He's family." He paused. "They're family."

Nick leaned away from the table as the rest of our dinner arrived. The waitress set down two heaping plates of beans and rice in front of us. Despite the gigantic cheeseburger I had eaten for lunch, I was starving and everything smelled fantastic. After a few heavenly bites of enchilada, I took a sip of my Diet Coke and studied Nick. His hair had long since lost its neatly gelled look of the morning, and the once neatly arranged curls had become unruly. He had ditched his tie before leaving the car, and the sleeves of his dress shirt were rolled to his elbows. I noticed for the first time how strong his hands were. He glanced up from his plate and caught me staring again. I flashed him a small, flustered smile and turned back to my own food. A few more minutes of slightly awkward silence followed before he spoke up again.

"So, if you don't mind me asking, I remember hearing something about a certain someone waiting around until you got home. Or was that just a rumor?" He smiled as he asked, but his voice was a little unsure, almost nervous.

"Yeah, I mean no," I stuttered. I sighed in frustration and Nick laughed. I tried again. "There was someone waiting. There isn't now."

"Can I ask what happened?" he asked slowly, keeping his eyes on his plate.

I laughed wryly. "What always happens, Nick."

"Dear John? Actually, I guess I should say Dear Jane." He laughed.

"Did you ever get one?" I couldn't help asking.

Nick shook his head. "She preemptively dumped me." There was no bitterness in his voice.

"I'm sorry," I replied.

Nick shrugged. "I had a companion get Dear Johned about three months before he went home." He made a face at me. "He was a mess. I think I prefer my way. I should probably thank her, actually." I wrinkled my nose at him. "No?" he asked, his eyes twinkling. I shook my head quickly, and he changed the subject. "Tell me this: was it at least a good breakup letter?"

I laughed. "Is there such a thing?"

Nick nodded. "I had the—well, I was going to say privilege, but I don't think that's the right word. A few of my companions showed me their letters and I was the judge of more than one 'worst Dear John' competition between a few elders. Some of them were awful. Some of them were actually kind of sweet. My favorites were the ones when they tried to slide in the news at an unexpected moment, like they were hoping no one would notice."

"I'm going to have to put mine in the tactless, abrupt, and a little bit heartbreaking categories." It had been almost six months, but I still had to watch the bitterness in my tone.

He studied my face. "I'm sorry. That really sucks."

I shrugged. "It did. Not as much anymore."

A smile tugged at the corners of his mouth. "I'm sure you're too good for him anyway."

I smiled back, returning to my enchiladas to hide my flushed face. We finished our dinners, still chatting long after our plates had been cleared. At a lull, Nick glanced at his watch, and started.

"We better go," he said, standing as he pulled on his coat. "It's almost nine."

"You're kidding," I laughed, pulling out my phone in disbelief. 8:51. I couldn't believe it. We had spent more than two hours just talking. I gave Nick directions to my parents' house and he pulled up to the curb. There was a car in the driveway that I didn't recognize. One of Annie's friends, I thought to myself. I pushed the car door open and turned to say good-bye.

"See you Monday?" he asked.

I wrinkled my nose at him. "Tuesday," I replied. "Funeral." I sighed. I wasn't at all looking forward to it.

"Right," he nodded, his voice a little kinder. I swung my legs out of the car but stopped when I felt Nick's hand on my arm. I turned back to him and he gazed at me seriously. "Call me if you need anything, Quinn. I mean it. Anything."

I could feel the shadow of a smile appear on my face. "Thanks, Nick." He let his hand fall away from my arm. I pulled myself out of the car and glanced back to him on a whim. "Same goes for you. You can call me. If, you know, you need to talk or anything," I blundered.

Nick smiled and I thought again what an amazing smile he had. "Thanks, Quinn." I closed the door and gave one last quick wave, then hurried to the front door, shivering slightly in the sudden cold.

I watched as he drove off, feeling, well, happy for the first time in what seemed like forever. I took a deep breath and turned to go inside, bracing myself for the mournful atmosphere. I pushed open the front door and jumped. There, sitting on the living room couch was Joshua. Alone.

Josh stood up when he saw me. My breath caught in my chest at the sight of him. It had been so long that I had forgotten, or maybe repressed, how attractive he was. He wore his hair longer than he had when I left for Florida, and it was a much darker shade of gold, the color of winter. He wore a fitted sweater and amazing jeans. I forced myself to remember that horrible email and the misery he had put me through. As the bitterness and pain coursed through me, I narrowed my eyes at him.

"What are you doing here, Josh?" I snapped, setting down my purse and turning to hang my coat in the closet. I could feel my heart pounding and I tried unsuccessfully to quiet my breathing.

"Quinn," he said softly. "I'm so, so sorry." I turned back to look at him, biting my cheeks to keep from crying, or screaming, or kissing him. "Quinn, I made a horrible mistake. I was stupid and selfish and . . ." He trailed off and looked at me helplessly. He shoved his hands in his pockets and pulled them back out again, obviously unsettled.

"Shallow and faithless and tactless and mean and horrible and . . . and . . ." I glared at him, unable to come up with a word awful enough to describe him. The last six months of anathemas seemed to have deserted me.

"All of those things," he agreed contritely. "More." He took a step toward me and I tensed. "I ended things with Jenny," he said slowly, carefully watching my reaction. I narrowed my eyes at him further, waiting for the other shoe to drop.

"I'm sorry," I replied hesitantly, wondering what would come next.

"I was hoping that maybe, well, you might be willing to give it another shot," he stuttered. "With me." I couldn't remember ever seeing Josh this nervous. He shifted his weight back and forth from one foot to another.

"You want to get back together?" I asked suspiciously, trying to comprehend what I was hearing. "Are you serious?" Josh nodded.

"I missed you," he breathed. "I—I miss you."

I bit my lip and studied him, deciding how to respond. Part of me wanted to fall right back into his arms, do just exactly what he wanted me to do, but the weeks of disappointment, and oddly, the day I had just spent with Nick held me back. “I can’t do this right now, Joshua. I’m not dealing with this today.” I pulled the front door open again, waiting for him to take the hint. He wasn’t quick enough. “You need to go.”

“Annie told me about your aunt,” he said softly, approaching me slowly. “I’m so sorry.”

The long day, the emotional week, and the shock of his sudden reappearance were taking its toll and I bit back a sob. “I can’t, Josh, not tonight.” I took a breath, willing my voice to remain steady. “Please, please go.”

Josh moved toward the door. “Don’t think I’m going to give you up so easily,” he said softly. “I need you to know that you are worth all the time that it takes.” He leaned forward before I could move and kissed my forehead gently, leaving me standing there, swaying on the spot.

9

It could have been the emotional upheaval of the week or simply the desire to have even a small break from the constant melancholy of my family, but on a whim I decided to try out the singles ward for the first time that Sunday. To be perfectly honest, I had never had much interest in attending the singles ward in general. After I graduated from high school, I stayed in my home ward for one major reason: Josh. He never went to the singles ward after his mission. He would, however, sit next to Olivia and me during Sunday School, and as our relationship developed, it was simply one more excuse to spend time with him. After I returned from my mission, I stayed in my home ward over the many vigorous protests of my mother. Josh was never there (I had researched that before my first Sunday), I knew everyone and was comfortable with them, and I was still licking my wounds.

Today would really be my first real venture into the singles ward world, and my nerves manifested themselves in how long I spent in front of the mirror before deeming my appearance acceptable and wondering how many of the horror stories were true.

The family ward began at 9:00, while the singles ward started at 11:00, so I had a good two hours to get ready in complete solitude, with no arguing over who got to shower first, scrambling for a prime spot with a mirror to do my makeup, or suffering the consequences of Annie's ridiculously long shower. And after the fourth wardrobe change, I was grateful for the absence of Nate's heckling. As I added the last few curls to my hair, I couldn't help but think that it might be worth it to go to the singles ward from here on out, just to have the bathroom all to myself every Sunday morning.

I slid shyly into an empty spot on the end of a pew near the back of the chapel, just as one of the counselors stood up to make the opening announcements. I scanned the room, searching for familiar faces. The boundaries of this ward matched the boundaries of my high school, and I would be shocked if this ward was made up entirely of strangers. What I didn't expect, however, was to see Nick Ryan in the congregation. Sitting right across the aisle from me, staring at me with raised eyebrows and a surprised smile on his face. I hadn't noticed him when I sat down. I smiled back and offered a little shrug, trying to say that I was just as surprised as he was. Our silent exchange was cut short by the opening prayer.

I spent the rest of the meeting self-consciously aware of Nick's occasional glances in my direction and regretting outfit number five, wishing instead for my pink sweater and suede boots. I determinedly kept my own gaze on the pulpit, with only the occasional glance, out of the corner of my eye, in Nick's direction. The first speaker, a tall, blonde young woman, did a great job, quoting from a recent conference address and making some insightful observations. She was obviously comfortable speaking in front of people, something I greatly admired, and I made a mental note to introduce myself after sacrament meeting.

The second speaker, a slightly heavier, bespectacled young man, however, was not quite as inspiring. He began by announcing that the Spirit had admonished him that his original talk was not what this congregation needed to hear this morning, so instead, he would be speaking from the heart led only by heavenly guidance. I had a hard time suppressing a groan. The following talk was a mixture of false doctrine and uncomfortably personal experiences concerning excommunication, pornography, and medical problems that probably shouldn't have been shared with anyone, let alone the entire congregation of the singles ward. By the end of the meeting, my face hurt from gritting my teeth in sympathetic embarrassment through the entire thing. I was seriously reconsidering my idea to permanently transition from the family ward by the end of it. There was an audible sigh of relief that swept through the chapel as speaker number two sat down and I couldn't stop myself from glancing over at Nick with a grimace. He coughed lightly to cover his laughter, causing heads to turn in his direction, and with a smile, I turned back to the pulpit.

Following the closing prayer, I found him standing next to my pew, smiling. "I didn't know that you were in this ward," he commented as he watched me gather my coat and get to my feet. His bright orange tie stood out vividly against his blue shirt. I brushed the wrinkles from my lap and stood to face him.

"Well, technically this is my first Sunday here, but it also may be my last," I replied, my eyes wandering to the stand where the unfortunate second speaker was shaking hands with the bishop. Even from the back of the chapel I could see the forced smile on the bishop's face. "Is that, um, common?" I jerked my head in their direction.

"I wouldn't say common," Nick replied through his laughter, his eyes following my gaze. "Just, you know, on special occasions." He laughed again. "It does take some getting used to. C'mon, I'll walk you to Sunday School," he paused and cocked an eyebrow, "Unless there's an oversized boyfriend lurking in the shadows to pummel me if I do?" He took an exaggerated step backwards, a comical look on his face.

I laughed and glanced surreptitiously around the chapel. "Does that happen to you a lot?" I asked.

"Only once." His face took on a look of mock severity.

"You're safe," I reassured him.

He offered me his arm and I slid mine through his. We made our way down the hall to the gym, where rows and rows of rapidly filling chairs awaited. I kept my eyes on the sea of faces, but no familiar ones jumped out at me. We got settled near the back and a thought occurred to me. "So, is there a maniacally jealous girlfriend I need to be worried about?" I asked.

"Does that happen to you often?"

"Only once," I replied, biting my lip to keep from smiling. "Maybe I should ask if sitting next to the new girl will ruin your chances with the rest of the girls?"

"In this ward?" he laughed. "I thank you for your service."

"Ohh," I replied, cuffing his shoulder and suppressing a giggle, "That's terrible."

"You're the one who asked," he shrugged lightly.

"I should go sit over there," I teased, pointing to an empty row across the room. "Make you pay for that one."

"Not if I can help it," he retorted, sliding his arm around my shoulders firmly, holding me in place. I laughed and elbowed him lightly in the side.

"Hey!" he yelped softly, leaning away from me. I just flashed him my most innocent smile and turned my attention to the front of the cultural hall, where the Gospel Doctrine teacher was getting his visual aids set up. It was clear that we were in for quite the multimedia event.

"You sound better today," he murmured softly as the Sunday School president stood up to welcome the class. I turned and gave him a sad sort of smile.

"It comes and goes," I shrugged. My chest rose with a deep breath. "I'm sure it'll be worse again tomorrow." Thinking of the funeral made my head hurt and I pushed the thought away.

"Probably," he agreed. He squeezed my shoulder gently, and I realized that his arm was still resting on the back of my chair. I opened my mouth to point it out and promptly closed it again as the teacher opened the lesson.

Sunday School had always been a problem for me. I tried really hard to focus, and I even thought about participating, but to no avail. As the lesson went on, a discussion that paralleled the story of the Rameumptom to our modern lives, I scanned the gym, studying the other members of the ward. Finally, a few familiar faces began to stand out: a couple of girls from high school, a guy a couple of years older than me that I knew from stake dances. But for the most part, I really didn't know anyone.

A lot of high school friends were already married, and even more had gone to school out of state. As I studied faces I noticed a few acidic glances in my direction, particularly potent ones from one platinum blonde in particular. For a few minutes, I wondered if maybe I knew her from somewhere, until Nick raised his hand and made an eloquent comment about padding our egos with the failures of others. I leaned toward Nick and asked in a low voice, "If you're so unimpressed with this ward, why do you keep coming?"

"Habit," he replied softly with a shrug. "Hannah has her Sunday 'family' she sits with and Dad doesn't go to church. So I come here."

I nodded and glanced back at the still unfamiliar blonde to find her eyes still on me. Or rather, darting between Nick and me. I realized that it was my first Sunday in this ward, and I was looking fairly cozy with one of the better-looking, still available guys in the ward.

As the closing prayer was said, I groaned inwardly at the thought of heading off to Relief Society with no allies and contemplated just skipping out on the whole thing.

"So," I asked reluctantly as the class began to get to their feet, "feel like pointing me in the direction of the Relief Society room?"

"Sure," replied Nick. "I'll walk you there." He pulled his arm out from behind me and offered me a hand. I took it and stood, once again glancing around the gym a little insecurely. I followed Nick across the gym and out the side door. Nick stopped me just before we arrived in the doorway of the Relief Society room. "Hey," he said, resting his hand lightly on my arm. "I meant what I said the other day. You need anything, tomorrow or whenever, you just call me, okay?" His brow furrowed in concern as his brown eyes focused on mine.

I gave him a quick smile. "I will. Thanks, Nick." I stood there awkwardly a moment longer, not sure if I should duck into the room or keep talking. He solved the problem, giving my arm a quick squeeze and leaving for priesthood with a little wave. I watched him go and turned back to the Relief Society room. I took a deep breath, squared my shoulders, and plunged in.

I scanned the Relief Society room quickly, looking for a friendly face to join. I spotted the opening speaker near the back, an open seat next to her. Deciding that now was just as good a time as any to introduce myself, I headed her way.

"Is this seat taken?" I asked quietly. I felt a little stupid and wished that I had just sat down.

She glanced up at me and smiled. "All yours," she replied with a little wave of her hand.

"Thanks," I sat down. "I'm Quinn."

"Kristen," she replied. "You here with your boyfriend?" She nodded to the door where Nick had left me.

"No," I replied. "No, no, no, no, no. No." Kristen began laughing at about the third no. "I work with him. Had no idea he was in this ward until I showed up this morning. Just relying on him for directions."

"I know several girls who will be happy to hear that."

I cocked my head in curiosity. "Really? Do you know Nick?"

Kristen shook her head. "He's been to a couple of family home evening group things, but that's about it. He kind of keeps to himself." She paused a moment, "So then, are you new?"

"Maybe," I smiled. "Test run."

"Wise," she nodded. "Opinion so far?" She narrowed her eyes in mock concentration.

"I'm on the fence," I answered slowly.

Kristen laughed. "Derek's talk have anything to do with that?" she asked shrewdly.

"Little bit." I smiled. "But yours was great."

She smiled. "Thanks!"

The Relief Society president had to practically yell to quell the chatter but finally got the meeting started. By the end of it Kristen and I had gotten to know each other well enough for her to invite me to her family home evening group the next night.

"I would love to actually, but I have a funeral tomorrow that might just kill me." I cringed. "Forgive the pun."

Kristen laughed. "Give me your phone and I'll put my number in. If you're still alive tomorrow night, you can text me and I'll give you details."

"Thanks!" I handed her my phone. Maybe the singles ward wouldn't be so bad after all.

"So, how was it?" Annie asked later that evening over her plate of French toast, Dad's specialty. Mom had gone to bed soon after they got home from church and it quickly became evident that she was not planning to reappear tonight. Dad and Nate had put together dinner—French toast, bacon, and hash browns, but I wasn't complaining.

"Not awful," I replied, scooping a pile of hash browns onto my fork. "Nick was there, so at least I knew someone. And I met this girl, Kristen, and she seems pretty cool."

"I thought you didn't like Nick," Dad asked around a mouthful of bacon.

"He's grown on me," I replied with a shrug.

"So it sounds like the singles ward was worth your while then," Dad continued.

"For the most part," I admitted. "Although it seems that heretical talks and deep, dark secrets are common during sacrament."

Nate laughed. "Welcome to the singles ward."

10

Lydia's funeral was at 11:00 a.m. Monday morning. We were up and out the door by 8:30, planning on being at the church for the short viewing before the services began. The morning was pale, the sun barely breaking through the thick layer of clouds. I couldn't help but think it appropriate as I opened the passenger door to get into Nate's car. As I turned to slide in, I happened to glance at the Civic that Annie and I shared. There was a note tucked under the windshield wiper. I closed the door again and strode across the driveway to grab it. As I got closer, I realized there was also a single lavender rose lying in the gutter under the windshield. I picked it up and plucked the note, a small white envelope with my name on it, out from under the wipers and held them up for Nate to see.

"Open it on the way, we have to go," he called impatiently. I nodded and headed back to his car, twirling the rose through my fingers curiously. I set it carefully on the console and slid a finger under the flap. A sympathy card fell out, adorned with a few lilacs.

"Who's it from?" Nate asked, as I flipped it open.

"You just worry about driving," I chided, pointing to the road where his focus should have been.

Inside, in small, scribbled handwriting, it said,

Quinn,
Just wanted you to know I'm thinking of you. I am so sorry for your loss. I know this card is kind of a cheesy way to say it, but let me know if you need anything. I mean it.
Nick

"It's from Nick," I said, smiling softly. I flipped the card over looking for more. I don't know what I was expecting, but it was unsurprisingly blank.

"From your office?" Nate asked, eyebrows raised.

"Yeah," I nodded.

"I thought he was a jerk? Jerks don't generally leave cards and roses on people's cars," Nate replied ironically.

"No, he's not a jerk," I murmured, picking the rose up from the dash. I was quiet the remainder of the drive to Salt Lake.

Nate sat next to me in the chapel as we listened to Lydia's daughter, Lizzie, struggle through "Be Still My Soul." I felt Nate's hand cover mine and squeeze. I flashed him a watery smile and leaned my head against his shoulder. The viewing had gone well, but it was strange to see Lydia like that. I had a hard time looking at her and I wasn't the only one. Ezra and Oliver had avoided the coffin altogether.

The chapel was warm and full of people, with folding chairs set up all the way back into the gym. The stand was decked out with gorgeous flower arrangements; friends had been generous. The planters were beautiful, but I hated the wreaths with the banner strung across the middle, "Mother" and "Aunt" displayed in glittered and fancy lettering. They just made the place look depressing.

As I watched Lizzie try to keep her voice under control, the tears streaming down her face, I couldn't help but think of Nick. Surviving something like this at ten. True, his mother hadn't died, but it must have felt almost the same. It was sad and horrible and amazing that he came through it as well as he did, and I silently prayed that Lizzie and Aaron and Jace would be as resilient. My eyes fell on Aaron, sitting on the stand. He had been given permission to come home from his mission in Canada, and there was no word yet as to when he would head back out. He looked like a missionary, with a tidy haircut and a worn suit and tie. He was only missing the name tag. Jace sat in the congregation with his dad. Neither would be speaking today. As Lizzie finished and returned to her seat, Nate leaned over to whisper in my ear.

"Do you think they'll be okay?"

I shrugged gently. "I hope so. I can't even imagine . . ." I trailed off and glanced down the row at Mom. She sat in a stunned sort of silence, her eyes dry and her face white. Dad had her hand tightly gripped in his. Next to her sat Annie, and my eyes welled just thinking about what it must be like to lose a sister. I reached across Ezra to take her hand in mine. She smiled briefly at me and then we both turned our attention to Aaron, who had stood to give his mother's eulogy.

"Lydia Ann Carson Smith was born June 30, 1970, in Ogden, Utah. Lydia—Mom," he amended, his voice cracking, "had two sisters and one brother. She was raised a member of The Church of Jesus Christ of Latter-day Saints and served in numerous callings throughout her life. She particularly loved serving in the Primary. She married Steven Smith on October 6, 1991, in the Logan Utah Temple and together they have three children, Aaron, Elizabeth, and Jace Smith." Aaron paused in his recitation to regain control of his voice. My throat tightened as I watched him fight back the tears and my own eyes overflowed at the pain of it all. My pain, Mom's pain, Aaron's pain, Lizzie's pain, the weight of them all pressed heavier and heavier on my weary chest, forcing me to take deep, cleansing breaths of air. I reached into my purse for some kind of tissue and cried silently for the remainder of Aaron's words.

The rest of the service was appropriately beautiful. Once I regained control, I heard stories about Lydia that I had never heard before. About the time that she had accidentally tripped one of the Apostles. About the time that she left Aaron at a gas station between here and Vegas. About the day that Aaron left on his mission to Vancouver. A lot of the stories were humorous, but a few used up the supply of tissue in my purse. The graveside service was even worse. The morning was cold and clear with a sharp breeze. A thin layer of snow covered the ground around the green mats laid down by the funeral home to protect the mourners from the mud. My grandfather dedicated the grave, offering a prayer of comfort on the family.

After the graveside service I found Lizzie. I wanted to tell her that I was there when she needed something, how much her mom meant to me, anything that might help ease her burden just the littlest bit, but I couldn't find the words. Instead, I wrapped my arms around her and asked, "How are you holding up?"

"I just want to go home," she replied. "I'm tired of being around people. They should really make the funeral like two weeks after a person dies. This is miserable." I offered a commiserating smile and she continued. "Everyone tries so hard to be nice, but honestly, I think that if one more person tells me that it's not 'good-bye,' it's just 'see you later,' I might kick them. It's not like she went on vacation. This whole 'see you later' business is crap. I have to wait the rest of my life to see her again, and I don't want to wait that long." Lizzie's voice broke. "It's too long."

I took her hand in mine and squeezed, but she didn't look at me. Instead, she pulled away and I watched her climb into her father's car and shut the door.

By the end of the day, we were all exhausted. The car was silent as we rode home from the dinner, and when we arrived, everyone headed in their own direction. Just as I collapsed onto my bed, my phone dinged with an incoming text.

—How was the funeral?

To my surprise, the message was from Nick. *That's sweet of him*, I thought as I texted him back.

—It was really nice. Hard, but nice. I got your card.

He replied almost immediately.

—Good. The florist said purple was the color for sympathy, so I went with that.

—Thank you.

—So you're doing okay?

I smiled.

—Yeah. I'll live. See you tomorrow?

—Of course.

It was almost 7:00 when the doorbell rang. "Quinn, it's for you," Annie called down the hallway. I padded down in the grubby pajama pants and thick socks that I had changed into and stopped. Joshua stood awkwardly in the living room again.

"I told you I wouldn't give up," he said softly.

"Josh," I began, gathering the strength to refuse him and send him home again.

"No, Quinn," he interrupted taking a step toward me. "I'm so sorry. You need to know how sorry I am. Even if that is as far as this goes and you really don't want me back, I need you to know. I was stupid and weak and I didn't realize what I had until I let it go. It was the biggest mistake of my life letting you go and I have regretted it every day since." Josh took several more steps towards me. I didn't retreat.

I shook my head, a mess of confused feelings. "I—" I began again, but he cut me off.

"Don't say no. Not yet. Let me take you out. If nothing else, then just to say I'm sorry. Tomorrow?" I shook my head. "Please, Quinn?"

I hated myself for being so weak. "Wednesday." Josh's face broke into a grin.

"I'll pick you up at seven. You won't regret it. I promise."

I watched silently as he let himself out and then went back to bed. The lavender rose lay across my nightstand, the lilac card behind it. I replayed the day in Price over again in my mind and tried to remember how I felt getting out of Nick's car but kept coming back to the shock of Joshua in the living room. I sighed and pushed both of them from my mind, my body desperate for sleep that was much too slow to come.

11

With Thanksgiving on Thursday, it was a short workweek. Wednesday afternoon was especially slow for showings, and Nick had taken up his perch on my desk earlier than usual.

"Do you stay here for Thanksgiving?" he asked, pretending to flip through some files in case Marie came out of her office. We had been rebuked several times now for spending too much time talking and not enough time working. On an afternoon like this one, however, there wasn't much work to be done.

"We usually go to my grandma's in Salt Lake for dinner. But this year," I paused, trying to phrase my answer without choking up, "with everything, we're staying home and she'll have just Lydia's family over." I glanced up at him, wondering what his first Thanksgiving was like without a mom. "What do you guys do?" I ventured.

"We used to go to my grandparents' every year, but they both passed away just before my mission. This is my first Thanksgiving home, so I'm actually not really sure," he replied with a shrug. "Watch, my dad will ask me tomorrow morning where the turkey is." He dropped the file on my desk and picked up a pen. I watched for a moment as he twirled it deftly between his fingers.

"Do you guys do Black Friday?" I asked, pushing the keyboard away. The calendar had been updated, the newsletter was ready to print for Monday, and I was officially out of tasks.

Nick wrinkled his nose and shook his head. "Black Friday is reserved for the seventh circle of hell," he replied sarcastically. I laughed.

"I take that as a no." I pulled my feet up under me in my chair.

He studied me. "Do you?"

I shook my head. "I have yet to see a deal that would inspire me to skip out on pie." Annie, on the other hand, would be up and out by 3:00 on Thursday afternoon.

He nodded approvingly. "So," he drawled, "If you're not shopping Friday and I'm not shopping Friday, it seems only appropriate that we boycott it together."

"Together?" I asked, eyebrows raised.

He shrugged nonchalantly. "Sure. We could get lunch or catch a movie or something. Somewhere far, far away from the mall."

I studied him for a moment, a little part of my brain wishing that he had suggested this a long time ago, slightly disappointed that he had not. Another little part of my brain suggested that this was more than just a request to hang out, and I felt a little thrill of delight. However, the answer had to be no. I had received a frenzied call from Olivia yesterday begging for all the latest developments between Josh and me, and so I had promised her all of Friday to catch up.

"I can't. I've already got plans with a friend for Friday. Sorry," I replied sincerely. Nick shrugged.

"No worries. Another time," he said with a forgiving smile. For a moment, I wished that he would ask me out for tonight, the thought tempting enough to cancel on Josh. "What?" Nick asked.

I realized that I was staring at him. My eyes widened in embarrassment. "Nothing," I mumbled, "just zoned out there for a second." I focused on my desk, looking for something to straighten up to diffuse the moment.

Marie walked out of her office and Nick quickly jumped off of my desk, scrabbling frantically for the file he had dropped. I braced myself for the rebuke, but Marie just glanced from the two of us to the clock on the wall. "Why don't you two take off?" she suggested. "I don't think anyone's going to be coming in for the rest of the afternoon."

I glanced at the clock. Barely 4:00. Well, at least I would have plenty of time to get ready for Josh. I glanced at Nick and caught a strange look pass between him and Marie. Unable to decipher, I turned to Marie. "Are you sure?" I asked politely, hoping that the answer would still be yes.

"Of course. No one tries to sell a house the day before Thanksgiving. Go have a little fun. I'll see you Monday," she called over her shoulder as she headed back to her office.

I stood and began gathering my things. I glanced at Nick with a smile, excited about the development.

"I honestly didn't see that coming," I commented as I shut down my computer. Nick glanced down the hall towards Marie's office.

"Nope," he replied in a strange voice. I gave him a look, then turned back to my desk, searching for my phone. I thought I heard him speak, and turned back to him.

"What?" I asked. "Did you say something?"

Nick looked embarrassed and quickly shook his head. "I guess I'll see you Monday, then," he said, slowly turning back toward his office as well.

"I guess so," I replied. "Happy Thanksgiving!"

"Happy Thanksgiving." He left the room and I grabbed my purse and didn't look back.

Annie put herself in charge of my date prep. She straightened my hair and pulled it up into a sleek ponytail. We decided casual was the way to go, and she helped me pair a cute button-down with my skinnies and boots. She was putting the final touches on my hair when the doorbell rang. She studied me momentarily in the mirror.

"Stay here. You need one more thing." She disappeared out of the bathroom.

I heard Nate answer the door and muffled voices in the living room. Annie reappeared with an adorable teal jacket that I had been eyeing for months. "Don't spill on it," she warned as she handed it to me.

"Why do I get to borrow it tonight, all of a sudden?" I asked with a smile, probably pushing my luck a little.

Annie shrugged. "He's totally hot, Quinn," she replied matter-of-factly, "You gotta up your game."

I laughed. "Gee, thanks for the confidence booster."

"You know me," Annie called over her shoulder as she headed back to her room. "I do what I can."

I shook my head and gave myself a final once over in the mirror. She wasn't wrong. With his golden hair and runner's body, Josh was way out of my league. I lifted my scarf off the doorknob, took a deep breath and headed out to greet him.

Josh and Nate sat across from each other awkwardly, their conversation long exhausted. The relief was evident on both their faces as I entered the room and they stood.

"Ready?" Josh asked. I nodded. "You look fantastic." As he smiled, I hated him just a little bit for being prettier than me. He wore a pair of high-end jeans that fit in all the right places and a pink pin-striped button-down.

"Bye, Nate," I called as Josh opened the front door for me. Nathan, by far Josh's biggest dissident, made a face. He was still angry with Josh for breaking it off with me in the first place and now he was astounded by my capacity to forgive.

"Remember who you are and what you stand for," he called sarcastically as the door shut behind me. Josh and I both laughed a little hesitantly.

"You really do look amazing," he repeated. I smiled.

"Thank you."

"Shall we?" Josh placed his hand on the small of my back and guided me to the car. For a split second I fought an internal battle: throw my arms around him or run screaming away. I settled on getting into the car and focused on being polite.

We had dinner at a tiny but delicious Italian restaurant. We were seated in a booth in a dark corner, away from most of the bustle of the main dining room. "So, you going to school at all?" Josh asked over a plate of ravioli. I nodded and swallowed.

"Just online classes right now. I'm working mostly." I took a sip of my Italian soda and bit back a sigh. It was that good. Josh had his faults, but his taste in restaurants was not one of them.

"Doing what?"

"Receptionist for a realtor." I twirled pasta around my fork. "How about you?"

"Right now, school mostly," he replied. "Accounting."

"How much longer do you have?" It was strange to think that I had known the answers to all of these questions a couple of years ago.

"I'll be done in April." I reached again for my drink and narrowly missed the bottle of balsamic vinegar. Josh quickly pushed it out of the way with a smirk.

"And then?" I asked, hoping to avoid the inevitable comment on my clumsiness.

Josh shrugged. "My dad wants to hire me full time to manage accounts for his dental practice, but I really don't think there is enough work at just the one practice. I'm trying to convince him that he just needs someone part time, but I'm not having much luck." Josh explained more about his relationship with his dad and their business dealings. I studied his face as he spoke. He was the same Josh, same golden hair, same big blue eyes, but it felt funny talking to him like this. It was almost like talking to a stranger, except I knew these things already. I knew that his dad wouldn't listen to him. I knew he was going into accounting. And yet, so much had changed in the last two years, I felt like I had to start all over again.

"You still run?" I asked at a lull in the conversation.

He nodded and told me about the last race he had run. "And I've done six marathons now, they're just not challenging anymore. I'm thinking about training for an Ironman." From there on out, he did most of the talking. He told me about his mom's latest diet craze: "Have you heard of paleo? It's awful." He told me about the idiot that Olivia had dated last: "She really has the worst taste, and I'm not just saying that because I'm her big brother." He really was the same old Josh, so I decided to ignore the nagging feeling that too much had changed.

For dessert, he took me to The Sweet Tooth Fairy to pick out a cupcake, and then we drove up Provo Canyon along the path of the first race we had run together. "We should do it again," he suggested as we headed home. The moonlight streaming through the windshield highlighted the contours of his face. I took a deep breath and decided to confront the elephant in the car.

"Joshua," I said softly. "Why do you want to do this again?"

"What, the race? I just thought it would be fun, but if you don't want to—" I cut him off.

"No, no. Us. What changed?" I kept my eyes on his face, looking for I don't know what. A reason to say yes.

"Quinn, I—I just . . ." he trailed off. "I was wrong. I made a mistake. I'm just hoping for a second chance."

"How do I trust you?" Even I could hear the exasperation in my voice. "How do I know that you won't change your mind again?" I studied his face as he answered. I hated to admit how much I had missed that face.

"I was an idiot to let you go once, I'm not stupid enough to do it again." I could hear the self-disgust in his voice

"Josh," I said again. "You can't just show up and expect things to go right back to the way they were. You hurt me. You emailed me and told me that I wasn't right for you. That it was *fun*, but never the real thing. How do I know that this is the real thing this time, and not just *fun*?" He winced at the bitterness in my voice.

"I was wrong, I was stupid, and it kills me to think about it. But, Quinn," he paused as he pulled the car off the road and came to a stop. He turned to face me. "I plan on spending as long as it takes to earn back your trust, and the rest of my life keeping it." His jaw was set and his eyes bore into mine.

We were silent for a moment. I needed to think, and his intense focus on me was unnerving. "You can't expect me to, I don't know, marry you tomorrow." I replied, flustered.

"I know."

"Can we go? I just need to think." Josh nodded briefly and pulled the car back out onto the highway.

I kept my eyes out the windshield and on the moonlit scenery. I wanted so badly to trust him again, to go back to the way things were, get back to my comfort zone. Out of the corner of my eye, I could see him glance in my direction more than once, trying to read my face.

"I don't know, Josh," I sighed, not quite ready to give in.

"If you don't believe me, let me show you." He took a hand off of the steering wheel and laid it on mine. "Let me show you how much I missed you and how much I care about you," he paused and squeezed my hand. "Just give me a chance. I love you, Quinn."

I bit my lip hesitantly. I still hadn't forgiven him. I hated even the memory of that day and I wanted him to know. I wanted to protest, to kick and scream and tell him how much he had hurt me, how mad I had been, and that I never wanted to see him again, but the feel of his hand on mine was intoxicating. My attempt to suppress the excitement and pleasure of simply being with him was becoming steadily more futile.

We didn't speak again until we pulled into my driveway. He opened my door for me and pulled me out of the car and into his arms. "Just a chance, Quinn," he whispered, his hand in my hair pulling me close to him. I couldn't count the number of times that I had wished for him to be here with me. He brushed his lips lightly across mine and I was gone.

When I broke the news to my parents the next morning, they were less than supportive of the development. Mom was so preoccupied by grief and Thanksgiving prep she could barely nod, but Dad was particularly vocal about it. "What makes you think," he emphasized more than once, "that he won't do it again?"

"Well, for one thing, Dad, I'm not going to be leaving on another mission anytime soon. So, I'm pretty sure that he'll stick around while I'm here." I retorted with more confidence than I felt.

"You know that is absolutely not what I meant," he shot back.

"I know. But seriously, if you think about it, that is the only reason we broke up. I was gone and he was lonely. It happens all the time." I raised my eyebrows meaningfully at him. He was one to talk. He had stolen Mom out from her missionary.

"Can you hear yourself?" Dad shook his head, choosing to ignore my comment. "I don't want to watch you go through the same thing that Nate has been through," he said gently.

"Dad, we're careful," I reassured him. "And we're not married; we're not even engaged. We're trying to figure out where we are exactly. Don't worry about me," I added, placing my hand over his. "I'll be fine."

"You forget who you're talking to, Quinn," he added dryly. "It's my job to worry." I smiled and hoped I was right.

Thanksgiving was small, only slightly more remarkable than a weeknight dinner. The somber mood of the prior week had only slightly lifted, so none of us were feeling very festive. Mom retreated to her room soon after dinner and Josh and Olivia came over. One of the fringe benefits of getting back together with Josh was the inevitable reconciliation with Olivia. There was little discussion about the apparent fragility of our relationship and much catching up. So much, in fact, we decided that we needed a sleepover, so when Josh went home that night, Olivia did not. As soon as Josh was gone, we pulled out the popcorn and ice cream and holed up in my room, filling each other in on the happenings of the past few months. I told her about Lydia, the funeral, everything. It was kind of cathartic to talk about it all, and I told her so.

"Honestly, the biggest help was talking to Nick. He's this guy that I work with," I explained. "His mom took off when he was a kid, so it was kind of nice to have that perspective. It's not the same, but you know." I dropped my empty carton of Ben and Jerry's in the trash.

Liv narrowed her eyes at me. "You're telling your family secrets to some guy at work?" she asked skeptically.

I shook my head. "It's not like he's just some random guy. He was actually in the mission with me, so I knew him before.

Plus, there are only three of us in my office, so you know, when you spend all day, every day with them, you're kind of forced to get to know each other really well."

"And you're sure that's all he is? Just some guy you work with?" she asked suspiciously, setting down the bowl of popcorn and reaching for the M&M's.

I glared at her in annoyance. "Are you kidding me, Liv?"

She smiled and readjusted the pillow under her head. "Yes," she replied with a laugh.

I smacked her arm. "Such a brat," I rebuked. Over the natural progression of conversation, Josh inevitably came up. "What happened? With Jenny, I mean?" I asked. I hadn't come right out and asked Josh, I had only hinted in that direction, but Josh was being either intentionally naive or simply oblivious.

Liv shrugged. "Honestly, I don't really know. Josh won't tell us what happened. He came home one night, didn't say anything to anyone, and then the next day Mom told me the wedding was off and I didn't see him until after he'd seen you. It was weird." Olivia popped another M&M into her mouth. "I've asked a bunch of times, but he really doesn't want to talk about it. But I don't really care. I never really liked Jenny."

I smiled and grabbed a handful of popcorn. Olivia lay back on the floor and kicked her feet up on my bed. "So," she said slyly, "tell me about Nathan." She pulled a blanket off of my bed and tucked it around her.

I studied her, suddenly wary. "What about him?"

"Quinn, he got married less than a year ago, and just up and moved back in with the parents without his wife? What is going on? Did they split up? What's the deal?"

I couldn't tell if she was asking for the gossip value or concern, and my sisterly defenses kicked in. "Nothing's final yet," I responded vaguely. "They're separated for now."

"But they're going to get a divorce?" she pushed.

I looked at her with eyebrows raised. "Why do you care so much?" I asked.

Liv shrugged awkwardly. "No reason. Just concerned about my best friend's brother, that's all," she replied with mock seriousness, her eyes innocently wide.

"Right," I responded in disbelief. I watched as she readjusted her pillow again and took a swig of Diet Coke. Was it really so hard to believe that she was interested in Nate? Wasn't I proof of the whole "best friend's big brother" cliché? I laughed silently at both of us and pulled my blanket more tightly around my shoulders.

For the rest of the night, the topic of our respective brothers was off the table by unspoken agreement. We fell asleep shortly before sunrise and when we woke up, we were both too exhausted to even think about shopping. I took Liv home after a late breakfast. As I was pulling the car out of the driveway, Josh ran out of the house to stop me.

"Dinner tonight?" he asked as I rolled down my window. He looked like he hadn't been up much longer than we had, his hair rumpled, in a T-shirt and flannel pants.

I smiled. "Love to. What time?"

"I'll pick you up at 6:30," he said.

"See you then," I called back and rolled the window back up. *Perfect,* I said to myself. That would give me plenty of time for a nap and a shower. I walked through the garage door to find Nate sitting at the counter, staring morosely at a pile of papers in front of him. I hung up my keys and peered over his shoulder.

"What is that?" I asked, standing on tiptoe to see better. He glanced up at me briefly and then down at the papers before him with a sigh.

"Divorce papers," he replied, hoarsely. I pulled out the stool next to him and studied his face as I sat down.

"I thought that you were expecting this?" I asked slowly, maybe not quite as sympathetically as I could have. "I thought you wanted this." We hadn't talked much about it since the night he had moved home, but I knew that both he and Sasha wanted to end things as quickly and painlessly as possible.

Nate sighed audibly. "It's different. It's real now." He looked up at me, his face tortured. "Quinn, I am a twenty-three-year-old divorcee. I am the pariah of the singles ward."

"It's not like you're the only one there." I shot back. "You're not the first person to get divorced at twenty-three."

Nate just raised his eyebrows. "You know the first thing people think when they find out you're divorced? 'What is wrong with him?' They never say it out loud, but you know it goes through their mind."

"Then go to Mom and Dad's ward. Everyone knows you there, they don't care."

"Do you really think Mom will let me sit on the same bench with everyone?" His self-deprecating tone was laced with bitterness.

"Nathan!" I chided, unwilling to admit that I was wondering the same thing.

"Maybe I'll just stay home, save the family from the embarrassment." He paused a moment. "This wasn't exactly what I had in mind for my five-year plan," he said sadly.

I was silent as I tried to see things from his view, thinking of what to say to him. I placed my hand on his forearm and looked up at him, studying him for a moment.

"So?" I asked. Nate raised his eyebrows. "You made a mistake. These are the consequences." I paused, deciding how to answer. "But now, you get a do-over. So, stop moping, sign the papers, and make a new five-year plan. And let's be honest, you're hardly the craziest person in the singles ward," I snorted. "You're not even the craziest divorcee in the singles ward. But you might want to wait at least until the divorce is final to test out that theory. Besides," I continued, "any girl out there worth having won't care that you're divorced once she gets to know you."

I hopped off my stool, grabbed a Coke from the fridge, and sat down on the couch. Nate was quiet for a long time. I watched him as I sipped my drink. Sure, it was easy enough for me to spout off about it all, but I had no idea what he was going through. I began second-guessing my speech, wondering if I had done more harm than good, wondering if maybe I should have been more understanding than I was. By the time that I finished my drink, he still hadn't moved. I decided that rather than take back what I had said, I would make an attempt to cheer him up.

"Hey, Josh is taking me to dinner tonight. You should come with us. I think Olivia's coming too." That was absolutely not the original plan but at least if I lost a few points with Josh, I would gain a few with Olivia.

He glanced in my direction. "Nah, I don't feel like seeing anyone."

"C'mon, Nate. We're both off this weekend, we should take advantage. You know you want to spend more time with your favorite sister," I teased.

He raised his eyebrows at me and a shadow of a smile crossed his face. "Oh, Annie's coming too?"

I wrinkled my nose and stuck out my tongue at him. "So that's a yes, right?"

"Fine," he said, gathering up the documents and pushing back from the counter. "What time?"

"6:30. Josh is driving. We'll go somewhere good." I carried my empty can to the garbage and came around the counter to give him a quick hug. "It'll be fun. I promise."

I called Josh and talked him into bringing Olivia and the two of them showed up on our doorstep at quarter to seven. "Blame Liv," Josh announced as I pulled the door open.

"I always do," I reassured him, going up on tiptoe to kiss his cheek. It was apparent he had been a bit heavy-handed with the cologne. "Thank you," I whispered while I was there. "I owe you one."

"Yeah, you do," he replied, but I couldn't decide if he was joking or not. "We will discuss repayment at a later time." I smiled awkwardly just as Nate came down the hall.

"Josh," Nate said in greeting, pulling his coat on over his shoulders.

"Nathan," Josh replied briskly with a slight nod. I grabbed Josh's hand and pulled him outside, eager to get this show on the road.

"Where we going?" I asked as we walked to the car, Nate close behind.

"Slab sound good?" Josh asked as he pulled the door open for me.

"Great."

Nate slid silently into the backseat next to Olivia and we were off. The evening was actually much less awkward than I thought that it would be. Liv commandeered most of Nate's attention, leaving Josh and I to focus on each other.

"So, Liv told me there's a guy at work that you served with?" Josh asked, pulling off a piece of pizza crust.

I nodded, my mouth momentarily full. "Yeah, we served in the same district twice."

"Is that how you got the job?" he asked curiously. His eyes were on his pizza as he asked the question, but traveled quickly to study my face as I answered.

"No," I shook my head and pulled a tomato off my pizza. "I had no idea he even worked there until after I had been hired."

Josh nodded and took a sip of soda. "So, you like it there?"

"Yeah, I really do. It was iffy at first, I mean, I didn't like that elder at all while we were in Florida, so I was kind of nervous about working with him every day. Lucky for me, it turns out he's not such a bad guy." I smiled, "Plus, Marie, our boss, is unique. I really like her, but she takes some getting used to."

"Maybe I'll stop by one day so I can meet her," Josh suggested.

My eyes widened inadvertently. "Oh, well, um, that might be kind of a problem. She's out most of the day with clients on showings and appointments and stuff, so it can be hard to catch her." I rambled.

Josh narrowed his eyes at me. "You don't want me to stop by?" he asked, the suspicion and offense obvious in his voice.

"NO!" I disagreed a little too quickly and loudly. Nate and Olivia stopped their conversation to look up at me. I lowered my voice in embarrassment and continued. "No, no, no, I mean, it's just that, you know she's gone so much—" I was saved by the arrival of our waitress, checking up on us. After I took a few more bites into my divine pizza, Josh looked back to me.

"Well, then maybe I'll just stop by one of these days to see you, not her," he said. His voice was light, but I could still see traces of jealousy in his expression.

"I would love that!" I replied with extra enthusiasm, hoping to make up for my previous hesitation.

"So this guy you work with . . ." Josh trailed off, obviously waiting for me to supply his name.

"Nick," I obliged.

"Nick," Josh repeated. "Is he gone most of the time on showings too?"

I shrugged. "Both of them are in and out of the office all day long. I swear, I'm there alone half the time!" I replied with a forced laugh. Josh's smile grew.

"Maybe I'll get lucky then, catch you all alone," he quipped suggestively, his voice low. I blushed and turned back to my dinner. We finished our pizza and hit Redbox on the way home. The four of us crammed onto the couch to watch *The Hobbit*, and I couldn't help but notice how comfortable Olivia got next to Nate. By the end of the night, I couldn't tell if Nate was uncomfortable or pleased.

13

Monday arrived much too quickly. After so many mornings of sleeping in as late as I wanted to, it was next to impossible to roll out of bed to get up for work. I stumbled into the office, blurry eyed and grumpy and already jonesing for a Diet Coke. I had just collapsed into my chair when Nick came strolling in.

"Someone had an exciting weekend," he teased, pausing next to my desk.

"Ha, ha, ha," I laughed sarcastically, glaring at him. He looked annoyingly chipper for this early in the morning. He had pulled out all the stops today, gray, pin-striped slacks, perfectly coiffed, dark curly hair, and a cornflower blue tie. He even smelled amazing. I mentally shook myself and tried to focus on what he was saying.

"Too much to drink?" he asked, laughter in his voice and a mischievous smile still on his face. I made a face at him.

"I'm just an idiot and stayed up way too late every single night," I moaned, dropping my head onto my arms.

"Right," he said slowly, lowering his voice and taking a step closer to me. I pulled my head up and wrinkled my nose at him.

"Just let me sleep," I retorted, throwing a paper clip at him.

"You weren't at church on Sunday," he commented, his voice neutral. I glanced up at him. Josh and I had gone together to our home ward.

"I just thought that with the holiday, I should go with my family." He nodded politely. "Plus," I threw in as an afterthought, "I haven't totally decided if the singles ward is for me."

He cocked his eyebrow at me. "You are single, are you not?"

"I just don't know if I can handle knowing the intimate details of every speaker's relationship, and/or their medical problems." I replied, dodging the question. He laughed and continued to his office without comment.

The rest of the day dragged along. There were fewer phone calls and appointments than usual due to the holiday season, according to Marie. I had plenty of time to sit at my desk and stare blankly into space, all the while fighting off the urge to lay my head on the desk and take a nap. Nick wandered out several times to chat, only returning to his office when Marie called him out on it. But after she left for her one and only appointment of the day around 4:00, he perched on my desk to stay. We had been discussing the merits of the Star Wars prequels versus the original trilogy, you know, intellectual conversation, when he paused for a moment, fixing his eyes on me.

"You busy this weekend?" he asked slowly. His eyes fell to his hands, which were frantically twirling a pencil through his fingers.

"Um, why?" I asked, suddenly tense. I reached, super casually, for my phone, but ended up knocking it ever so elegantly off the edge of the desk. I then proceeded to bang my elbow on the corner of the desk in the process of picking it up and sat up wincing in pain, to find Nick biting back a laugh. He cleared his throat before speaking again.

"I was just wondering if maybe you wanted to maybe catch a movie or something with me. Maybe get some dinner." He looked at me hopefully. And there it was. There was no question about it this time. He was asking me out.

"Um," I stuttered, trying to gather the words to explain. I opened my mouth to say more, but the office door opened.

Nick bolted off my desk, hoping to avoid another rebuke from Marie, but it wasn't her.

Josh strolled in with a smile on his face and a bouquet of daisies in hand. He looked like he had just completed a shift at his father's dentist office. He wore a bright blue button-down that made his eyes look electric and a pair of slacks. I had to admit, he looked good.

"Josh!" I exclaimed, jumping out of my chair in surprise. "What are you doing here?"

"I told you I was going to drop by," he replied with a smile, his eyes darting between Nick and me. I smiled back faintly, wondering if he could have chosen a worse time to drop in. Josh leaned forward and planted a kiss overtly on my lips. I pulled away hastily and glanced at Nick with an awkward and slightly apologetic smile.

"Josh, this is Nick. Nick, Josh."

Josh turned to Nick, holding out his hand in greeting. "Nice to meet you," Josh said shortly. "I hear you served in Florida with Quinn." Nick's face had gone blank. He shook Josh's hand and nodded shortly.

"Nice to meet you too," Nick replied in the same tone. He looked at me. I saw his jaw clench, but I couldn't read his expression. "Quinn, can you please let me know when Marie gets back? I need to discuss something with her."

I nodded quickly and Nick turned on his heel and disappeared into his office. The door slammed a little louder than usual and I jumped at the sound. I tried to shake it off and smiled brightly at Josh, hoping to dispel some of the tension his entrance had created.

"Thanks for the flowers!" I gushed, reaching for them. Josh offered me a smile and handed them over.

"I think you should leave them here," he advised, glancing around the room. "This place could do with a little personality."

"If I can find a vase, sure," I placated, putting the bouquet to my nose and taking a deep breath. And I remembered why daisies are not my favorite. Daisies don't smell good.

Josh studied my sparsely decorated desk as I set the flowers down on it. "No pictures?" he asked, an eyebrow raised. "Is it against the rules?"

I shook my head. "No, I just haven't brought any." I smoothed my skirt and quickly glanced back to where Nick had disappeared, wondering if he was upset or just surprised, and not knowing how I was going to smooth things over.

Josh's eyes followed my gaze and then swiveled back to the desk. "You know that picture of us right after the marathon? You should bring that one." That particular photograph of Josh and me had formerly resided on my nightstand. Josh had poured water over my head at the end of the race and my face was bright red and splotchy, but we were both smiling broadly at the accomplishment of running for twenty-six miles.

I raised my eyebrows and laughed. "Seriously? That is possibly the worst picture of me in the history of the world." Not to mention the fact that I wasn't sure whether or not it still existed. There had been a ceremonial burning of all things Josh after I got home. If I remembered correctly, that picture had been in the doomed pile.

Josh leaned closer to me. I could feel his breath on my cheek as he spoke. "Trust me, babe," he said softly. "It's not."

I smiled at his tone. "We'll see," I replied. He leaned forward and kissed me again. I took his shoulders and pushed them gently away. "Josh," I rebuked gently. "I am still at work."

"Take off early," he suggested. I glanced at the clock. It was 4:30, only thirty more minutes left in my workday. It wouldn't be totally unreasonable for me to sneak out, especially with things so slow, but I just couldn't leave things with Nick the way they were. *He must think I lied to him*, I thought, remembering his question in the restaurant. And his question about the singles ward this morning. And his unanswered invitation.

"I really shouldn't," I wavered, gazing at my desk. I didn't have anything left to file, the few appointments had long been confirmed, but I couldn't do it.

"You still have a bunch of stuff that needs to be done?" Josh asked.

"Well," I hesitated, "yeah, I just need to finish a few things up first," I lied. "But I'll see you tonight?" I asked with a hopeful smile.

"Yeah," he answered, obviously disappointed. "I'll be over around seven to pick you up."

"Perfect," I replied with a smile and a peck on his cheek. "Thank you for the flowers. I love them."

Josh softened and gave me a hug. "See you tonight." As the door closed behind him, I looked back toward Nick's office, working up the courage to go talk to him and trying to figure out what to say. I spent a few more minutes in indecision and then hesitantly headed back.

I knocked lightly and then opened the door, as I had done dozens of times before. "Nick?" I said quietly, sticking my head into his office. He glanced up at me from the computer screen briefly and then back. His jaw was set as he stared at the screen blankly.

"What?" he asked, his voice short. I still wasn't exactly sure what to say to him.

"Um, I just—I was going to, um—"

"What is it Quinn? I've got to get this stuff done," he snapped impatiently. Immediately I was taken back to Florida and I was dealing with Elder Ryan again.

"I'm sorry about all that," I said awkwardly.

"About what?" he said, intentionally making the moment that much more uncomfortable.

"I didn't get to answer your question, and I'm sorry, but I don't think that I am available this weekend." I switched tactics. It didn't seem to help.

"Yeah, I figured. Is that all?" His eyes were still focused on the computer screen.

"Yep, that's all," I replied, backing out of the doorway, fighting back the urge to be antagonistic. "See you tomorrow?"

"Sure," he replied shortly, still focused solely on his computer.

I returned to my desk, feeling a little idiotic. Sure, it's always awkward turning someone down for a date, but I shouldn't feel the need to explain my relationship to him. True, I hadn't mentioned Josh at all, but still. It was still really new. I shook off my uncertainty and the slight disappointment at having to turn Nick down. I decided that if I didn't make it a big deal, it wouldn't be a big deal.

Driving home, I thought about Okeechobee for the first time in a long time. Elder Ryan and I arrived in Okeechobee on the same transfer. Half the district did. I came down from Winter Park, and my companion, Sister Giles, came from Harrisburg. Shortly after transfers, there was a zone conference at a building in Fort Pierce. President Jacobs spoke, and as usual, Elder Ryan was the special musical number.

After the meeting, the Relief Society served us lunch in the gym. I was sneaking a second piece of chocolate cake from the kitchen when I noticed Elder Ryan corner President Jacobs. I was too far away to hear what they were saying, but Elder Ryan was very intense about whatever it was. After a few moments, President Jacobs glanced up and noticed me watching them. Elder Ryan followed his gaze and he and I shared a very awkward split second of eye contact. I made a show of looking for a fork, but fooled no one. He put his arm around Elder Ryan and led him out of sight. I was curious, but it didn't take me long to forget the scene, aided by the chocolate cake. That is, until the next transfer two weeks later.

Elder Ryan was the only missionary to leave Okeechobee that transfer, and unexpectedly too. President Jacobs was a firm believer in the missionaries really getting to know the members in their areas and developing relationships. He tended to leave missionaries in the same area for long periods of time and explained regularly that in his experience, missionaries had more success when that was the case. Elder Ryan was in Okeechobee a total of four weeks, while the average transfer was at least twelve weeks long. I couldn't help questioning Elder Trevan about it when I met his new companion.

"Elder Ryan was transferred? Already?"

"Don't sound so excited about it," Elder Trevan laughed.

"No, I just—that's weird, right? For him to get transferred so quick?" I glanced at Elder Trevan's new companion, a greenie who looked as if he might actually be scared of Sister Giles and me.

"I don't know," Trevan shrugged. "Not gonna call the mission office and ask about it though, am I?"

"No, no, never mind." And somehow, at the back of my mind I knew Elder Ryan left because of me. I don't know how I knew, and I never told anyone. Sister Giles would call me paranoid, and maybe I was, but I knew it. He left because of me.

Later that night, Josh and I sat snuggled together on my couch, finally alone in the living room. The conversation had died a while ago and I was fighting the urge to close my eyes and drift away. He was so warm and comfortable.

"So," began Josh, startling me out of my doze, "you really like working there, huh?"

I pushed myself off of his chest to look at him. "Yeah," I murmured. "I do."

"You know, my dad's secretary is retiring at the end of the year." There was something in his voice as he said it that I couldn't quite place.

"Oh?" I replied, wondering what this had to do with me.

"They've already started interviewing for her replacement, but so far, they haven't found anyone organized or experienced enough to deal with all the paperwork of a dentist's office."

"That's too bad," I agreed.

Josh shifted position slightly. "I bet if I asked my dad, he could get you the job."

I sat up to look him in the face, eyebrows raised. "I already have a job."

He shrugged sheepishly. "I know. But who knows? Maybe the pay will be better. Maybe you'll like it more? Maybe you'll see me more often? I'm there a couple days a week." He listed the virtues in the most convincing tone he could muster, and still his voice had a strange edge to it.

I smiled. "It would be fun to see you more, Josh, but I really do like my job and the pay isn't bad at all. Plus, I have my system worked out and I don't know if it would translate to a dentist's office." His face fell. "But thanks for the offer," I planted a kiss on his cheek. "It was really sweet of you." I nestled back into him and he rested his arm lightly across my shoulders.

"How about this," he began again. "Don't say no just yet. Think about it. You wouldn't have to start until January 2. Plenty of time to decide."

I let out a short laugh and squeezed his hand. "I'll think about it," I promised. I changed the subject to something much more exciting: I had finally saved enough to buy my first car.

"What about an SUV, Quinn?" Josh asked, pulling my laptop toward him to search classifieds. I shook my head with a laugh.

"Not gonna happen, Josh." We quickly found the used car section of Craigslist. I found a Nissan that I had been admiring from afar for a totally reasonable price.

"They're great in the snow," Josh continued to sell the whole SUV idea on me, clicking over to a page featuring a fairly new Honda. I shook my head without even looking at it. "You know you need a good snow car," he urged.

I glanced over at him. "You can't be serious, Josh. I can't afford half of that car."

Josh shrugged. "I worry about you driving in the snow. You're out of practice."

I laughed again. "Are you calling me a bad driver?" I asked teasingly.

"I almost forgot," Josh said, changing the subject. "Guess who was pulling up at my house tonight just as I was leaving?"

"Who?" I asked, turning away from the pictures of cars in front of me.

"Nate," he said with a strange smile.

"Seriously?" I asked. "To see Liv?"

"Well, I don't think he's stopping by to see my mom," Josh laughed. "At least, I hope not."

"Wow, Nate and Olivia. Gonna have to wrap my mind around that one."

"I know how you feel," Josh replied. "Come on," he said, "look at this one."

We spent the rest of the night online until we found the perfect car. A three-year-old Prius without too many miles that was right in my price range. Josh still pushed for the SUV, but I was sold. I called the owner the next day and by that night was the proud owner of a new-to-me Prius. Annie would be thrilled to have her Civic back.

Over the weekend I talked Josh into coming to the ward Christmas party with me.

"Free dinner," I taunted in a singsong voice. "Even better entertainment." I had a hard time keeping a smile off my face as I said it. Josh rolled his eyes at me.

"Fine. Let's go." His tone was barely resigned. Although Josh and I had gone to church together last Sunday, there was a large portion of the ward that didn't know about our reconciliation. The first half of the evening was spent explaining that no, Josh was no longer engaged to Jenny, yes, we were back together, and no, we were not engaged to each other. It was awkward, to say the least, and barely worth the free dinner.

I was relieved once we had our food and were sitting down, surrounded by my family and Joshua's. Olivia and Nate sat across from us, obviously unsure how to act around each other while trying to hide their relationship from the nosier members of the ward. We chatted through dinner, and I had just begun to enjoy myself when the entertainment took the stage.

The bishopric had booked a barbershop quartet from BYU and they were moderately talented. Ezra and Oliver particularly enjoyed their rendition of "Rudolph the Red Nose Reindeer," complete with updated echoes. After they closed with "Like Obama!" one of them approached the front of the stage.

"For our next number, we need a volunteer from the audience." Little hands shot up all over the gym. The singer smiled and amended, "A lovely young lady, please." There was an audible groan as the disappointed boys dropped their hands, leaving only an eligible few in the air. I turned to comment on this to Josh and realized he was waving his arms over me and pointing at my head. My stomach dropped.

"What are you doing?" I hissed, grabbing for his arms. My nightmares were made up of two scenarios: being swarmed by spiders, and being forced in front of large crowds to perform against my will. It was the reason I had shied away from choir or drama or any kind of scenario that would put the spotlight on me in any form.

"I'm volunteering for you," Josh laughed.

I glared at him, knowing that we were both making a scene, and therefore, were that much more visible to the performers on stage. Josh only laughed harder, thinking it all a great joke. I swiveled in my seat to glance toward the stage and found, to my horror, that the speaker was looking directly at me with a horribly mischievous smile on his face.

"This young lady right here will be perfect." He announced gesturing directly at me. His bandmates behind him wheeled a rolling desk chair to the center of the stage and spun it around a few times.

I blanched and looked at Annie in desperation. The polar opposite of me, and luckily a sympathetic sister rather than a sadistic one, she bounced out of her chair and onto the stage without a second thought, as though he had been pointing at her all along.

I turned back to Josh, my mouth set in a line. "Please, don't ever do that again," I asked quietly.

"What?" he replied. "You would have had fun!"

I shook my head shortly. "You know I hate stuff like that." Josh leaned down and kissed my cheek quickly as the singing began again.

"You're no fun," he whispered in my ear. I could hear the smile in his voice and I knew he hadn't done it to torture me, but I still had a hard time relaxing enough to bring my pulse down.

The performers slid Annie all over the stage, each pretending to fall in love with her as they sang, "All I Want for Christmas Is You." I promised her silently that I owed her big time, at least a new pair of shoes, if not more. In the end, it worked out for everyone. The tallest of the four singers asked for Annie's number after the show and I managed to forgive Josh before he took me home.

14

Sunday morning I woke up with a frog in my throat, but by that evening it had evolved to chills and a fever. I barely slept that night with all the coughing and inability to breathe through my nose, and when I woke up Monday morning my voice was gone completely.

I wasn't entirely sure that Marie would be able to hear me, let alone understand me, over the phone, so I texted Nick and asked him to let her know that I wouldn't be coming in. I got a brief acknowledgment in response and crawled back under the covers to try and sleep a little more. I woke up several hours later, coughing and feeling like I had been run over by a truck. I could barely drag myself out of bed, but I knew Mom had stashed some herbal tea somewhere in the pantry that was supposed to practically cure a cold, so I stumbled into the kitchen and searched until I found it.

I was just pulling my mug out of the microwave when I heard the doorbell ring. My first response was to ignore it. It was almost surely a delivery or a salesman. I dropped the tea bag into my cup and warmed my hands on the mug while I waited for it to steep. And the doorbell rang again. I rolled my eyes with a sigh. This was not the day for an obnoxiously persistent salesman. And then he started knocking. I set my tea on the counter and marched to the front door to get a glimpse of this jerk, and maybe even give him a piece of my mind. I peered through the peephole and was immediately glad I had left my tea in the kitchen, because I'm pretty sure I would have dropped it.

Nick stood on the other side of the door with several bags in hand. I shook off my shock and pulled the door open.

"Hey," he said. "I didn't wake you, did I?" I shook my head.

"What are you doing here?" I whispered. Almost no sound came out of my mouth. He held up the bags in his hands.

"When Marie heard you were sick, she asked me to bring you a few things. Can I come in?"

I nodded and opened the door wider to let him in.

"She would have brought them herself, but she actually has a pretty full day today." I stopped as we reached the kitchen and he set the bags on the counter. He turned to study me. "How are you feeling?"

"Awful," I rasped. "I kind of just want to die. And my voice is completely gone."

"I can tell. So, that's why you texted me?" he asked. "Instead of just calling Marie?"

I nodded and he turned back to the bags on the counter. He began pulling items out.

"Honey and cinnamon. You mix them together and take it three times a day. It's supposed to boost your immune system or something." He pulled out a bag of cough drops and a jar of Vicks. "Obvious," he said, holding them up. And then he took a take-out container from the last bag. "Chicken soup from Kneaders. The best possible medicine." He smiled at me.

A wave of dizziness hit me, and I gripped the edge of the counter to keep from falling over. I hoped Nick wouldn't notice, but alas, he darted around the bar and pulled a chair out for me. I sank into it gratefully. I closed my eyes to steady myself and jumped when I felt a hand on my forehead. My eyes flew open and I pulled back in surprise.

"Quinn!" Nick exclaimed, "You are burning up."

"I'm fine," I mumbled.

"You need to go to the doctor," he announced, pulling his phone out of his pocket.

"Nick," I whined, "I just need to go back to bed." I cradled my head on my arms on the counter.

"Is your mom or anyone else here that can take you?" I was a little surprised at the concern in his voice.

I shook my head without lifting it.

"Come on," Nick coaxed, wrapping his arm around my waist and pulling me gently out of the chair. "I'm taking you to urgent care."

I stumbled to my feet, leaning heavily on him.

"I'm fine," I repeated. My nonexistent voice wasn't helping me make my case. To say I sounded like a sixty-year-old chain smoker was an understatement. "I just need to sleep. Then I'll be fine."

"Sleep in the car. We're going." He was pushing me out of the kitchen and toward the front door, his arm still around my waist.

"Shoes," I protested in resignation. Nick stopped pushing.

"Where are they? I'll grab them."

I pointed down the hall to my room and collapsed back into the chair. He reappeared a moment later with a pair of boots and then led me to his car and drove me to the nearest urgent care office. I lay across three chairs in the waiting room until they called me back. Nick stood to follow me.

"Uh-uh. Sit." There was no way he was going into the exam room with me. I pointed at his chair. He did so obediently, with a concerned smile on his face.

During my exam, the doctor determined that I had strep throat on top of the flu and I left with three prescriptions. Nick stood when he saw me re-enter the waiting room and hurried over, reaching out to support my weight again. I shrugged him off.

"I don't have a broken leg, I'm just dying," I thrust the three scripts at him and he laughed as he plucked them from my hand. He drove to the nearest Walgreens and after dropping the prescriptions off, he sat in the car with me while we waited for them to be filled.

"Did they tell you what your temperature was?" he asked after a few minutes of silence. I nodded. "And?"

"One hundred and five." I was annoyed at him for being right.

Nick let out a low whistle. "I always knew you were hot, but—"

"Shut up," I rasped, leaning my head against the cold window. Nick chuckled.

"So, uh, you still seeing that guy?" he asked hesitantly a few minutes later.

"Yeah," I replied without opening my eyes.

"You guys pretty serious, then?"

I peered at him through my eyelashes, "I guess so, why?"

"It just seems kind of fast, is all." He kept his eyes determinedly out the front window.

My throat hurt, and all I wanted was to go to sleep. "Long story," I whispered and settled against the window again, hoping he would take the hint. And for a few silent minutes, I thought he had.

"Wait," he exclaimed, "Quinn, he's not the guy, right? The 'Dear Jane' guy? The one who got engaged?"

I nodded again.

"Are you serious? What happened?" His tone was less than encouraging.

It literally felt like there were knives stabbing me in the throat, and the last thing that I wanted to do right now was get into this with Nick. "He's not engaged any more and we got back together." I pressed my forehead into the window turning away from him.

"So, did he come crawling back or did you go after him?"

I looked at him incredulously. "Are you kidding me right now?" I began to push the car door open. "I'm getting my drugs and then you're taking me home." I pushed myself out of the car much more slowly than I would have liked for the dramatic effect, and by the time I was standing he had jumped out and run around the car.

"Quinn, sit. I'll go get them. I'm sorry, I just—I'll go." As much as I would have liked to brush past him defiantly, I sank gratefully back into the car without another word. I closed my eyes and pulled the lever to lay the seat down. A few minutes later, I heard the driver's side door open and close and the car start. I didn't move as we drove in silence for a few minutes before he spoke again.

"Um, I'm sorry about what I said earlier." He sounded sincere, but I was still super annoyed.

"Whatever," I mumbled.

"You deserve better than that. Than him." Nick sounded more like he was talking to himself than to me.

"And you know that because you've met him once," I retorted.

"I know you."

I was silent for a moment. "No second chances then?" I asked.

"Not for him," he muttered.

"You really don't know him," I shot back. "And to be totally honest, you don't know me that much better." The car pulled into the driveway. "Thank you for taking me and everything, but I think it would just be better if you stayed out of my business."

"Just trying to look out for you." Nick put the car in park.

"Well, don't," I replied, grabbing the bags of medicine.

"Won't bother," he snapped.

"Great." I stood, took a deep breath, and turned back to him. "Please thank Marie for the stuff she sent. And for sending you." I steadied myself and walked into the house alone. I dropped the bags on a kitchen chair and collapsed on the couch.

"Where've you been?"

I jumped, surprised by another person in the house. Mom had arrived home from work early. "Doctor's. I have the flu. And strep. I think I'm dying."

She ignored the dramatics. "Who was that?"

"Nick. From work. Can you get me my medicine?" The trip to the doctor and the argument with Nick had drained every last ounce of energy.

"Why did he take you? Why didn't you call me? Or Josh?"

"Mom," I moaned. "Please?"

She grumbled under her breath, but I could hear the bags from the pharmacy rustling. I took everything and then fell into a drug-induced stupor for the next several days.

As I walked through the kitchen on my way to bed a few nights later, I could hear them murmuring softly in the living room. I couldn't see them; they were either on the floor or lying on the couch. I paused, not trying to listen, but letting it sink in. I wondered if this was how Olivia felt when I had started seeing Joshua. She had always seemed so happy, so supportive. I wondered if it was weird for her at first, seeing the two of us together. I wondered if she worried about the two of us hurting each other, the repercussions that would have for her, like I was now.

When I thought about Olivia and Nate together, it was strange. I was worried about Nate coming off of his divorce so quickly, and throwing himself into something that he wasn't ready for. I was worried about Olivia getting hurt if she was just Nate's rebound. Our friendship had floundered when Josh had cut things off with me; what would happen to it if it didn't work out between them, no matter who was at fault?

I shook my head quickly, trying to clear my mind and leave before they saw me, but before I could move, Nate appeared, reaching down to pull Liv to her feet. He saw me and offered an awkward smile. I raised my hand as if to say "don't mind me," but Liv saw me first.

"Quinn! Hey!" I could hear the embarrassment in her voice and I just wanted to get out of there as quickly as possible.

"Hey, sorry, I was just going to run downstairs real quick. Don't mind me." I made a beeline for the stairs keeping my eyes straight ahead.

"Nah," drawled Nate. "Don't worry about it. I was just about to walk Olivia out."

I offered her a half-hearted smile and wave and darted down the stairs. When I came back up, with every intention to walk directly to my room without looking around, Nate was sitting at the counter, a bowl of cereal in front of him.

"That was a quick good-bye," I couldn't help commenting, kicking myself as soon as it was out of my mouth. Nate shrugged, his mouth full of Captain Crunch.

"Yeah," he said slowly, after swallowing. "I don't think it's going to work out with Olivia."

Honestly, I wasn't sure if I should be relieved or upset. "Why?" I asked, trying to sound completely neutral.

Nate stirred his cereal with his spoon. "It's just not," he responded vaguely.

"You're going to need a better reason than that to get out of it, you know that right?" I asked, eyebrows raised.

Nate nodded. "I know. I've actually been trying to come up with something for a little while."

"Nathan!" I chided. "You can't drag this out forever! You'll just make it so much worse."

Nate guiltily dropped his eyes to his cereal bowl and rubbed the back of his neck awkwardly.

"Nathan," I rebuked in a low voice, "How long have you been stalling?"

"Just, you know, a couple of weeks." He was difficult to understand around the mouthful of cereal.

"You've only been dating her a couple of weeks!" I barked indignantly. "Why did you even let it get this far? Why did you ask her out again?"

"Well," he raised his hands in self-defense, "she kept calling me. I just . . . didn't say no," he finished lamely.

I sighed. "This is what you're going to do. Tomorrow, you're going to take her out to lunch. You are going to tell her that it's just too much so soon after the divorce and you still need to get your head on straight. You are going to tell her that you think that she's great, it's just the timing, and you need to take a break, get grounded, and adjust. You tell her that it's nothing that she did, that it's all your fault, that you jumped in too quickly without thinking about it. And so help me Nathan, you will do this tomorrow. I will not let you ruin my friendship with her." My finger was inches from his chest by the end of this little speech, driving home the point. Nate hung his head like a guilty little boy and nodded.

"I'm going to bed," I announced. "You call me when it's done." I turned on my heel and marched away, slightly disgusted with myself for sounding so much like my mother.

"Quinn," he called after me softly. "I'm sorry."

I stopped without looking back at him. "I know, Nate. Good night."

"Night."

15

Over the next few weeks, Josh's job offer became more and more appealing. Did you know that the slowest time of year in a realtor's office is over the holidays? No one wants to buy or sell a house over Christmas. Which meant that the phone was quiet, appointments were few and far between, and all three of us were at the office almost all day every day.

Never one to sit still, Marie thought of jobs to keep us all busy. The old and smelly fridge in the break room was cleaned top to bottom one day. All of the cabinets were emptied out and wiped down. Light fixtures were changed out, desks were rearranged, and everything from paper clips to pencils was organized.

For the most part, I didn't mind it. I would rather stay busy than sit twiddling my thumbs day after day. But after my argument with Nick, it was as if a cold breeze had blown through the office, particularly Nick's half of the office. He no longer perched on my desk to chat during the slow parts of the day, he always had somewhere to be at lunchtime so we never ate together, and when I did try and strike up a conversation with him, his answers were short and curt. I resigned myself to the change, and though the thought of starting over somewhere new was tempting, I really did enjoy working with Marie. And Nick. I hoped that the tension would wear off over time, but I was so horribly wrong. And it all came to a head about a week before Christmas.

Nick and Marie were both out on a rare appointment. A new housing development was being zoned and they were interviewing with the builder to become the exclusive real estate office for the neighborhood. I was alone in the office with the task of going through extra files and documents on the computers and deleting unnecessary ones. I was sifting through a particularly old file, trying to decipher what were obviously scanned brochures from the 90s when the front door opened.

A gust of cold air and sunlight streamed in. I glanced up expecting to see Nick, but instead there was an unfamiliar young man in an old T-shirt and torn jeans standing there. His hair was short, but fairly unkempt, and a pungent odor hung heavy around him. I surreptitiously reached into my desk drawer where I kept my cell phone, ready to speed dial 911. This was not the typical real estate client.

"Hi," I said warily. "Can I help you?"

He jumped as if noticing me for the first time. His eyes landed on me and narrowed. There were shadows beneath both of them and the lower half of his face was covered in a short and scraggly beard. "I need to see Nick," he said. His voice was lower than I expected and grating. I tensed at his tone and tightened my grip on my phone.

"He is actually out of the office at the moment, but if you leave your information with me, I can give him the message that you stopped by," I replied as professionally as possible. His eyes narrowed even further.

"Who are you?" he asked.

"I'm the secretary, my name is Quinn," I supplied, instantly kicking myself for giving him my real name. "Can I give him a message for you?"

"When's he coming back?" He took another step toward me.

"I'm not quite sure, but it should be in the near future. Are you sure I can't give him a message?" I asked again, trying to keep my voice level.

"No, I'm going to wait for him. Where's his office?" he asked brusquely, peering down the hallway.

"Oh, well, you can have a seat right over there until he comes," I offered, pointing to the chairs in the corner.

"I'm his brother, damn it, I'm going to wait in his office!" he yelled. I paused and studied him for a moment.

"Oh, you're his brother? It's Blake, right?" I asked, hoping that this was the right tack. Blake's eyebrows rose.

"He told you about me?" The surprise in his voice was obvious.

"A little," I continued. "That he has a brother and a sister. Hannah, right?" Blake's face visibly softened at the sound of her name. "He'll want to see you," I said. "Can I get you anything while you wait?"

"You have any food here?" he asked hopefully. I nodded.

"Follow me. You can wait in Nick's office and I'll see what I can find in the kitchen."

"Thank you," he replied, as I stood to lead the way. I got him situated in a chair in the corner and went to scour the kitchen for leftovers. There were a couple of sodas in the cabinets, a box of crackers, some yogurt in the fridge, and a bowl of apples. I grabbed one of each and took them back to Blake.

"Help yourself," I told him, setting it down on the chair next to him. "I'll just be out front if you need anything." He nodded, gazing at the pile of food hungrily. I strode out of the room straight for my desk and pulled out my phone. I texted Nick.

—Blake is here, he's waiting for you to get back.

It was only moments before a reply came.

—I will be right there. Do not leave him alone.

I read the message and set my phone down on the desk. I returned to the office and found Blake where I had left him, most of the food now gone. "I just got a text from Nick. He's on his way back." I paused, trying to come up with a reason to stay. "Is there anything more I can get for you?" I asked. Blake opened his mouth to respond, but the phone at my desk began to ring. I glanced between him and my desk and decided to risk it.

"I'll be right back," I said, darting for the phone. It was a stupid telemarketer. I hate being rude, but when a simple "no" wouldn't do the trick, I hung up on them and headed straight back to Nick's office, almost crashing into Blake as he was coming out of the doorway.

"I have to go," he announced, continuing briskly to the front door. "I can't wait around for him anymore."

I almost had to jog to keep up with him, trying in vain to get in front of him. "Blake, wait. He really will be here any minute. He's on his way. He really wants to see you," I attempted, but Blake wasn't convinced. He pushed the front door opened and glanced back at me momentarily.

"Thanks for the food," he said and was out the door. He opened his mouth to say something else but then apparently thought better of it and turned away from me. I followed him out on to the porch, but he quickly turned a corner and was gone. I stood there shivering for a moment, wondering if I should go call Nick and tell him what had happened or just wait for him, when his car came screeching into the parking lot. Nick jumped out, slammed the door, and ran to the porch.

"Where is he?" he demanded, taking the porch steps two at a time.

I shook my head. "Gone." I pointed to the corner where he had disappeared. Nick turned and ran in that direction and disappeared after him. Unable to stand the cold, I returned to the office and pulled my coat over my shoulders to warm up. I headed to Nick's office to clean up the mess of wrappers and crumbs left behind and was just finishing up when I heard the front door slam.

"Quinn?" Nick called.

"In here," I replied, sticking my head out into the hall. He came in and watched me brush the rest of the crumbs into the trash.

"What happened?" he asked brusquely.

I shrugged. "He came in looking for you. He told me who he was and I got him some food; he ate it, obviously," I gestured to the mess in the trash can, "and then he left."

Nick's eyes scanned the office. "Did you leave him alone in here?"

"Um, yeah. When I got the food and then when I had to answer the phone."

Nick muttered a curse under his breath and strode to his desk. He started ripping open drawer after drawer. His mouth formed a tight line as he rifled through his things. "It's gone," he muttered angrily.

"What's gone?" I asked hesitantly, instantly regretting the question as his focus shifted from his desk to me.

"Every bit of cash I had in this desk, plus the office check book," he barked glaring at me.

"He's only been gone a few minutes, Nick. Call the bank. They can stop the checks."

Nick laughed ironically. "Knowing Blake, he's already spent a few hundred." He ripped the phone off his desk and punched the numbers in violently. I stood, listening as he reported the theft to the bank and not realizing that I should have left when I had the chance. As soon as he hung up the phone, his gaze shifted back to me.

"I can't believe you did that," he muttered angrily.

"Did what?"

"Exactly what I asked you not to do, Quinn. What is wrong with you?" Nick yelled. I pulled back in shock. It took a split second for me to decide that this wasn't a flight kind of day. I had not escaped inheriting at least some of my mother's temper.

"What is wrong with me?" I countered. "I don't remember being stupid enough to leave a wad of cash just sitting in my desk." I was on the balls of my feet, my body tensed as if anticipating a physical blow.

"No," Nick shouted back, "You are just stupid enough to leave a drug addict and a drunk alone in my office. You should have called the police; you shouldn't have let him past reception." His jaw was hard set and his hands were gesticulating wildly.

"It was your brother, Nick. If you wanted me to call the cops on your brother, you should have said so."

"You knew about him, Quinn. How stupid can you get? Anywhere else and you would have been fired for that."

I set my own jaw and narrowed my eyes. "So fire me, Nick. I could use a break from you and your drama."

Nick scoffed. "Really? I thought that's why you were with Mr. Metrosexual. Will they? Won't they? Don't tell me you don't love that drama."

"Grow up," I shot back.

"Me grow up? That's *hilarious* since you're the one who just realized that life isn't all sunshine and daisies. I'm really sorry that bad stuff keeps happening to EVERYONE ELSE, Quinn. Is that hard for you?" His voice was horribly mocking and the last straw of my restraint broke.

"You know, for a few minutes, I thought you weren't the worst person I had ever met. Obviously I was wrong about that. Do us all a favor and just go live under the bridge with your pothead brother." I clapped my hand over my mouth, sorry as soon as I said it.

Nick's eyes widened slowly. He looked as if I had slapped him across the face. "Get out," he said slowly, his voice icy.

I backed away, the bile rising in my throat. I had never said anything so horrible in my life, and I wanted to apologize, but I knew if I opened my mouth I would vomit or sob, and I didn't want to do either. I managed to ignore the burning behind my eyes and at the back of my throat until I got to my car and then couldn't hold back any longer. I sobbed in the front seat for longer than I wanted to. As soon as I could see clearly, I pulled out of the parking lot, and once my voice had steadied I was dialing Josh. By the time I got home, I had a new job.

The next morning I headed straight to Marie's office, refusing to so much as look at Nick, out of equal parts anger and humiliation.

"Can I talk to you for a minute?" I asked, closing the door behind me. Marie looked up from the paperwork before her and nodded. I sat in the chair opposite her.

"I was offered a job," I began. I had practiced this speech several times last night. Marie raised her eyebrows and I shifted my gaze to my lap. "I start January 2. So, I guess, this is my two-week notice. I appreciate everything that you have done for me," I continued focusing again on Marie, "but it's just time for me to make a change." She was studying me, brows furrowed.

"Can I ask why you have decided to take this job offer?" she asked, her tone brisk. I had come up with a dozen answers to this question last night. Do I tell her about the fight with Nick? About the awkwardness of the past few weeks? At the last second, my mind drew a blank. I opened and closed my mouth several times before answering.

"I just felt like this was an opportunity that I couldn't pass up," I replied slowly. I glanced at Marie, trying to determine if she believed me and hoping she wouldn't see me as ungrateful. She nodded shortly.

"Well, we will miss you, but if you're committed, then I suppose that's the way it will have to be." Marie pulled open a desk drawer and produced a short list. “Will you please place a want ad for a secretary with these publications?” she asked, handing it to me.

I nodded. “Anything else?” I asked.

“Just your usual responsibilities,” she replied, turning her attention back to her desk. On second thought, I stopped in the doorway.

“And Marie, I never thanked you for sending that stuff with Nick while I was so sick.”

She looked up at me, her head tilted in confusion. “What?”

“When I was out sick a few weeks ago. Nick brought by a bag of remedies from you. I just wanted to thank you.”

Marie shook her head. “I didn’t send him with anything, Quinn. I’m sorry.”

“Oh,” I replied, surprised. “Well, um, never mind then, I guess.” She nodded briefly and turned back to her computer.

I headed back to my desk, turned on the computer, and tried not to think about anything but work.

16

"Quinn, you have got to get it checked." Nathan followed me into the house and slammed the door behind him.

"I don't have any money, Nate," I snapped, throwing my coat over a kitchen stool.

"I guarantee the medical bills will be more expensive than the car repairs," he shot back. I wrinkled my nose at him, annoyed that he was right. We had just gotten home from a quick drink run to Sonic, and Nate was concerned about the odd noise my car was making, the same noise that I had been trying to ignore for about week.

"If you go right now, I'll go with you, make sure they don't try to rip you off," he offered.

"Seriously, Nate, I spent all my money on the stupid car. There's not much left." It was killing me that this stupid car that I had been so excited about would be the death of me, physically or financially, and probably both.

"You know Dad will lend you some. Plus, Dad will probably hide your keys until you get it fixed."

"Dad doesn't know about it."

"Yet." The threat hung unspoken in the air.

I growled at Nate and gathered up my coat and keys again. "Let's go," I muttered, grabbing my drink and brushing past him. We pulled up in front of Stan's a few minutes later. My parents had been bringing their cars here for as long as I could remember. I was fairly confident that they wouldn't attempt to rip me off, but I was still begrudgingly glad to have Nate there with me. I knew nothing about cars. Someone could easily convince me to replace my *dufendorfer* and I wouldn't know I'd been scammed until I told my Dad about it.

I pushed the painted glass doors open to an empty office. This whole situation was becoming more irksome by the second. Nate found a bell on the counter and dinged it a couple of times, just to be obnoxious. The swinging doors behind the counter opened and a familiar smiling blonde appeared.

"Kristen!"

"Hey," she replied with a flash of recognition on her face. "Quinn, right? I haven't seen you at church, so I guess you decided the singles ward was a no-go?"

I wrinkled my nose. "It's complicated." I was interrupted by a loud "ahem" from behind me. "Oh, this is my brother, Nathan. Nate, this is Kristen. She's in the singles ward."

"Hey," he greeted her with calculated nonchalance. I rolled my eyes at his apparent attempt at coolness and he edged his way between the counter and me.

"So," he continued, "you work here?"

"Kind of," Kristen replied, pulling out the desk chair. "My dad owns the place. I help out on weekends." She pulled a clipboard and a pen out and looked between the two of us expectantly. "Car problems?"

I nodded. "It's been making this weird noise for a while and *somebody*," I looked significantly at Nate, "made me bring it in to get it checked out."

"Well, I hate to say it, but somebody is probably right," she responded, throwing a smile in Nate's direction.

"I like her," Nate replied, smiling back.

I rolled my eyes as Kristen stood. "Give me your keys, I'll have them check it out. Here," she handed me a clipboard, covered with several forms and a pen. "Fill these out and I'll be right back."

"Thanks," I said, taking the clipboard and settling in a chair. Nathan plunked down next to me. I hated filling out forms. Year. Make. Model.

"So," he muttered, "she's in the singles ward, huh?"

"Yep." Mileage? Insurance information? Ugh.

"But you don't know her very well?"

"Nope." I glanced at him and realized he was staring intently out the front window of the shop. I followed his gaze. Kristen was visible talking to one of the mechanics and pointing to my car. I watched his eyes follow her until she disappeared from sight. He pulled out his phone, but kept glancing out the window and toward the swinging doors until Kristen returned a few minutes later with the announcement that the diagnostics should only take about a half an hour.

Rather than return to her spot behind the desk, she took a seat opposite us and struck up a conversation. The longer we chatted the more I liked her, and I could tell Nate felt the same. I was almost disappointed when the mechanic appeared to announce that it was a small fix, "only a slipped belt, we fixed it in about a minute and a half. Kristen can process you out." Apparently the feeling was mutual, because after I had paid a very reasonable bill, Kristen invited me to hang out with her and a bunch of friends.

"We might go to a movie. I don't really know what we're doing, but you should come. I think you'd get along great with everyone." She handed me my receipt.

"I would love to," I replied. "Text me details?"

"Of course! And, uh, Nate," she called over my shoulder, "you should come too."

Nate perked up when he realized she was talking to him. "Oh, um, yeah, sure." He tried so hard to sound casual that he sounded a bit ridiculous. I smirked at him as we left the auto shop.

"So, you really want to hang out with your little sister tonight, huh?" I teased as we got into my newly repaired and quiet car.

"Something like that," he muttered.

"You know," I continued obnoxiously, pulling out into traffic, "it's good you have a sister. Otherwise, you'd never meet any girls." Nate smacked my arm as I laughed. It was good to have my brother back.

"So, are you going to marry him or not?" Annie asked bluntly as she scrubbed Christmas dinner off a plate. I scowled at her.

It had been a very long day and I wasn't in the mood. Christmas is supposed to be the most wonderful time of the year and holly jolly, but Lydia's death and Nathan's divorce had us all subdued. We had a tree, we had lights outside, but most of the Christmas decorations still resided in their home in the garage. There had been presents under the tree this morning, but most had been purchased and wrapped by Dad, and therefore most were gift cards and cash.

Grandma had somehow convinced Uncle Steven to join the festivities, but I could tell from the moment he arrived that he regretted it. Most of us spent the evening trying to avoid any topic that would remind anyone else of Lydia, which gave us little to discuss. Aaron hadn't returned to his mission just yet, and he and Nate and I managed to forget everything for a little while with a long mission conversation. Uncle Steven left shortly after dessert, and my grandparents followed soon after. Mom went to bed, leaving Annie and I in charge of clean up.

The house was quiet now, with the boys occupied in the basement by their new video games, and Nate hiding in his room to avoid any clean up responsibilities. I turned my back on Annie and stuck a glass into the dishwasher.

"You know, we've barely been back together for a month. It seems a little too soon for that. And it's really none of your business," I replied venomously.

"Sorry," Annie snapped back. The truth was, I was wondering the same thing. Actually, "wondering" might be understating it. I hated this relationship limbo, neither one of us willing to risk saying anything that might scare the other away. True, we had only been back together for a month. But we had been together for almost a year before I left on my mission, and if I hadn't gone, I couldn't see a future that didn't involve marrying Joshua. We danced around the subject of our future now and then, but I didn't want to ruin the already slightly precarious relationship we had by jumping the gun. And already, things were a little rocky since my bout with the flu. Josh couldn't seem to get over the fact that I let Nick take me to the doctor.

"Why didn't you just call me?" he had complained a few days after the fact.

I rolled my eyes and responded the same way I had the first six times he asked. "You were at school, Josh. Plus, I wouldn't have called anyone. If he hadn't shown up, I would have just stayed in bed all day. My dad probably would have just taken me that night."

I sighed in exasperation. "I'm not blaming you Josh. It's fine. It happened. I'm better. And to top it all off, I quit. I will never see him again after December 31. We're all good, okay?"

However, we had started to run together again. His suggestion to run another race together had become reality, and Josh had signed us up to run a 10k together in February, "an easy one to get you back into the swing of things, and then we can do another marathon in the spring!" We were running together several days a week, and I loved having a partner to motivate me to put on my running shoes more often. I really hoped that would make up for the whole sick day awkwardness.

Despite all of the bumps and false starts, a little part of me had secretly hoped that Josh would propose to me on Christmas. Christmas Eve, at least. I could have used a romantic night out, just the two of us. But no such luck. Josh showed up this morning after his family's Christmas brunch to exchange gifts, and the moment I saw the size of the box he handed me, I knew that it did not contain a ring. I hid my disappointment well and exclaimed over the beautiful sweater that he had picked out for me, wondering where we would go from here.

Annie stuck the last few spoons into the dishwasher and stalked to the couch where she collapsed dramatically. I dropped the soap into the dishwasher and turned it on before following her. The Christmas tree lights were still on, and a few newly opened presents still strewn beneath it. A garbage bag full of wrapping paper still sat in the corner of the room next to a small pile of empty boxes.

Annie gazed at the tree lights for a moment before speaking. "I need a job, Quinn." Apparently I had been forgiven for snapping at her and I sank into the armchair next to her.

"So go get one," I advised snarkily. She glared at me. I flashed a fake smile in her direction and dodged a well-aimed kick.

"Since you don't drive the Civic anymore, Dad is making me pay for all the gas. Gas is expensive," she whined. "Plus, this is the worst time in the world to get a job," she barked irritably, propping herself up on her elbows. "The holidays are over, which means everyone is firing all of their extra seasonal workers and no one is looking to hire."

She was right about that. I gazed at her for a few moments, thinking. "You could babysit?" I suggested. Annie cocked an eyebrow at me incredulously.

"Really, Quinn?" she asked. "Most people want their children alive and their house intact at the end of the night."

It was funny, because it was true. Annie really never was good with kids. She managed with Ezra and Oliver because they were her little brothers, but outside of them, there were very few children that she was willing to tolerate. I babysat all through junior high, and I think the neighborhood families all expected her to follow in my footsteps and were pretty disappointed when she turned down pretty much every job offer she ever received. That, and the one time she had accepted a babysitting job, she almost burned down the house with a bag of microwave popcorn.

"Shoveling snow?"

She just glared at me for that one. And then it hit me. "You know, I'm quitting the real estate office," I began, sitting up straight in my chair.

"So?"

"Well, they haven't found anyone to take my place yet. Things are pretty slow right now, but there's a possibility that they could get by with a part-time secretary for the next month or two. It'd have to be temporary," I explained, "but it would be better than nothing."

Annie's eyes were wide as she sat up. "Do you really think they would hire me? That would be so much better than fast food or something."

I shrugged hopefully. "I think if Marie likes you, there's a good chance. The office reopens tomorrow. You can come with me and we'll ask her then." I picked up a book Dad had given me for Christmas and started flipping through it.

Annie studied me thoughtfully. "Will that be weird?"

"What? Working for Marie?" I looked up from my book.

Annie nodded. "And me working with Nick."

"Why would that be weird?"

"Well," Annie hesitated. "You and Nick aren't exactly on good terms. Would it be weird if your sister started working there?"

I had given Annie the watered-down version of the events surrounding Blake's appearance. She knew that Nick and I had fought, but I didn't tell her what either of us had said. Or that he hadn't actually spoken to me directly since. Or that I couldn't quite bring myself to look him in the eye.

"Weird for him or for me?" I asked with a laugh, trying to lighten the air.

"Me!" she responded, smacking my arm.

I pursed my lips, considering, and let the book drop onto my lap. "No," I said slowly. "No, I think it will be okay. You don't have a history with him, so you'll go in with a clean slate."

"Except that I'm your sister. That's kind of a history right there." I couldn't deny that she had a point there.

"I don't think he'll hold it against you," I announced slowly with more confidence than I felt.

"I *would* love it," Annie murmured.

I nodded my agreement. "It's a good job." I picked up the novel again, and began to read, focusing my attention away from just how good a job it was.

The next morning Annie rode to work with me. I was impressed at her attempt to look professional. She wore a purple button-down shirt that made her eyes almost glow and some slacks that I didn't even know she owned. The purple streaks had mostly faded from her hair, and much to Mom's relief, she hadn't had a touch-up lately. She definitely looked older than sixteen. As we pulled into the familiar parking lot, I breathed a little sigh of relief that Marie's was the only car there. I had told Annie that it wouldn't be weird, and I didn't think it would be after all was said and done, but I was worried that Nick would oppose the whole idea from the start.

After dropping our things off at my desk, the two of us walked back to Marie's office. Annie grabbed my arm nervously as we approached. "Are you sure this is going to work?"

"You want a job or not?"

Annie took a deep breath and nodded. Marie was in her customary plum suit and sensible shoes, standing at her filing cabinet, her back to us. "Knock, knock," I called through the open doorway. She glanced over her shoulder and smiled at us.

"Good morning, Quinn." She peered at Annie, "And this must be your sister. I can see the resemblance." Marie smiled and held out her hand. Annie stepped forward and took it.

"Annie Matthews," Annie introduced herself.

"Nice to meet you," Marie replied.

"Nice to meet you too," said Annie.

Marie turned to look at me expectantly. "And to what do I owe this pleasure?"

I tried not to look too nervous. I hated asking for things, especially favors like this. "I know that we haven't—" I hesitated, hoping that I wasn't doing Annie a disservice by reminding Marie that I quit, "that you haven't hired a replacement for me. And Annie is looking for a job. We were wondering if it might be," I paused, looking for a suitable word, "feasible that she might replace me."

"Really?" asked Marie, studying Annie more intently.

Annie jumped right in. "I would love to work with you, but I am still in high school so I would only be available on a part-time basis. That being said, I am willing to work as hard as necessary to keep up with the demand. Quinn mentioned that things were slow right now, so until they pick back up, a part-time secretary could handle the workload." Annie continued before Marie could speak. "I know that it would only be on a temporary basis, but very few people are hiring right now, and I would really appreciate the opportunity and the experience."

I regarded Annie with respect. Marie shared my appraising look. She studied Annie momentarily before inclining her head in a slight nod. "I think that we might just be able to work something out."

Annie's face split into an enthusiastic smile. "Thank you so much! Quinn can train me for the next couple of days, and then I can start on the second."

Marie nodded with a smile. "If you're anything like your sister, I think we will get along just fine. Quinn, I'll pull out the employment papers tomorrow for her to fill out."

I recognized the dismissal and beckoned to Annie. "We'll get started. Thanks, Marie."

She just nodded and turned back to her work. Annie followed me back out to the front, the huge smile still on her face. As soon as we were in the lobby, Annie threw her arms out and danced around silently in victory. I laughed quietly as I pulled a chair over from the waiting area to my desk, and once Annie finished celebrating, the two of us sat down in front of the computer. I began to walk her through the system, beginning with an explanation of how the appointment book worked, when the front door opened and Nick walked in. I glanced up briefly, but turned back to the computer as soon as I saw him. Annie was not so discerning.

"Good morning," she said. "How can I help you?"

I looked over at her, eyebrows raised.

"What?" she asked. "I'm just practicing." She looked back up at Nick, who was now standing in front of the desk.

"You're the new secretary?" he asked, his eyes darting between the two of us. I focused on the computer and let Annie deal with it.

"I am," she replied with a smile. She held out her hand, "Annie Matthews."

"Matthews?" he asked, ignoring her hand. "You're Quinn's sister?"

"Guilty," she joked. Nick shifted his gaze to me, back to her, and then strode purposefully to Marie's office. I heard the door slam shut and Nick's raised voice trickle out. Annie turned to me, her eyes wide.

"You said it wouldn't be weird," she accused. I offered her an awkward smile.

"Apparently, I was wrong," I offered with a shrug. "He'll get over it." I turned back to the computer and picked up where

I had left off. Annie was slightly disgruntled, particularly when we heard Marie's door fly open and Nick's slam, but she got over it quickly. Nick left the office shortly thereafter without another word and we spent a successful day going over the inner workings of the office. She didn't mention Nick again until the ride home that afternoon.

"You know, you never mentioned how cute he is."

I pulled myself out of musing what I would wear for my date with Josh that night. "What?" I asked distractedly.

"Nick. You're right, he's totally a jerk, but he's really cute." She shifted her gaze out the window. "It always seems such a waste to me when such a hot guy is a jerk."

"He's not a jerk," I replied softly. "Most of the time." I could feel Annie's eyes on me, but kept my own focused on the road.

"Well, that's interesting," she said. I glanced at her quickly, but she looked away and didn't elaborate. She was quiet the rest of the way home.

Annie picked up on everything at the office surprisingly quickly. Luckily, there really wasn't a lot to learn. On my last day of work at Jonas Realty, I went over everything quickly again, just to make sure that she didn't have any questions, and was confident that she could handle everything without me. At the end of the day, Marie appeared with a card and a hug. I pulled away from her, surprised by the amount of emotion I felt. "Thanks for everything, Marie," I told her, my voice thick. "This job has been incredibly val—" I stopped short as Nick made his way down the hall. He brushed past us without so much as an acknowledgment of our presence. Marie watched as my eyes followed him out.

"Don't worry about it," she reassured me softly, squeezing my arm. "There's more there than you realize." I studied her for a moment, wondering how much she knew and nodded briefly, unsure how to respond. I gathered up my things and

Annie, and we left. "See you next week!" Marie called after Annie.

As we pulled out of the parking lot, I glanced back at the little house one last time, wondering if I had made a mistake.

"What are you waiting for, Quinn? I've got a date tonight, let's go!" I shook off my doubts and turned my attention to the rest of my life.

Joshua did not ask me to spend New Year's Eve with him. He just showed up at my door around 5:00 that night and announced we were going out. I scrambled to get ready, a little annoyed at him for the lack of communication. He took me to Provo for First Night at the mall, which had been our traditional New Year's Eve date before my mission. The mall was packed to capacity and the air was thick with live music, the smell of fried food, and an energy that only exists on New Year's Eve.

Provo had been throwing this party for years, and it has gotten bigger and better every year. Neither of us had eaten dinner and so we bounced around to all the different food vendors, feasting on pizza, caramel corn, giant Icees, fudge and, my favorite, cotton candy. Josh handed me the largest cotton candy that I had ever seen with a smile.

"I got enough for both of us," he announced. I just shook my head sadly at him.

"I'm really sorry to tell you, but you didn't." I pulled a giant tuft from the bright pink mass and let it melt on my tongue.

"You aren't seriously going to eat all of that alone? Aren't you worried about calories or something?"

I pursed my lips. "Josh, there are a few things you need to know. Number one: calories eaten on a holiday don't count.

Number two: I don't share cotton candy. Pretty much everything else, sure, I am happy to share with you. But you're going to need to get your own cotton candy." Another huge wad of the stuff went into my mouth to prove my point.

"Okay," Josh said slowly, looking at me like he thought I was crazy. He was quiet a moment, gazing around the mall. "Dancing or karaoke?"

"Let's start with dancing," I grabbed Josh's hand and pulled him toward the dance floor.

We danced for a while at the big band stage, where we discovered that I have two left feet and Joshua not a ton of patience, and then headed over to the karaoke stage to take a break and make fun of the participants. We stood at the back of the crowd, far enough away that no one would be able to hear our mocking. I nestled my head against Josh and watched as the worst singer I had ever heard finished up his song.

"That's just sad," I commented, shaking my head. "I don't even have the heart to mock him." Josh laughed. "No, really," I defended. "I bet he has no idea how terrible he just sounded."

Josh leaned closer to me to be heard over the din. "I bet his friends dared him to get up there and do that and now they owe him money," he said knowingly.

"I hope it's a lot," I laughed, pulling Josh's arm around my waist. I shifted so my head was leaning against his chest. I loved that he was so much taller than me.

"Hey," he said suddenly, "isn't that the guy from your office?"

"What?" I asked distractedly, pulling my attention away from the current performer, who actually had some talent. "Who?"

"That guy. The one from your mission."

He had my full attention now. "Where?"

"Front of the crowd."

I scanned the audience looking for Nick's dark head of curly hair. I found him standing next to the stage, the next person in line to perform.

"Um, yeah, I think that's him," I muttered, studying him.

"Does he sing?" Josh asked.

I shrugged. "I think so," I replied vaguely, knowing full well the magnificence of Nick's voice. He had been the star performer at many a zone conference.

The singer on stage ended her song and bounded down the stairs to enthusiastic applause. Nick took his place on stage, microphone in hand, and smiled at the audience. There were several catcalls in response. The first few bars of the song began and Nick's eyes scanned the audience. He spotted me and his eyes widened for a fraction of a second before he began to sing. He was better than I had remembered. Better by far than any of the other performers we had heard. And he sang Dylan's "Make You Feel My Love," one of my favorites.

Goose bumps ran up and down my arms and I was grateful for my long-sleeved sweater to hide them. I felt Josh tense behind me every time that Nick's eyes wandered in my direction, and they wandered my way often. As the last few bars of Nick's song faded, the audience, particularly the female contingent, exploded with cheers.

"Not bad," commented Josh icily, as Nick exited the stage. "And you know what? That gives me an idea. Stay here," he said as he pulled away from me.

I knew immediately what he was thinking and I also knew that it was the last thing on the planet that I wanted him to do.

"Josh," I called after him, "let's go do something else. We could go dancing again," I suggested hopefully. "Or see a movie. I thought you said there was a new one out that you wanted to see?"

Josh just flashed me a confident smile and swaggered toward the karaoke line. I cringed, knowing what was coming.

Josh loved to sing. He sang in the shower. He sang in the car. He sang while he was cooking. At some point in his life, he got it in his head that he had a great voice. The thing was, he didn't. Olivia had teased him all his life, but he had brushed it off as his annoying little sister making fun of him, and therefore, not viable criticism. In high school, he had been too much of a jock to try out for anything that would place him firmly in the geek camp, like theater or choir, so no one had the opportunity to bust his bubble then.

And now, he was headed to the stage to make an idiot of himself in front of, oh, eight thousand people or so. I debated seriously about making up some kind of emergency. Was I willing to do myself physical harm? And to what extent? Just as a plan began to form in my mind, I heard my name behind me.

"Quinn." I turned to find Nick, his arms intertwined with a slightly familiar, gorgeous blonde standing next to him. Plastering a smile on my face and ignoring the shock that he was actually speaking to me, I greeted him.

"Hey, Nick, how are you?" I asked heartily. I kind of wanted to kick myself for sounding like an idiot.

"Great." Despite the smile on his face, his voice was slightly clipped. "I just wanted to say hi. Oh, and introduce you to my date. This is Tori." He nodded toward the girl next to him. "Tori, this is Quinn. We used to work together." There was a definite emphasis on "used to."

Tori giggled and gave a little wave. "Hi!" Her platinum hair was big and solid, and she bounced strategically as she spoke.

I bit the inside of my cheeks. "Hi," I replied stiffly, resisting the urge to ask her if she needed some hairspray.

"So, you used to work for Nick?" she asked. I bristled.

"No," I corrected primly. "No, I used to work *with* him." My condescending tone was obvious, but she didn't seem to pick up on it. Nick, however, raised his eyebrows, whether in surprise or annoyance, I wasn't sure.

When I turned back to Tori, her attention was on the stage. "Ooh, he's cute."

Nick and I both looked up. Josh was adjusting the microphone. He had apparently sweet-talked his way to the front of the line. He caught me looking and winked loudly. I grimaced, but gritted my teeth and hoped it looked like a smile from this distance.

The song began and I braced myself against the noise. An 80s power ballad. Fan-freaking-tastic. Tori seemed captivated by the performance, but Nick turned to look at me, eyes wide and a delighted smile on his face. He caught my expression and his smile grew.

"That's him, isn't it Quinn?" he asked snidely, knowing the answer full well.

"What?" I shouted, feigning deafness over the music. Who am I kidding? It was just noise.

"Your boyfriend."

Tori whipped around so fast I thought her hair would fall off. "He's your boyfriend?" she asked incredulously. Her eyes gave me the once over, head to toe. "How'd you pull that off?" Possibly the most hurtful part of that comment was the genuine sincerity in her voice. It wasn't an insult. She was obviously amazed and astounded by the coupling. When she realized that I would not be answering the question, she turned back to the stage as if nothing had happened.

After scraping my jaw off the floor and blinking back the tears that were stinging my eyes, I tried to focus on Joshua and ignore her. Moments later, I was surprised to hear Nick tell her off for it.

"Seriously, Tori, was that necessary?" he muttered.

She turned to him with a confused look on her face. "What?" she asked blankly. I watched them out of the corner of my eye, trying to keep my obvious focus on the stage.

"You don't have to be like that." He lowered his voice, but not far enough.

"What? I just meant he's way hotter than she is, so I'm just trying to figure out how *she* got a guy like *that*. I wasn't trying to be mean or anything. I was just curious." Tori turned back to the stage. Nick looked back to me, a horrified expression on his face. She kept talking loud enough for pretty much the whole crowd to hear her. "And you know that thing, where there's always one person in a relationship that is hotter than the other? Well, he's hotter than she is. She's the reacher. That's just the way things work," she continued over her shoulder.

Nick just stared at her, appalled, as she bounced away to the music, his jaw set. He turned back to me; his brow furrowed and gripped my arm roughly. He pulled me toward him and spoke directly into my ear.

"She's an idiot. He's the one reaching, not you." I felt his warm breath tickling my ear as he spoke. He smelled of cologne and cotton candy. He backed away and grabbed Tori's hand, pulling her away without looking at me. I watched him leave, utterly confused and a little out of breath.

"Quinn Matthews, would you come to the stage please?"

My head swiveled away from the crowd where Nick had disappeared and back toward the stage. There stood Josh, a huge smile on his face. His song had finished, but the karaoke music played in the background and the crowd began to cheer. I shook my head the tiniest bit, hoping he would notice and just come down. He didn't.

"C'mon, Quinn! She needs a little encouraging. Help me out guys."

My stomach dropped as the crowd cheered louder. I shot him a pleading look but it didn't help. He was too focused on the cheering crowd and the microphone in his hands. The first wave of nausea hit and I took deep breaths, hoping it would pass. I plastered a smile on my face, holding back the tears of embarrassment, and moved slowly toward the stage. Josh met me at the top of the stairs and pulled me into center stage. My breathing was panicked now, and I was pretty sure that if he asked me to start singing, I would pass out.

Josh shot a smile to the crowd and then lowered himself to one knee. The crowd exploded.

My eyes widened with panic. This was not the way I was supposed to get engaged. There should be flowers and candles and chocolate and privacy. This was my worst nightmare. This had to be a joke. He had to be pulling a prank on me. That was the only explanation. I bit my lip and fought back the anxiety attack that threatened to overpower me.

"Quinn, will you marry me?" Josh spoke into the microphone and held up a ring.

This wasn't a joke. He was totally serious. Choking back the bile rising in my throat, I nodded quickly and smiled, hoping to get off the stage as fast as possible. The noise from the crowd grew even louder as Josh shoved the ring onto my finger and kissed me.

As I pulled away, hurrying off the stage as fast as I could, I caught sight of Nick and Tori again. They watched from the back of the crowd, Tori with blatant amazement on her face, but Nick's face unreadable.

Josh led me off the stage, and excited girls surrounded us, clamoring to see the ring. It was pretty, I had to admit: a marquise-cut diamond on an embellished white gold band. It took a long time to get my heart to stop pounding and I excused the few tears that escaped as tears of joy.

Josh paraded me around for the rest of the night. We ran into several acquaintances, and by the time fireworks were exploding in the sky, I felt like matching explosions were happening in my stomach. Rather than linger, I asked Josh to take me home, citing exhaustion and a slightly upset stomach from all the cotton candy. After an "I told you so," he left me on the porch with a kiss and an argument that we should wake my parents and tell them the news right now. I promised an official announcement at dinner the next day and escaped into the house.

I was still reeling. It was strange. I had thought I had wanted a proposal, I had been hoping for it, but now that the ring was on my finger, I didn't feel the way I thought I should. I loved Joshua. I should be thrilled. This was the life I had dreamed about and then mourned when I thought it impossible.

As I stared at the ring, Nick's face floated unbidden through my mind. I shook it off and comforted myself with the thought of the new job that I would be starting, well, technically, tomorrow. Nick officially wasn't a part of my life anymore, and I had to accept that.

Working in a dentist's office wasn't all that different from working in a realtor's office. I was still making and confirming appointments, filing patient records, and keeping track of office supplies. I also had to deal with insurance companies on a regular basis, which I quickly decided was not my favorite thing. True, there were more patients than we ever had clients at Jonas, but there were three secretaries rather than one to keep up with the workload, so it didn't seem quite as overwhelming as it could have.

The other two secretaries, Amanda and Betty, were so sweet and wanted to know all about me, particularly my relationship with Josh. Betty had been working for Josh's dad since Josh was about eight and loved him like a son. She told me more than once that she was thrilled to meet me and get to know me so well. Amanda hadn't been there quite as long. She was married with three kids and only worked part time.

The biggest difference between the two offices was the amount of personal interaction. At Marie's, clients coming into the office were few and far between. Marie and Nick saw most of their clients at showings and at title companies, and most of my interaction with them was over the phone. But here, patients came in constantly all day long. I decided that while I was great at the whole appointment and organization thing, I didn't love having to be cheerful all day long. And I missed the solitude and quiet of my desk back at Jonas Realty. But otherwise, I liked it. And Josh was there a few times a week, which meant more time that I got to spend with him.

Wedding plans began in earnest once the date was officially set: June 29. We would be married in Salt Lake and spend the following week on our honeymoon in Florida, at my request. I was looking forward to the return visit, as well as a chance to be a tourist instead of a missionary. Mom took over the arrangements zealously, reserving a beautiful reception hall and picking out the flowers without consulting me. She spent an entire day calling friends and family to share the news.

"She's thrilled to have something to make up for the disgrace that is me," Nate said in a low voice as we watched a movie and listened to Mom call her second cousins with the news.

"Nate," I chided, nudging him with my shoulder. "That's not true." I spoke reassuringly, but we both knew that he was right.

Annie was almost as excited as Mom was. At first. She was thrilled when I told her the news and demanded final say in the bridesmaid dresses. "You have mostly good taste," she explained, "but sometimes you need a little help." But as the weeks wore on, she became less and less interested in wedding plans. I chalked it up to time and, well, the fact that it was the major and sometimes only topic of conversation at our house and Annie was tired of hearing about it. February rolled around and I offered to take her dress shopping with me, but she brushed it off with excuses of having made plans.

"Well, we don't have to go right now. We could go tomorrow instead," I suggested. To be honest, I didn't really care what the dresses looked like, I mostly wanted to avoid Annie's wrath if she hated them.

"Nah, I've got some stuff I need to get done," she turned back to her homework, spread across the kitchen table.

"Next weekend?" I pressed.

She wrinkled her nose. "No good."

"Seriously, Annie," I barked in frustration. "I thought you wanted a say in this?"

She shrugged and looked up at me. She hesitated a moment before speaking. "Are you sure you want to marry Josh?"

"What?" I asked, my mouth dropping open in surprise. "Where did that come from?" She looked at me expectantly. "Seriously?"

Annie nodded.

"Do you think I would waste my time shopping for bridesmaid dresses otherwise?" I asked, hedging the question. The truth was, I hadn't been sure about anything since the day that I stood on the stage, staring down at the glittering ring in shock. Everyone had just seemed so happy with it that I thought it must be the right thing. And I loved Josh. "Why are you asking me?" I pushed. Annie shrugged again.

"I just don't want you to make a huge mistake," she said slowly, shifting her eyes off of me and back onto her papers.

"Do you think I'm making a huge mistake?" I pulled out the chair next to her and sank into it.

She shrugged again. "I don't know. But what if you are?"

"Seriously, Annie, where did this come from?"

"What if there was someone else out there? Who was perfect for you and who was already in love with you? Would it change anything?" She kept her eyes down as she spoke, avoiding my gaze.

I narrowed my eyes at her. "Is there someone else in love with me?" I asked skeptically.

"Just hypothetically," she replied.

"No," I replied slowly, hesitantly. My mind was whirring. Did someone say something to her? And then the name I had been avoiding quickly jumped to my mind. "Nick?"

She glanced up at me. "He didn't say anything. I don't

know. It's just, Josh treats me like a five-year-old. Like your annoying little sister. But Nick treats me like a person."

I laughed ironically. "Why don't you marry him, then?" I asked, standing to leave, done with this conversation.

"He doesn't want to marry *me*," she muttered. This wouldn't change anything. My decision to marry Josh had nothing to do with Nick. Nothing. I paused in the doorway, the doubts trickling in again. *No*, I said to myself, and pushed past them and into my room.

—Is Nate dating someone?

It was from Olivia. I stared at my phone for a moment in confusion before texting back.

—I don't think so. If he is, he didn't tell me. Why?

A reply came almost immediately.

—He broke up with me because he said he wasn't ready to date anyone. But that was crap, wasn't it?

I rolled my eyes. This was exactly what I was worried about when Nate and Olivia started going out.

—No! I'll corner him when he gets home, but I really don't think he is.

I didn't have to wait long. I heard the front door slam and the jingle of keys landing on the kitchen counter less than an hour later. I found Nate with his head in the fridge, rummaging for leftovers.

"There's nothing in there. We just had sandwiches for dinner," I announced. "I got a text from Liv tonight."

He threw a package of cold cuts on the counter. "Yeah?"

"When you broke up with her, you told her that you weren't ready to date yet, right?" I watched as he pulled the rest of the sandwich condiments from the fridge.

"I did what you told me to." He pulled out a couple slices of bread and dropped them on a plate.

"That only works, Nate, if you're not seeing anyone. Are you?" Nate stuck his head back in the fridge and his response was muffled. "What? Are you?"

He reappeared, his face sheepish. "Not really."

"Not really?" I repeated. "What does that mean?"

"We just hang out. Kind of a lot." He finished piling on the cheese and began putting things back into the fridge.

"Who?" I was torn between irritation, on behalf of Olivia, and curiosity.

"Kristen." He replied simply, keeping his eyes down.

"Kristen? Singles ward Kristen?"

Nate nodded and took a bite of his sandwich. "I like her a lot, Quinn." He picked up his plate and carried it to the couch. I followed him over and plopped down next to him.

The curiosity was winning. "How long?"

"Since we met?" I heard the uncertainty in his voice, and I knew it wasn't about the timing.

"Does she know?" I asked softly.

Nate shook his head.

"About any of it?"

"No," he replied softly. "I don't know how to tell her."

I pulled my legs up to my chest and studied him. I tried to see the situation through Kristen's eyes and everything suddenly seemed so much bigger. I wished there was something I could say that would help him. "The longer you wait, the worse it will be."

"So what are you going to tell Liv?" he asked with his mouth full, obviously wanting the change the subject.

"The truth. You're not dating anyone. Not yet."

I got home late. There had been a dental emergency, and I had spent the last hour and a half on the phone with the insurance agency, dealing with a stupid typo on our patient's record. I was tired and I was starving. I dumped my bag and coat over the kitchen counter and yanked the fridge open, praying for leftovers. I scowled at the tiny little container of chicken that had once been dinner and scoured the fridge for something more substantial.

"Hey, what took you so long?" Dad flipped on the rest of the kitchen lights as I slammed the fridge shut. "Whoa, someone's blood sugar a little low?" he joked.

I gave him an annoyed smile and moved my search to the pantry.

"Want to take a drive?" he asked, jingling his car keys.

"To where?" I asked, still searching for a meal. "Cafe Rio?"

"We could make that happen, I suppose," he replied, handing me my coat. "Let's go." We got in the car and pulled out of the driveway. "Hey, call your order in now. Then you won't have to wait in line."

I pulled out my phone and did as requested, finishing the call just as we arrived at the edge of the neighborhood.

"Right, left, or straight?" Dad asked.

I groaned. It was a game we had played all the time when I was little. We would go for a drive and I gave Dad directions, and he had to follow them, no matter where we ended up. We hit a lot of dead ends, and once even managed to make it to the other side of Utah Lake. If I hadn't felt faint from the lack of food, I would have laughed.

"The direction of Cafe Rio," I muttered. I wondered if he could hear my stomach growling.

"You're pick up time isn't for twenty minutes. It'll only take us ten to get there. Give me ten minutes, huh?" He glanced at me and then into the rearview mirror, noticing the line of cars that had formed behind him.

"Blargh," I moaned, annoyed that he was right. If we went straight there we'd have to sit in the parking lot for ten minutes.

"Right, left, or straight?" he asked again.

"Right." He followed my command. After a few turns I realized this game was more fun when I didn't know where everything was. I closed my eyes and he asked again.

"Straight."

"You like your new job?" Dad asked as I leaned my head back against the seat, my eyes still closed.

"Mmmhmm," I mumbled.

"Better than your old one?"

"Eh." I didn't really want to talk about it. It hadn't taken me long to realize that I preferred working with people instead of insurance companies and drugged patients. I wasn't quite ready to admit that, however; nor was I ready to admit how much I missed my former coworkers.

"Things still going well with Josh?" I held up my ring in response. "Yes, you're getting married," Dad droned, obviously biting back his annoyance. "But how are things going?"

"Fine." I shrugged. "Straight."

"Fine?"

"Fine," I repeated, wondering if it was time to start heading in the direction of food.

"You're marrying the man in three months and all you can say is fine?"

"What do you want, Dad? We're madly in love. We're soul mates. My life would mean nothing without him." The sarcasm was dripping.

"Apparently, I've hit a sensitive spot."

My eyes flew open. "What? No! We're good, we're fine, I was being stupid."

"Okay, let's try this. How's school? Are you still taking classes?"

"Left. Yes." I let my eyes close again and felt the car turn as I leaned my head against the cold window.

"Any epiphanies lately on your future degree? Which way?"

"Maybe. Straight. "

"Care to share?" This was what I loved about my father. He was always interested, but never pushy.

I glanced at him, debating about how much I wanted to explain. "I started a couple of business classes in January."

"Really? Which way?"

"Left. Really. I don't know, I think I might want to get a degree in business."

"Can I ask what caused this particular epiphany?"

I hesitated wondering if I wanted to tell this story. It hadn't really been an epiphany; I don't know what I would call it. "Remember back in the fall, when I went to Price for the day?"

"With that missionary?"

"Nick, yeah. Well, it was fascinating. He took me to all the meetings and negotiations with the contractor and the builder and I really liked it. So, after that I just kind of started asking Marie questions about the business side of things. And it was really interesting. So, when I registered for classes this semester, I thought I would try out some business classes with my generals and, so far, I really like it."

"I'm glad you found something that you like." Dad pulled into the Cafe Rio parking lot. "You run in and pick it up, I'll just wait here."

I had ordered some extra chips and pico, and I ate them in the car on the way home.

"So, do you get to see the business side of things at Dr. Adams's office?" Dad asked as I piled a chip with tomatoes.

"Meh," I replied with my mouthful. "I spend a lot of time on the phone, more than I did at Marie's, and most of that time I'm talking to insurance companies." I turned to look at him. "That is one very clear epiphany that I had: I'm *never* working at an insurance company. I couldn't handle that for a single minute."

Dad laughed. "Do you think you'll stay there long?"

I shrugged. "It's a good job. And I don't hate it."

"But you don't love it either," he pointed out sagely.

"No," I agreed, shaking my head. "No, I don't love it."

Dad was quiet for a moment. "Annie seems to like her job. I'm glad you set her up there. She says it's mostly the people she likes. Nick is it? And Marie, they're good people."

"They are," I agreed almost wistfully.

"You sound like you miss working with them," Dad commented quietly.

"Yeah, maybe," I murmured. He pulled the car into the garage.

"You think you could humor me just for a second, let me give you a bit of fatherly advice?" He turned the ignition off. I gazed blankly out the windshield at the neatly ordered shelves that I had spent so long organizing, not so long ago.

"Sure," I muttered, still not looking at him.

"Don't stay there for Josh. I know you love him; you want to spend as much time as possible with him, but don't work there because he wants you to work there. If you want to be doing something else, do something else. And if he truly loves you and wants what is best for you, he'll agree with me." Dad smacked the steering wheel. "Sermon over, you are free to go."

I smiled at him and pushed my door open. He pushed himself out of the car just as I opened the door to the house.

"I love you, Quinn," he called after me.

"Love you too, Dad."

19

I was just getting ready to close up shop at the dentist's office one Tuesday night in March when the text came through. Betty and Amanda were already gone for the day, the last patient had long ago left, and I was in the middle of filing the last stack of patient charts, so I ignored the beeping phone until I was done. I grabbed the phone off my desk on my way to my next task and stopped.

— Call 911 nicks bro knife

The text was from Nick's phone number, but it was obviously not Nick texting. "Annie," I whispered unconsciously. I dialed 911 and gave them the address to Jonas Realty as I ran to my car. I sped frantically across town, arriving just in time to see Annie come bursting out of the front door of the little red brick house. My car lurched into the parking lot and I jumped out of the car.

"Quinn," she yelled, running to me. She threw herself into my arms, sobbing. Her hair was falling out of her ponytail on one side of her head.

"What happened?" I asked. Several sirens screeching into the parking lot interrupted me. We both whirled to watch a police officer jump out of his car and run over to us.

"What's happening?" he asked urgently.

"Inside," Annie gasped through the sobs. "He has a knife."

"Is he alone? Is there someone else in there?" Annie nodded. "How many?"

"Just one," she replied, and the officer didn't wait for more information. He and his partner headed quickly for the front door.

"Marie? Nick?" I asked frantically. Annie shook her head.

"Just Nick." A paramedic approached Annie and for the first time, I realized that she was bleeding.

"Annie!" I exclaimed as the paramedic led her to the ambulance. "He hurt you?" A mixture of rage and fear was coursing through me. Before Annie could speak there were muffled shouts from the house and the officers burst through the front door with Blake in handcuffs.

"We need a medic in here," yelled one of the officers.

"Nick," I whispered, realizing what that meant. Without thinking I began heading for the house. The paramedic brushed past, stopping me.

"Stay here," he demanded and turned and ran into the house. I watched as the police officers shoved Blake into their patrol car. His left side was covered in blood, but other than a small cut on his cheek, he didn't seem injured. He wasn't limping or favoring one side while he walked. I glanced back at Annie. Her arm was cut, but the bleeding was minimal. My breathing turned shallow as I looked back to the house in horror, realizing whose blood covered Blake.

"Quinn?" Annie called softly. She was sitting just inside the ambulance holding a piece of gauze on her arm. I turned to her blankly.

"Nick?" I asked weakly. I felt sick and put my hand on the side of the ambulance to steady myself.

She shook her head. "I don't know." Her face was streaked with tears and watery mascara. I could see a raised welt above her left eye.

"What happened?" I asked again, desperately.

She gave a shuddering sigh. "I was at the desk. Marie's gone showing houses. It was just Nick and I. Blake came in. I didn't know who he was, but he just started yelling 'Where's Nick? Where is he?' and waving a knife around. I didn't know what to do, Quinn. I couldn't think." Annie's voice cracked as she explained. "I just ran to Nick's office. Blake was faster and he, he, uh, threw me against the desk. I hit the corner. That's what this is from," she gestured at her arm and continued. "Nick pushed me behind the desk after I fell and dropped his phone next to me. He went after Blake. I texted you. I didn't want to call." Annie began crying again. "I was scared that if he heard me calling for help, he would come after me again."

I wrapped an arm around her good shoulder and squeezed. "You did good, Annie. What about Nick? What happened after that?"

"They yelled at each other. I guess Blake's mad at him for not giving him money, or something. They fought. I know Nick hit him, and after a few minutes he got Blake to drop the knife. Nick tackled Blake and then he started yelling at me, telling me to run." Annie shuddered. "There was a lot of blood, Quinn, but I didn't know whose it was. I just ran."

A new wave of sobs overtook her and I let her cry into my arms, keeping my eyes steadily on the front door. It seemed like forever before the paramedics carried out the stretcher. I carefully unwound myself from Annie's arms and ran across the parking lot. The paramedics cleared the stairs and were wheeling him across the asphalt. Nick was conscious, but his face was a frightening shade of grey.

"Are you okay?" I asked frantically, and without waiting for an answer, I turned to the paramedic. "Is he going to be all right?"

Nick took my hand. "It's just a flesh wound," he grinned weakly. "I'll be fine." He winced involuntarily as they rolled the gurney over a bump in the parking lot. "Annie?" he asked.

"She's fine. Stitches, maybe, but fine." We reached the ambulance. "Which hospital are you taking him to?" I asked the paramedic.

"IHC. In Provo." The paramedic began to collapse the legs on the gurney.

"I'll follow you there," I said, pulling away from Nick as they began to load him.

Nick shook his head on the pillow. "Quinn, no," he said. "You should stay with Annie."

"She's coming too," I replied firmly. "I'll see you there." The ambulance doors shut and I backed away and hurried back to Annie.

After reassuring her that I would follow and see her at the hospital, the second ambulance followed and I drove behind the convoy in silence. The adrenaline rush of the last half hour was beginning to wear off and I could feel the exhaustion begin to overwhelm me. I took a deep, shuddering breath as we pulled into the hospital parking lot. I saw Annie checked into the ER, where Mom and Dad stood waiting anxiously. I left her in their concerned but capable hands and went in search of Nick. He had been admitted immediately, and it didn't take me too long to find his room. Unfortunately, it was empty.

"They took him down to radiology," a nurse informed me kindly. "You can wait here for him, if you like."

I nodded and sat in an uncomfortable chair opposite the bed. The room seemed to spin around me and I took a deep breath and focused on a machine on the opposite wall. The tears came then, slow and hot. I kept imagining the scene. The knife, the terror that Annie must have felt. I should have been there. It should have been me. I couldn't help but think about what could have happened. I could have lost her. I could have lost him.

The thought stopped me cold. It had wormed its way in unwittingly, but I couldn't shake it. The thought of this world without Nick in it was devastating. I stared around the room, focusing on the mauve walls, the geometric print curtain hanging next to the door, the window that looked out over a shopping center next to the hospital. I watched people getting in and out of their cars, loading bags of groceries, carrying pizzas, and wished that I was one of them, wished that it was yesterday.

The loud clattering of a hospital gurney startled me from my reverie. Nick was wheeled in, followed closely by a young woman. She was beautiful, hovering over him solicitously, her hand on Nick's arm, and suddenly I felt ridiculous. I hadn't spoken to him in weeks, months even, really not since the day that we had screamed at each other. I could hear Nick's voice in my head, yelling at me for leaving Blake alone, and I realized I had no place here. I stood, ready to leave. The nurses slowly cleared the room and as I tried to follow them furtively, Nick looked up and noticed me for the first time.

"Quinn," he began, but I interrupted him.

"No, I just wanted to make sure you were okay," I stuttered. "I'll go now. You probably need to rest." I offered a half smile and made my move for the door.

"No, Quinn, wait," Nick called after me. I turned. "I want you to meet my sister, Hannah." I bit back a sigh of relief and embarrassment as I looked at her again. She was tall and thin, the perfect frame for a dancer, with hair a few shades lighter than Nick's and bright green eyes. When she smiled I could see the family resemblance.

Hannah waved. I smiled back.

"Hannah, it's really nice to meet you," I said, hoping that my embarrassment wasn't too obvious.

"You too," she replied. "I've heard a lot about you."

I glanced back at Nick in surprise and as I studied him, he kept his eyes on me as well. "They said you would be okay?" I asked, my voice wavering slightly. I hadn't been entirely successful in quashing the emotions from a few minutes ago.

He nodded. "He didn't hit anything major," Nick replied soberly. "It wasn't deep. Some muscle damage, but it would have been so much worse if—" He broke off and cleared his throat. "How's Annie?" he asked again.

"She's fine," I replied, taking a step toward him. "I think a few stitches, but otherwise . . . She's downstairs in the ER with my parents getting checked out."

Nick studied me for a moment, his face solemn. "Quinn, I'm so, so sorry. I had no idea that Blake would resort to that. I feel terrible for putting her in harm's way." His voice broke and my heart ached for him. I closed the gap between the bed and myself and took his hand tentatively in mine. It was cold and I instinctively gripped it tighter, trying to warm him.

"You couldn't have known, Nick. She'll be fine. It's not your fault," I reassured him. I bit my lip, debating what to say next, wishing for some way to ease his guilt.

Hannah finally broke the silence. "I'm going to go call Dad again, and Aunt Marie. I'll be back in a bit." She brushed Nick's legs with her fingertips as she swept out of the room. I looked back at him and found a grimace of pain on his face. He squeezed my hand.

"Are you in pain? Should I get the doctor?" I asked nervously.

"No, it's not that. It's fine, I'm fine." His voice was strained, and immediately my urge to flee returned.

"Do you want to rest? I can go." I tried to leave, but Nick tightened his grip on my hand and pulled me back.

"Stay," he said hoarsely. "Please."

I nodded and grabbed the nearest chair and pulled it closer to the bed. We sat silently for a long time, neither of us sure what to say next.

"Nick," I asked, gathering my courage, "what happened?"

Nick sighed and looked out the window. "Last week, I told him I couldn't pay anymore. That I wouldn't pay anymore. I told him that I couldn't help him, unless he got clean. He swore up and down that he would." Nick's voice became emphatic. "That he would get help or go to rehab or something. But I told him that I needed proof before I would give him another dollar." He swiveled his head back to me. "Jim finally got him evicted just after Christmas." Nick sighed and glanced down at his hand. He wove his fingers through mine and didn't look back at me as he finished his story. "Of course he ran out of money. It was inevitable. He called this morning to threaten me if I didn't pay him, but I didn't take him seriously. He's done it before, he usually just disappears for a couple of weeks and when he surfaces again, he's worse off than ever. I thought that, you know, he would do the same thing." Nick paused, his face drawn. "I couldn't protect her," he whispered, his eyes full of tears. "I'm so sorry, Quinn, I did my best, but he hurt her. I wasn't fast enough."

"Shhh," I breathed, "She's all right. It's a cut and a bruise and a fantastic story for her to go back to school with. It's not your fault. And you got her out," I continued, squashing the urge to reach out and push an unruly lock of hair off of his forehead. "Before he could do anything else, you got her out."

"Quinn," he said softly, "Quinn, I'm sorry. I'm so sorry."

I shook my head. "Nick, stop it. It's not your fault," I reprimanded gently.

"No," he disagreed. "No, I'm sorry for yelling at you. For saying those things to you." He looked sheepish. "I didn't mean it. Any of it."

I offered him half a smile. "Neither did I. Nick, I—I was awful. The things I said—" I broke off as a wave of guilt washed over me. "I wish I had never—" I paused for a moment looking for the right words, but finally gave up. "Forgive me?"

"Done." He returned a watery smile and squeezed my hand. Our eyes locked for a long moment. "Quinn," he asked quietly, "why are you here?"

Before I could answer the door swung open. Hannah came in, followed by an older man with grey hair: Nick's father. His nose and his stature made that glaringly obvious. He wore a stiff button-down shirt and a stern look on his weathered face. Once again, I felt out of place and tried to leave, but once more, Nick tightened his grip on my hand before I could and held me tightly.

"Nick," his father said formally with a nod.

"Dad," Nick replied in the same tone. His dad looked blankly at me. "Dad, this is Quinn Matthews; Quinn, this is my father, Jackson Ryan."

Mr. Ryan simply nodded at me and turned back to Nick. "How long do they want you to stay?" he asked shortly.

"Overnight at least, Dad," replied Hannah. "They're pretty sure that the bleeding has stopped, but they don't want to take any chances that it will reopen."

"And your insurance will cover that?" Mr. Ryan asked. My eyes widened and a little sound of exasperation came from Hannah's direction, but Nick simply nodded.

Mr. Ryan nodded again. "It was Blake?" he asked simply, as if asking the weather. Nick just nodded in reply. "Well, maybe you'll listen to me now you've learned your lesson."

I rocked back on my heels in surprise. Nick had told me about his father's attitude toward Blake, but watching it in action was disturbing.

I watched Nick's jaw tighten in anger at his father's response. Nick took a breath and turned to Hannah. "Did you ever get ahold of Marie?" he asked tautly, deftly changing the subject.

Hannah shook her head. "She must be out on showings. She puts her phone on silent. I've left enough messages, though, that her purse has to be practically vibrating off of her shoulder."

Nick offered her an appreciative smile. Hannah's crack had lessened the tension in the room slightly.

She moved closer to the bed and spoke again. "Nick, the

police want to talk to you. They need a statement." Her voice matched the pained look on her face.

Nick cringed. "When?"

"They're waiting outside."

Nick turned to gaze at the closed door, seemingly deciding whether or not to allow them in. I watched his jaw set and his face harden. He nodded shortly.

"I'll go get them," Hannah offered softly and disappeared again.

I studied Nick's face. "Do you want me to stay?" I asked hesitantly.

"Yes," he breathed. "But you probably shouldn't," he added resignedly.

I nodded and gathered my coat and bag. He still didn't release my hand.

"Don't go far," he requested.

"I should go check on Annie. I'll be right back," I promised.

He gave my hand one last squeeze and released me. I nodded to Mr. Ryan and slipped through the door just as two uniformed police officers came in. I paused in the doorway and glanced back at Nick, half reclining in his bed, surrounded by three very stern-looking men. Part of me was glad that I was leaving, but the other half wanted to stand between the officers and Nick, shielding him from having to relive the nightmare all over again. Nick caught my eye and I tried to encourage him with one last smile before allowing the door to close.

Hannah stood in the hallway, leaning against the opposite wall. She smiled as I approached. "Thanks for being here for him," she said. I stood next to her.

"I don't mind," I replied. She studied me intently for a moment.

"I don't think that there is anyone else in the world that he would rather have next to him," she admitted.

"Not Tori?" I asked sarcastically. Hannah laughed out loud.

"I still can't figure out why that boy asked her out in the first place." Hannah shook her head.

"I can give you two pretty big reasons why," I joked, wryly. Hannah laughed again.

"Touché." She shot me a questioning look. "Wait, how do you know Tori?"

I made a face. "I had the privilege of meeting her on New Year's. Delightful girl," I quipped. Hannah laughed again and then grew quiet.

"I'm really sorry about your sister," she murmured a moment later.

"Me too." I fingered my purse. "I was going to go check on her. You want to come?"

Hannah shook her head. "I'll stay here. If Nick and Dad stay in the same room alone together for too long, bad things could happen and we don't need both of them spending the night in the hospital."

I smiled. "I'll be back in a little bit."

Hannah nodded and waved.

I pulled out my phone in the elevator and texted Josh.

—Sorry, can't make it tonight. Something came up.

I had almost reached the ER when I got the reply.

—My mom said there was something on the news about a stabbing at Annie's work. Is she okay?

—Yeah. She's in the hospital now, but it should only be a few stitches and she'll go home tonight.

—You there too?

—Yep.

—Want me to come be with you?

—No. You're sweet, but I'm okay. It sounds worse than it is.

—Call me when you get home?

—Sure.

I flipped my phone off, slid it in my purse, and went to find Annie.

20

It took a surprising amount of research and a little bit of pleading, but I finally managed to track down Annie and my parents, waiting somewhat impatiently to be discharged. They were still in the ER; my parents huddled next to Annie's hospital bed in her curtain-drawn little stall. The gash on her arm had been stitched up neatly: five stitches in all, plus a bit of glue on a smaller cut, and all of it was covered with a huge bandage. There was an ugly bruise blossoming over one eye as well, taking the place of the red welt. The remainder of her face was pale and exhausted, but there was relief on it when she saw me as I pulled back the curtain.

"How's Nick?" she asked urgently as soon as she saw me.

"He'll be okay. Blake didn't hit anything vital; it wasn't too deep. They're keeping him overnight just to be safe. How're you?" I rubbed her blanketed leg. She was hooked up to an IV, I assumed either painkillers or saline, maybe both, and the TV was on above her bed, reruns of "Friends" playing out in silence.

"Great!" she smiled. "They doped me up and I feel awesome!"

Relief flooded through me as I laughed at her reaction, and I glanced at Dad. "She really is fine?" I asked him.

He nodded. "They said everything should heal up quickly. They took an X-ray on her arm to check for any hairline fractures, but it looked good. We need to keep an eye on her tonight for any concussion symptoms, but otherwise, she's perfect." He laid his hand on Annie's uninjured arm and his brow furrowed in concern as he focused his attention on me. "Did Nick tell you what happened?"

I nodded. "Did Annie tell you about Blake?" I asked, not wanting to repeat the backstory. Dad nodded, so I continued. "Nick had to cut him off financially. He's been supporting Blake for a while now, paying his rent, getting him food, but he told Blake last week that he wouldn't do it anymore unless Blake went into rehab. Blake ran out of money, food, and whatever else today, and came after him. The police are with Nick now. Have they been down to talk to Annie?" Dad shook his head while Mom scoffed quietly.

"Just a piece of human trash," she muttered.

I raised my eyebrows in annoyance, but Dad looked at me pleadingly. I took a deep breath and looked back to Annie. "I don't know what the plan is yet for the office. They still haven't been able to get ahold of Marie. But I wouldn't plan on going in to work tomorrow." I teased with a wry smile.

Annie nodded, but Mom snorted. "Tomorrow?" she snapped. "Try never. Neither one of you are ever going back to that office."

"Mom!" Both Annie and I turned on her with exasperation. Mom threw her hands up.

"I refuse to allow my daughters to be in a situation where they are put in danger for no reason. Who knows when that degenerate is going to lose his temper with his brother again or just get bored and come barging in with a gun!" Our mouths were both gaping.

"Mel," Dad began quietly, laying his hand gently on her arm. "This isn't the time for that discussion." She ignored him.

"Have you two thought about what could have happened today? What he could have done if he been any less lucid?

I refuse to allow either of you to further associate with that family in any way. If they had been able to keep that boy under control, I might feel differently, but they have been irresponsible and completely negligent and I will not allow you to be put in such a dangerous situation again!" My mother's voice rose with every word until she was shouting.

My anger roared in my ears, drowning out the beeping monitors and low hum of conversation from the surrounding patients. I couldn't swallow my temper this time. "Seriously Mom?" I hissed. "Keep him under control? It's not like he's a rebellious little boy. Honestly. It's like you kept Nathan under control, right? Sure, he's never threatened anyone with a knife, but according to you, he might as well have." I turned to stomp out of the room. I yanked the curtains open and turned back to her. "I am twenty-one years old. I will spend my time with whomever I want to and work wherever I please, and there is nothing that you can do about it." I shot an apologetic look at my dad and Annie and I headed for the elevator, fuming. I could hear my parents arguing behind the curtain as I stalked away.

I couldn't believe her. That woman had said a lot of judgmental and intolerant things in her life, but this went above and beyond. How dare she judge Nick's family, when ours had just as many problems? The last year had proven that repeatedly. Nate's divorce. Lydia's suicide. Her denial was staggering. In my haze of anger and frustration, I hit the wrong button on the elevator and wandered around the wrong floor of the hospital for a good ten minutes before I realized I was lost. I was still bristling when I finally arrived back at Nick's room on the fourth floor. The door was closed and I knocked softly and cracked it open.

"Can I come in?" I called softly. The curtain was drawn around the door and I couldn't see into the room.

"Please," came the answer. I walked in and found Nick alone, a tray of food on the table in front of him. Despite the reputation of hospital food, the smell was intoxicating and I realized how long it had been since I had eaten.

"Where is everyone?" I asked, resuming my seat and doing my best to keep my eyes off the plate of French fries.

Nick sighed. "Well, the police left about ten minutes ago after the privilege of hearing my dad and I try to rip each other's heads off. Then Hannah thought it would be best to take Dad home to keep him from finishing the job, seeing as I'm at a disadvantage." Nick scowled to himself.

"Well, if it makes you feel any better," I interjected, "my mother and I just had a screaming match in the middle of the ER. So, you know, I feel you." I tried to brush the fight off as nothing, like a funny little anecdote, but I was having a hard time quelling the rage in my chest. I deliberately shifted my thoughts away from her and onto Nick.

"It does a little, actually." He smiled, noticing my hungry gaze on the dinner tray. "You hungry?" he asked, waving a fry at me. "I'm not."

"Shouldn't you eat something, though?" I asked, pulling my feet underneath me as I gazed longingly at the tray.

Nick shrugged. "The painkillers are kind of killing my appetite."

"You sure?" I asked hopefully.

Nick nodded. "It's yours," he said, pushing the tray towards me.

"I'm starving." I admitted and popped a French fry in my mouth. Nick smiled and winced. One arm went unconsciously to his stomach, where I knew he was covered in bandages underneath his gown.

"Annie okay?" he asked, still grimacing. He shifted uncomfortably under the thin hospital blanket.

"Do you need anything? Can I get you anything?" I asked anxiously around a mouthful of fries. Nick shook his head and motioned me back into my chair.

"Annie?"

I nodded and swallowed my mouthful. "She's drunk, but okay. They're just waiting for the okay to go home."

"Drunk?" he asked with eyebrows raised.

"The painkillers. I don't know what they gave her, but I kind of want some." I offered a sardonic smile and unwrapped what looked like a turkey sandwich. Nick laughed and watched me pull the onions out. "Any updates about when they're going to let you go home?" I asked.

Nick shrugged. "Apparently tomorrow isn't my lucky day. The doctor came in for a few minutes before my dad took off. It looks like they have to do surgery."

My eyes widened. "It's that bad?" I asked softly, setting the sandwich back down.

Nick shrugged, trying for nonchalance, but the tense muscles of his jaw betrayed his anxiety. "It's not awful. He said it's a simple surgery, just kind of stitches one layer down. Then I should be able to go home the day after that."

I stared at him silently, biting my lower lip anxiously. Surgery. It was kind of an ugly word, when you looked right at it. I swallowed my anxiety. "What time?"

"The surgery? I don't know exactly. First thing, I think."

I nodded. "I'll be here."

Nick shook his head. "You shouldn't, I mean, you don't need to do that, Quinn."

"I'm coming, Nick, unless," I paused awkwardly, "unless you don't want me to?"

"No, no," he reassured me quickly, "I just—"

I cut him off. "Then I'll be here." I picked the sandwich back up off of the plate and took a bite, trying to defuse the moment. "You're sure you don't want any?" I asked again, holding out the sandwich and hoping to change the subject.

"Nah." He was quiet for another moment, his eyes on me, making me feel self-conscious. "Thanks for staying, Quinn." I offered him a small smile. He watched as I threw yet another fry into my mouth. "Why did you stay?" he asked quietly.

I was suddenly grateful for a mouthful of food, because I had no idea how to answer. I chewed slowly, thinking. "I don't know," I shrugged, hoping to deflect. The question had been bothering me too. I hadn't spoken to this man in almost three months. And the last time that we did speak, we screamed horrible things at each other. But, here I was, still sitting next to his hospital bed, and I was beginning to realize that I had been lying to myself for a long time. That didn't mean I was ready to admit it out loud, however.

"You don't know?" Nick repeated. "Seriously, Quinn, why are you still here?"

"I, you know, I have to be here for Annie, and since I was here anyway . . ." I fumbled, keeping my eyes on my hands.

"Oh," Nick replied softly, "so you came to the hospital for Annie, but you've only spent like ten minutes with her. She's about to go home. Why are you here?" There was a note of impatience in his voice.

"I don't really know what you want me to say here," I snapped, beginning to get a bit impatient myself.

"I want you to answer the question," Nick snapped back, raising the volume. "Didn't think it was a hard one, but maybe I was wrong."

"What do you want to hear, Nick?" I barked. I was on my feet and across the room before I knew what I was doing. Between my exhaustion and exasperation, my temper was quick and hot. "You want me to tell you that for the few minutes I thought you were dead, I couldn't breathe? You want me to tell you that I'm a little terrified to let you out of my sight? That something will happen, and I'll never see you again? Is that what you're looking for?" I was full out shouting at this point. I took a deep breath and wondered just how far down the hall my voice had carried.

Nick's eyes were wide. "Quinn—" he began, but broke off as the door opened and a nurse came bustling in.

"Oh, hello, dear. Have you finished your dinner?" Her scrubs were brightly colored, the top covered in yellow Minions.

Nick nodded silently and pushed the table toward her. The nurse gathered up the tray and set it on the counter next to the sink while she checked Nick's charts and the monitors. I quietly resumed my seat next to Nick's bed without looking at him.

"Just need to check your vitals and I'll be out of your way." She wrapped the cuff around his arm and waited for the machine to get a reading. She stood back and studied the two of us. "You two make a cute couple, if I do say so myself," she laughed. I smiled awkwardly at her and turned to face Nick, my heart in my throat. His brown eyes were already on me. I couldn't read them.

"Looks good," the nurse announced, ripping the cuff off loudly and tucking it into its wire container. "I'll be back to check on you in a bit, and you let me know if you need anything."

Nick nodded and the nurse picked up the tray and left, closing the door behind her. As it latched, Nick struggled to sit up.

"Wait!" I exclaimed. "What are you doing? You'll hurt yourself!" I stood and pushed gently on his chest. He lay back and covered my hand with his own. "Here," I said, finding the button to move the bed. It was comically slow, watching it push him into a sitting position, his eyes on me the whole time.

"Come here," he murmured, gesturing to the edge of the bed and shifting slightly to make room for me. I sat down awkwardly, the guilt beginning to set in as it inevitably does after a tantrum.

"Nick, I didn't—" I began.

"Quinn," he cut me off, but I talked over him.

"No, I'm sorry, I just—"

"Quinn," he tried again. His face was only a few inches from mine.

"Nick, just let me apologize!" The irritation was beginning to set in again.

"Quinn," he said firmly. "Shut up."

I closed my mouth. And he leaned closer and kissed me. I pulled back in surprise, realized what I had done, and kissed him. And kissed him. He wove the fingers of one hand through my hair and gripped my hand with the other. He kissed me harder and tightened his hand around mine until I could feel my engagement ring pinching . . .

I pulled back with a gasp. "I have to go," I breathed, jumping to my feet.

"Quinn!" he protested.

"I have to go. I have to go." I repeated stupidly, gathering my things. I paused and glanced at him. "I'll see you tomorrow." I offered him the ghost of a smile and swept out of the room without another word.

21

I found Annie on the couch at home that night, regaling the boys with her heroism. Nate had given them permission to stay up until she got home from the hospital. He told me later they were both terrified that she was going to die. It was only that explanation that had assuaged Mom's wrath when she saw the boys still wide awake at 11:00 p.m. Annie's bandages, along with her story, mesmerized them.

"How is he?" she asked over their heads as soon as she saw me.

I threw my purse over a kitchen chair and shed my coat. "Same. He has to have surgery tomorrow."

Annie narrowed her eyes at me. "How are you?" she asked.

"Fine," I said hesitantly, pulling open the fridge. I wrinkled my nose at the lack of anything appetizing.

"What happened?" she asked intuitively.

"Annie," Ezra protested. "You weren't finished."

"What?" she asked, turning back to look at him. "Oh, well, and then the brave Nick saved me from the bad guy and the police took him away to jail. Now go to bed," she ordered them, turning back to me. "Okay," she demanded over Oliver and Ezra's protests. "What happened?"

I grabbed an orange off of the counter and flopped onto the couch next to her. Turning the fruit over and over in my hands, I watched the boys shuffle slowly to their room, grumbling all the way. I glanced at her expectant face and gave in. "He kissed me," I admitted. Her expression didn't change.

"And?" she said impatiently. She fingered the gauze on her arm unconsciously.

"And?" I asked incredulously. "That isn't enough?"

"Quinn," she replied with an air of explaining something obvious to a four-year-old. "He likes you. A lot. It's not news."

I sighed. "I'm engaged, Annie. It's kind of a complication." I took a chunk of peel off the orange. "Plus, he was just slashed in the stomach by his own brother. Why are we even talking about this?"

"Talking is not going to make him heal faster. But it might make you come to your senses sometime this century. And, just so you know, engaged isn't married, Quinn." She left me alone in the living room.

I threw the orange onto the coffee table, cursing her wisdom. She was right, engaged wasn't married. And I couldn't just ignore the way that I felt. Not just when he kissed me either. The terror that I felt when I didn't know if he was alive or dead was surprisingly overwhelming. And the need to be near him that he had forced me to express was now out in the open. Nick meant more to me than I was willing to admit. And was it really fair to marry Joshua if I felt so strongly about someone else?

I got up early the next morning and called in sick. My running shoes were calling my name and I answered, hoping to clear my head a little before heading to the hospital. I tried to sort my feelings as I ran, forcing myself to be honest about the reasons I had said yes to Joshua. I had to admit, our relationship had changed since before the mission. We were both so different, but it seemed, at least in my case, that I was trying to be the person I was before to fit with him. *That* Quinn had been more concerned with the blond hair and the blue eyes.

That Quinn hadn't lost her favorite aunt to suicide. *That* Quinn hadn't had her heart broken. *That* Quinn was still so sure that life was fair and simple and straightforward. *That* Quinn belonged with Joshua, but I was beginning to realize that *this one* belonged with someone else.

As soon as I had showered and dressed, I drove to the hospital, but when I arrived at Nick's room, it was empty. I stood in the doorway a moment, trying to decide what to do, wondering if he was already in surgery or if maybe they had sent him home.

"They took him down about an hour ago," said a voice behind me. I whirled around to find the nurse who had taken his blood pressure last night, still sporting her Minion scrubs. She had a kind smile on her face as she watched me.

"Down?" I asked.

"To surgery," she supplied. "It's a minor one, sweetie, don't worry. He should be out in another hour or so. Waiting room's down on the third floor, if you want to wait for him there. They'll give you updates."

I smiled at her gratefully. "Thank you."

She returned the smile. "Of course, sweetie."

I returned to the elevator and found the waiting room easily. Only three of the chairs were filled, one of them by Hannah. She smiled when she saw me and gestured to the empty seat next to her. "They had already taken him when I got here too," she commented as I got situated.

"Have you heard anything?" I asked.

Hannah shook her head. "There's a nurse who has given me a couple of updates, but just things like, 'it's going well, the doctor is confident, things look good.' Encouraging, but nothing really useful." She dropped the magazine she had been reading into her lap. I gave a frustrated sigh and gazed out the window.

"You're engaged?" Hannah asked. I glanced at her and noticed her staring at my ring.

I nodded awkwardly. "Um, yeah," I responded, glancing at my ring self-consciously. I focused on my lap, but I could feel her gaze on me. "How much did Nick tell you about me?"

Hannah studied me. "Nothing for a while, actually. He was really excited when Marie hired you, said he had known you from Florida. He talked about you a lot for a couple of months, actually, and then he just stopped. I asked him about it once, but he said you had quit and he didn't want to talk about it. So, I left him alone." I recognized the look on her face. It was the same one I generally had when Nate started dating anyone. The sisterly concern expression.

Nervously biting my lip, I contemplated where to start. "Um, yeah, I did quit, after Christmas. We, Nick and I, had a—" I paused, looking for a word to describe what had happened, "a misunderstanding and I thought it would be better if I left. I got engaged about the same time. But," I shrugged unconsciously, "I think I made a mistake."

We were quiet for a long time. I stared out the huge windows of the waiting room, watching cars speed past on their way to work. Most of the winter's snow had melted over the past couple of weeks, leaving only dirty gray patches scattered in the corners of parking lots. The early March sun streamed into the room, warming my legs.

"Is that why you're here?" Hannah asked me suddenly. "You want to apologize? You want to be friends?" I looked over to find her studying me. "I'm sorry," she muttered, "I just, I don't want to see Nick get hurt."

I bit my lip as I studied her. "I don't either," I replied sincerely. We didn't get a chance to finish our conversation.

"You're Nick Ryan's family?" Hannah and I looked up to find a doctor, his hair still covered in a surgical cap, standing in front of us. We both stood up.

"Yes," she replied, "Is he okay? Did everything go okay?"

The doctor smiled. "Everything went perfectly. There were no surprises once we got in, and there should be no permanent damage, as long as he gives himself a chance to heal. We'll keep an eye on him, but he should be able to go home tomorrow."

"Can we see him?" Hannah asked, as the doctor turned to walk away.

"He's still under, but once he wakes up they'll bring him into recovery and you can see him then." He looked at us, silently waiting for more questions.

"Will they tell us?" I asked. "That he's awake?"

"I'll make sure that they do."

"Thank you," Hannah called after him, as he returned to the surgical ward. Both of us sank into our chairs and I could hear Hannah's ragged sigh of relief. She leaned her head back against the headrest and a tear slipped from the corner of her eye.

"Hey," I said softly, resting my hand on hers, "he's fine. He's going to be fine. It's done."

"I know," she replied, turning to look at me. "I just couldn't handle it if I lost him too."

I offered her a sad smile and wrapped an arm around her.

"I'm glad you're here, Quinn," Hannah said softly after a little while.

"Me too."

It didn't take Nick too long to come out of the anesthesia, and he was only a little disoriented when he did. A nurse called Hannah in, but I wasn't able to see him until they wheeled him back to his room. I was there first.

"Hey," Nick called from his gurney, his voice slightly slurred, "you're here."

I smiled. "I told you I would be."

The orderlies got him situated in his bed again, careful not to disturb the row of stitches along his abdomen. Hannah and I pulled up chairs on either side of the bed and spent the rest of the afternoon chatting about everything and nothing, while Nick napped off and on. None of us mentioned Blake or Annie or even Marie, and I kept the discussion off of me as much as possible.

Lunch came from the vending machine down the hall, supplemented by a few stolen crumbs off of Nick's tray. As the day wore on, his face gradually lost the ashen sheen and began to look almost normal again. Hannah and I both teased him about the unruly state of his hair until he demanded a mirror and some gel. Hannah told us about her latest piece of choreography and Nick goaded her into telling us about the guy who, according to Hannah, was just a friend. Around 4:00 that afternoon, Hannah got up to leave.

"I called Dad when you got out of surgery, but he should be getting off work soon. I'll fill him in and see if he wants to come visit." Nick nodded brusquely, and Hannah leaned down to kiss his forehead. "He'll come get you tomorrow. I don't know if they'll trust you to me." She smiled and ruffled his hair gently. "I'll come with him."

"You better," he said with a smile. Hannah flashed me a farewell smile and I returned it with a wave. Nick and I were quiet until the heavy door latched behind her.

I turned back to look at Nick.

"You missed work," he commented.

I shrugged. "Yeah, I have a few sick days that need to get used up," I smiled. He laid his hand over mine, and I could feel his fingers running over the jagged edges of my ring. He twisted it absently on my finger.

"So, when's the big day?" he asked slowly, his eyes locked on mine.

I took a deep breath. "Nick, please don't."

"What?" he asked, feigning innocence.

"I don't think that there will be one." My voice was low, my eyes on the floor.

"Really?" he asked softly, eyebrows raised. "And why is that?" His hand closed tightly around mine as he waited for an answer.

"I, um," I began, hesitantly annoyed at his persistence, "I don't think this is the right ring for me."

"So," he posited with a smile and a cocked head, "you're saying you need a bigger ring?"

I laughed. "Not bigger. Just . . . different."

"Different how?"

I studied Nick. His usually flawless hair was a mess. There were shadows under his eyes and his face was a shade paler than usual, making the two days worth of stubble on his chin and cheeks look even darker. Blankets covered him to the waist and a too-big hospital gown hung loosely around his neck. I studied my engagement ring one last time, then pulled it off and slid it into my pocket.

"I need a ring," I said slowly, deciding it was easier to speak in metaphor, "that fits me better than that one. One that's a little less shiny," Nick snorted softly, "but a little more valuable."

"More valuable?" he repeated, taking my hand again.

"Almost priceless," my eyes held his. He pulled me close until my forehead rested on his.

"You deserve the best this world has to offer."

"I'm in luck, then," I breathed. "He's sitting right in front of me."

As I walked out of the hospital doors an hour later, I pulled out my phone. Marie was the first on my list.

"This is Marie."

"Marie? This is Quinn Matthews."

"Quinn? Are you still at the hospital? How's Nick?"

I pulled out of the hospital parking lot and headed out. "Pretty good. The surgery went well. They think he will be able to go home tomorrow. He'll have to take it easy, but he'll be home."

"Good." I could hear the satisfaction in her voice. "What can I do for you, Quinn?"

"Well, with Nick out for a while, I know you'll need some extra help. And I was wondering, well, if you'd be willing to have me. I'd be so happy to come back to work." I finished awkwardly, wondering just how lame I sounded.

"Temporarily?"

"Um, well, I guess that's up to you. If you only need help temporarily, I can do that, but," I hesitated, "I'd love to come back long term."

The line was quiet. I tapped my fingers nervously on the steering wheel.

"You and Nick worked out your problems, I take it?" Marie asked slowly.

"You know about that?" I stuttered in surprise.

Marie laughed. "Didn't take a genius to pick up on it, Quinn."

"Oh," I replied, embarrassed. "Well, yeah, um, we did."

"Good." I could hear the smile in her voice. "What about your new job?"

"I'm going to take care of that right now," I replied with more confidence than I felt. "I can start again on Monday."

"See you on Monday, then."

I smiled in relief. "Thanks, Marie. Really. Thank you."

I hung up as I pulled into Josh's driveway. I counted to ten, taking deep breaths to calm my nerves. Confrontation was not my strong suit. I gathered my courage and got out of the car. Olivia opened the door.

"Hey, Quinn, what's up? How's Annie?"

"She's totally fine," I replied. "Just a few stitches."

"I'm glad," answered Liv. Things had been just a bit off since Nate had ended things with her.

"Hey, is Josh here?" I asked, stepping inside. Liv closed the door behind me and nodded.

"He's downstairs. You can go down, if you want."

"Thanks, Liv." I headed for the staircase.

"Hey, Quinn? About Nate, did you ever talk to him?" Olivia asked, her eyebrows raised.

"What?" I asked, distracted. "Oh, um, yeah, no, I don't think so."

"So he's not dating anyone else?"

I had difficulty hiding my irritation. "I don't think so, Olivia."

"Okay," she replied, obviously sensing my annoyance. I turned to go again and paused.

"Hey, Liv? I'm sorry." I grimaced.

"For what?" she asked.

I shook my head. "Just everything." I took a deep breath and ran down the stairs.

Josh sat alone on the couch, his Xbox controller in hand. He was so focused on his game that he didn't notice me. I studied him for a moment. My resolve began to waver as I watched him. I was giving him up, and most likely Olivia as well, but this was the right thing and I knew it. Josh looked up from his game and saw me. A smile spread across his face and he patted the couch next to him, inviting me to join him. I swallowed my fear, as well as the sob that was threatening to ruin everything.

"Where have you been?" he asked as I approached. "I've been calling you since yesterday. Is Annie okay?"

I perched on the edge of the couch, tensed for a quick getaway. "Annie's fine. She's just got a few stitches and a bruise."

"So, what's going on?" he asked, a hint of impatience in his voice. "Where've you been?"

"I need to talk to you about something," I said slowly, ignoring his question.

"Okay," he replied hesitantly. I sucked in my breath and looked down at my empty finger. I bit my lip, willing myself not to cry.

"I'm so sorry," I began, my voice cracking. "But I can't, I mean, we can't . . ." I paused, looking for the right way to say it, and pulled the ring out of my pocket.

Josh's eyes dropped from my face to my hands. "Quinn—" Josh began, his confusion evident. "Everything was fine a week ago. What happened?"

"We've never been fine, Josh. We're just not meant to be," I said softly, standing up and handing him the ring. He raised his eyes and met mine again, his mouth set in a hard line. I began to leave, but he grabbed my hand and stopped me.

"It's him, isn't it?" Josh asked roughly. I pulled my hand out of his grip. I wasn't sure how to respond, but I didn't want to lie.

"It's not just that, Josh, it's me. I'm not the same girl I was two years ago. I'm sorry." Once again I headed for the stairs.

"I don't get it, Quinn," he called after me. "His brother just attacked your sister. You really want that to be your life?"

"He's not his brother, Josh. He's—" I stopped myself. I could feel my temper rising, and I knew I had to keep it under control to get through this. "It's just what I have to do."

Josh smirked. "Whatever, Quinn. Just don't come crawling back and expect me to welcome you with open arms." His tone was acidic.

"What, like you did?" I snapped back before I could stop myself. Josh's eyes widened in shock. "I have to go. I'm sorry." I ran up the stairs before he could say anything else and out the front door without even looking at Olivia. I threw myself into my car and slammed the door as if it would protect me from the pain. First thing in the morning, I would call the office and give my notice. I drove home slowly, second-guessing the entire day and hoping that I had done the right thing.

22

The hospital was quiet as I walked through the main doors the next morning. A wave of unexpected butterflies washed over me as the elevator reached Nick's floor. I tried to shake them off, but they followed me down the hall and through the door of Nick's room.

"You awake?" I called softly through the pulled curtains surrounding the doorway. There was no reply. I pushed the door all the way open, trying not to wake him, and slipped inside. I pushed the curtain to one side and stopped short at the sight of the empty bed. My stomach dropped and I backed out of the room, searching for the handwritten nameplate that had been on the wall yesterday. It was gone. I looked up and down the hall frantically and almost ran to the nurse's station in a panic.

"Nick, Nick Ryan," I stuttered, "he's—he's, did he . . ." I took a breath. "Was he released?" I didn't recognize the nurse sitting at the desk. She spun her chair to the computer and typed in his name.

"Ryan, Nick. Nope. Not released. They moved him to a different floor last night."

Relief flooded through me. "Okay. Okay. Can you tell me where?" The nurse tilted her head to one side as she studied the screen and then shook her head.

"Um, I can't. He requested that no one be given the information beyond immediate family." She gave me a sympathetic smile.

I stared at her in confusion. Why would he do that? "I'm sure it's fine. I was here yesterday, and there wasn't a problem."

"I'm really sorry, there's nothing that I can do." She turned back to the pile of paperwork and picked up her pen. I stood there stupidly, not sure what to do next. She glanced back up at me. "If you talked to him, I'm sure that he would give you the information. But I am not allowed to."

I nodded, still unsure why this was happening. I turned slowly and walked back down the hallway to the elevator, pulling out my phone as I went. I texted Nick and watched the screen of my phone stay black the entire elevator ride to the main floor. I stepped out of the elevator and called him. It went straight to voicemail. I stared at my phone for a few moments, willing it to light up. I debated calling Marie, wished I had Hannah's number, and began second-guessing everything that had happened in the last twenty-four hours. I exited the lobby and almost ran into Hannah. She began to apologize, but her eyes focused on me and widened. "Quinn, hi," she said, a little too loudly.

"Hannah, did you know?"

"Know?" Something was off with her voice.

"That they moved him. Nick. He changed rooms." I searched her face, trying to figure out what was going on.

"Um, yeah. I, uh, he called me last night to tell me." She wouldn't look at me as she spoke. I tried to move into her field of vision.

"They won't tell me where they moved him to. I tried to go see him, but—" I stopped, growing more and more frustrated. "Hannah, what is going on?"

She sighed and stared hard at her feet. "He just doesn't want to see anyone right now."

"Did something happen?" I pressed.

She shrugged noncommittally. "I think he just needs some space."

"From everyone?" I paused, hating the words as they left my mouth. "Or from me?"

Hannah finally looked up at me. I couldn't read her face. It was somewhere between anger and pain. "You said you didn't want him to get hurt." Her face hardened. "You should have tried harder." She brushed past me and walked quickly toward the elevator. I watched her go, more bewildered than ever. Hurt? I replayed the conversation from the night before as I walked through the parking lot. As I slid into my car, I began to despair that anything would ever work out the way that it was supposed to. I shut the door and put my head down on the steering wheel. This was not how my day was supposed to go. I allowed myself ten minutes of self-pity crying, then pulled it together and headed home to deal with the collateral from the cancelled wedding.

I was surprised to find Kristen in the kitchen when I woke up. I felt a little stupid padding out there in all of my bed head glory.

"Kristen?" I said stupidly. "What are you doing here?"

She turned and gave me an embarrassed look. "Nate came and got me this morning. He's taking me to breakfast, but he forgot something, so we stopped here for a couple of minutes." She was almost apologetic about it.

"Sounds fun. Where are you guys going?" I pulled a bowl out of the cabinet and set it on the counter. Kristen shrugged.

"Nate won't tell me anything. He just said that he wanted to take me out because he wanted to talk to me about something." She looked surreptitiously around the room. "He's not going to propose, is he?" She lowered her voice. "I like him, but we've only been out like four times." Her expression was somewhere between embarrassment and anxiety.

I snorted. "He'd better not." Relief spread over Kristen's face.

"Oh, hey, Quinn, I almost forgot. My roommate is moving out in a few weeks and Nate said you might be looking for a place."

My eyebrows shot up and I nodded. If that apartment was even remotely reasonable, I wanted in. "Details?"

"End of the month, semi-furnished, free cable." And then she told me the price and I had to refrain from dropping to my knees in joy.

"I'm totally in. Wait," I paused on second thought, "Would that be weird with you dating my brother? Or, heaven forbid, if it doesn't work out with him?"

Kristen's smile widened. "I'm not too worried about it."

"You like him?"

She nodded, the smile still on her face.

"Good. Will you do me a favor? Just hear him out today? He's a good guy."

"Now you're freaking me out again. Are you sure he isn't going to propose?"

I laughed. "No, this is just in case he's stupid. I love my brother, but he's an idiot."

"Who's an idiot?" Dad came in through the garage door just as I finished speaking.

"Nate," I replied. Dad laughed at looked at Kristen.

"We haven't met. I'm Quinn's dad, Dan." He held out his hand to her. She took his and shook.

"Kristen. It's nice to meet you."

"Wait, Kristen?" Dad glanced at me. "Nate's Kristen?"

I nodded with a grimace, hoping that Kristen wouldn't be put off by his classification of her.

Dad looked back to her. "Well, I have to tell you, young lady, I am very pleased to meet you." Kristen grinned shyly as he continued. "Nathan is very impressed with you."

"He's not the only one," I quipped with a wink. Kristen waved her hands humbly, warding off further complements.

"Well," she replied, "he's not too bad either."

Dad nodded in agreement. "Nate's a good kid. He just needs to get his head on straight after the last year."

"The last year?" Kristen asked. I froze, begging him silently not to say it.

"With the divorce and everything. His history makes me appreciate you even more." Dad patted Kristen's shoulder gently and disappeared into the hallway without noticing the pale, distraught expression on Kristen's face. She turned to me.

"Divorce?" Before I had time to respond, Nate appeared from the basement.

"You ready to go?" Nate asked, slinging a small backpack over his shoulder. He glanced between Kristen's somewhat shell-shocked face and my wide eyes and stiffened. "What?"

Kristen slid slowly off of her chair. "Can we, um, talk outside?" Nate nodded and led her out the front door. I watched them go with a sinking sensation in my stomach.

I ate breakfast slowly, waiting to see if Nate and Kristen would return. They did not. In fact, I did not see Nate for the rest of the day. I texted him before I went to bed that night, asking where he was and if everything was okay. He didn't respond.

Anxious to put Joshua and possibly Nick behind me, I decided to return to the singles ward Sunday morning. I was a little nervous about running into Nick, but almost positive that he wouldn't be going to church anywhere so soon after being discharged. Sacrament meeting was a little less blasphemous this time around, and therefore more enjoyable. I couldn't help casting a few furtive glances around the chapel looking for Nick or Kristen. It seemed that I was correct; I didn't see Nick anywhere. Kristen, however, was in the far back corner of the chapel. After the meeting closed, Kristen approached hesitantly.

"Giving the singles ward another chance?" she asked with a smile. I nodded.

"Sunday School still in the gym?" I asked.

"Yep," Kristen replied.

"You mind if I come with you?"

"Sure," she replied. We walked silently into the gym. After finding a seat and a somewhat awkward pause, we both turned to each other and began speaking.

"I don't know what Nate told you—"

"I don't know what happened—"

We both laughed quickly. She began again. "I don't know what Nate told you about what happened—"

"Nothing," I cut in. "Absolutely nothing."

She let out a sigh and made a pained face. "I was kind of a jerk," she muttered. I waited for her to continue. "Nate, he told me about everything. And I, um, I could have handled it better."

"It is a lot to swallow," I empathized.

"It honestly wouldn't have been as bad if he had told me sooner. I mean, we've been hanging out for months, and I had no idea. If he had just been up front . . ." she trailed off with a sigh.

I hesitated a moment. "If he had," I began slowly, "if he had told you when you met, would you have kept hanging out with him? Or dated him?"

Kristen kept her eyes on the whiteboard at the front of the gym. The Sunday School teacher was scribbling a list of questions in a squeaky red marker.

"What would you do?" she asked me, avoiding my question. "If it were you?"

I was quiet for a moment. "I don't know," I answered honestly. "He's my brother, and I love him, but I was really upset when he told me everything. I don't blame you for a little shell shock."

"How long has the divorce been final?" Kristen asked quietly.

"About three months."

"I really do like him, Quinn," she said quietly.

"Did you tell him that?"

She shook her head. "I overreacted. I was so caught off guard." She paused. "And then, I said some things. And then he said some things."

I just nodded. "Come home with me after church. Talk to him."

Kristen shook her head again. "Not yet. It's too soon. I think maybe we both need a little space." I wrinkled my nose at her.

"So, space probably doesn't translate to having his sister as a roommate?" I asked. Kristen laughed.

"My roommate doesn't move out for about three more weeks. I think that's probably enough space, don't you?"

I smiled. "We can only hope," I laughed and turned to the front as the Gospel Doctrine teacher began his lesson.

23

I began work with Marie again on Monday. It was a relief to pull into that familiar parking lot. The grass on either side of the building was the brilliant green that only late March brings with it, and a border of tulips and daffodils edged the building. I pushed my way through the front door and got settled into my old desk. Annie hadn't changed much, and I hadn't personalized it much while I was there.

Marie came out to greet me and announced that I would be training as a realtor. "Nothing better than on-the-job training," she explained. Annie, apparently, had already agreed to stay on part time, and Marie would take me out on appointments and showings in the afternoons.

"Nick?" I asked hesitantly.

"He quit. Friday," Marie reported. I nodded, more in resignation than surprise.

"Marie, when I called . . . When you asked about Nick and me—"

She held up her hands, silencing me. "I talked to Hannah, you don't need to explain anything."

"What's he going to do?" I asked quietly.

"He'll figure it out. He always does." She patted my arm reassuringly.

"And Blake?" I asked. Marie sighed.

"Jack's pressing charges. And I assume your family as well?"

I shrugged in response. I had been avoiding my mother and hadn't bothered to ask Annie how her interview with the police had gone.

"Well, Blake's pleading guilty anyway, so, he's been charged with assault and battery and we're waiting on sentencing."

I nodded briefly. Marie opened her mouth as if to say something more, but after a moment, she closed it and retreated to her office.

The next few weeks were a blur. I tried calling Nick a few times and texted him more than once, but there was never any response. I kept my phone in one hand almost constantly at first, hoping that he would change his mind, or at least explain his sudden change of heart. Luckily, there was a lot of catching up to do at the office, so I stayed as busy as I could. I quickly realized how much weight Nick had carried while he was Marie's partner. Annie had kept up with the secretarial side of things, but with Nick gone, and with the onset of spring, Marie had more clients than she could handle on her own. She was swamped without his help. So swamped, in fact, that I had only been on two initial appointments and one day of showings when she sent me out to do my first solo showing.

"You'll be fine," she soothed as she pushed me out the door.

"Are you sure this is okay? I'm not a real realtor. I don't know anything!" The panic in my voice was obvious. I grabbed the door frame dramatically, preventing her from pushing me any farther.

"Quinn, everything you need to know is on the info sheets. Really, you'll be fine, but you need to go." Marie practically shoved me out the door. I walked to the car as if it were my execution chamber and sat without moving until I got a phone call.

"You'll be fine, but go now or you'll be late." Marie didn't even bother with a greeting when I answered, just got right to the point.

I looked back toward the office and saw Marie's face peering out the window, an impatient look on her features. I sighed and waved and reluctantly started the car.

I pulled up at the address written on my paper and drove to the tiny duplex. I stood and smoothed my blouse and skirt, hoping that I looked professional enough. I stared at the blue door and took a deep breath before heading up the walk.

I knocked on the door hesitantly and a beautiful redhead pulled it open. "Hi!" she said brightly. "You must be Marie!" She smiled and opened the door wider to let me in. I returned the smile.

"No," I matched her tone. "I'm Marie's . . . associate, Quinn."

"Hi, Quinn, I'm Jenny. Nice to meet you."

"Come on in. My fiancé will be here in just a minute, and then we can head out."

"Great," I smiled, stepping into her apartment. It was as tiny as it looked from the outside, but obviously well-decorated and cared for. She invited me to sit on her worn couch and offered me a drink.

"No, no, I'm fine, thanks," I replied. "So, I've got all of these sheets here with prospective homes." I held up the packet that Marie had given me. "But what type of place are you looking for?"

Jenny sat in a chair across from me. "Something for newlyweds," she smiled. She was wearing a pair of designer jeans and such a cute top that I couldn't help but wonder where she got it. I wanted one.

"When's the wedding?" I asked, trying to keep the conversation going.

"June," she replied. "It was supposed to be over Christmas, but there were some complications. We had to move it." A shadow crossed her face as she said it.

My stomach dropped an inch or two and I nodded politely. Something was off. Where had I heard the name Jenny before? "Can I see the ring?" I asked with exaggerated cheerfulness.

"Sure!" she replied, holding out her hand willingly. I bit back my gasp. Luckily, Jenny mistook it for awe. "I know, it's gorgeous, isn't it?"

I nodded, trying to catch the gasp, trying to escape. Marquise-cut diamond, platinum band, with swirling designs on either side. That little rat. I had regifted a time or two in my life, but this was ridiculous. Suddenly, the last traces of guilt from ending things with Josh melted away. Things may not have gone the way that I wanted them to, but I was so very, very glad that I was not the one who would be marrying Joshua.

Jenny continued to tell me about the ring and I tuned back into her just in time to hear her tell me that it was custom-designed for her.

"Really?" I squeaked. I cleared my throat quickly. "It's beautiful."

"I actually just got it," she elaborated. "We designed it together, but before it was ready, we—" she paused, looking for the right word, "we took some time off."

"Wow," I managed. I swallowed the rage/pity that was roaring through my stomach. "Could I maybe get a drink of water after all?" I asked, regretting my decision to ask about the ring at all.

"Sure!" she responded brightly and disappeared around the corner into the kitchen. I took several deep breaths, hoping to be able to keep it together. If I could make it through today, I could make it through anything, I told myself.

There was knock on the door just as Jenny reentered, carrying a glass of water. She pulled the door open and bright sunlight streamed in.

"Hey, babe." I was pleased that the familiar voice did little to further disrupt my outward calm. Oh, yes, this day would be awkward, possibly the most awkward in the history of the world. But I would survive. And have one heck of a story to tell for the rest of my life.

I stood to greet him, a plastic smile frozen across my face, grateful that he was the one who had to deal with the shock and not the other way around.

"Josh, this is our new realtor, Quinn. Quinn, this is my fiancé, Josh." Jenny slid her arm through his and stood on her tiptoes to plant a kiss on his cheek. The color slowly drained from his face, and it took a few moments for him to react.

"Hey, sweetie," Josh began slowly, "You know, I think today might not be the best day to do this. I've got a lot of stuff to get done. Do you think we could reschedule?" He raised his eyes hopefully at her.

"Josh," she whined, "this was the only time that you were available for weeks! And finals are coming up. If we don't do it now, there won't be time to get everything taken care of so we can move in right after the wedding. Plus, Quinn's already here. We can't waste her time like that." Jenny shot me a smile and I simpered back.

Josh glanced once between the two of us and I could almost read his mind. Would I tell Jenny who I was? And about the ring? Was the risk worth taking? For a moment, I wondered the same things myself. All at once, I made up my mind.

"We will keep this as quick and as painless as possible," I reassured him, hoping he would get the message that I wouldn't be the one to give up his secret. He sighed and nodded shortly and the three of us headed outside to my car.

I got home late that night. It had been horribly awkward, terribly uncomfortable, and absolutely unpleasant, but we made it through. Both of us feigned ignorance, pretending to meet for the first time, trying to ignore our history and the fact that I was the complication that had pushed the wedding back. It was obvious that Josh hadn't given her the details. A name like Quinn would have given it away in a second. But we made it through, and I was incredibly proud of myself for not backing down and running away.

Mom was cleaning up dinner when I walked through the garage door. "Leftovers are in the fridge," she barked over her shoulder. She was still mad at me for breaking it off with Josh, and I was really looking forward to the day when she could talk without sniping at me. Things had improved, slightly, since the breakup, however. A few weeks ago, she would have thrown the leftovers out just to keep me from eating them.

I pulled them out and heated them up. Chicken enchiladas were never my favorite, but I was starving. Nate appeared from the basement while I waited.

"Have you talked to Kristen yet?" It had become my new greeting. Nate hadn't seen Kristen, nor had he called her since their last encounter. And as much as I tried to convince her during Relief Society every Sunday to talk to him, she hadn't made a move either. I could just feel the apartment slipping slowly through my fingers.

"Leave me alone, Quinn," Nate called over his shoulder as he disappeared down the hallway. I pulled my enchiladas out of the microwave and I was just sitting down to eat when Annie walked in carrying her books. She plopped down at the table across from me and opened them up.

"You will never guess what happened today," I told her, unable to help myself. I explained how I had spent the afternoon showing Josh and his fiancée houses. Looking for the perfect little cottage that Jenny wanted. And when I told her about the ring, she actually yelped.

"You. Are. Joking," she replied, her eyes wide in amazement. "I can't believe him!"

"I know. It was a narrow escape," I joked. She laughed.

"It's not funny," barked Mom from across the kitchen. I realized for the first time that she had been listening to the entire conversation. I looked up in surprise. "That could have been your ring, your house, but you threw it all away, didn't you, and for what?"

"For me, Mom," I retorted, my temper flaring. "I didn't want to marry him, and so I didn't. And I'm pretty sure I made the right call."

"No," she disagreed. "You didn't. You did it for that boy, who at least had the sense to realize how above him you actually are. Though he doesn't deserve the credit for being able to come to that without help."

I stared at her, the meaning sinking in slowly. "What do you mean, 'help'?" I asked slowly. "He didn't come to that without help?" I paused, "Mom, what did you do?"

Annie's eyes were wide, darting back and forth between the two of us.

"You were too blind to see what was good for you. So I took care of it." Mom turned to leave the kitchen.

"What did you do?" I yelled, my temper completely gone.

She turned back to me. "He needed to be told. He needed to understand that you are worth more than he could give you. That every minute that you spent with him put you in danger. If he cared for you, he should have seen that coming a long way off." Her voice was acidic as she listed Nick's offenses. I could feel the rage in my chest. I was devastated and utterly mortified.

"Are you serious?" I asked furiously. My mother had done some embarrassing things over the course of my life, painfully even, but this went above and beyond what I thought she was capable of. "When?" I demanded.

"The hospital," she announced unapologetically.

"How could you do that?" I yelled, the intensity of my anger bringing tears to my eyes.

"You refuse to listen to me, Quinn." Mom slammed her hand down on the countertop. "No one in this house listens to me. He is not good enough for you," she punctuated each word with a stabbing finger in the air.

"You don't even know him," I spat.

"I know enough," she shot back. I was too stunned to reply. Mom took advantage and slid out of the kitchen and down the hall without another word. I sank back into my chair and looked silently at Annie.

It made so much sense. The overnight change. Ignoring me. Avoiding me. I felt sick. What she must have said to him, I couldn't even imagine. She was the most tactless woman alive. She must have humiliated him. She was capable of making a person feel lower than dirt, and I had a feeling that she had pulled out all the stops for Nick. Annie stared at me wide eyed from across the table.

"I can't believe she did that," Annie whispered incredulously. "She's never gone that far before. What are you going to do?" she asked slowly.

I shook my head. "I have to call him. Something." I put my head in my hands, trying to calm the pounding that was making it hard to think.

I was breathing hard, trying to form a plan, a way to fix this. Before anything reasonable formed in my mind, my cell phone began to ring.

24

I frantically dug through my purse on the chair next to me and barely managed to answer in time. Marie's name came up on the caller ID.

"Hello?" I was surprised to see Marie calling me in the evening. Rarely was anything so important that it couldn't wait until the next morning at work. I wondered nervously if maybe Jenny, or worse, Josh, had called to complain about how awkward their realtor had been at their showings and demand a new one.

"Quinn?" Marie's usually sharp voice was uncharacteristically soft. "I thought I should call you. Something's happened." She paused and the line was silent.

My heart began to pound and my train of thought instantly shifted away from the business. "Nick?" I asked apprehensively, a million horrible possibilities running through my brain. Annie looked up from her homework, her eyes curious.

"No, no." She paused again, and this time I could hear her taking deep breaths before continuing. When she did, I heard the pain in her voice. "Blake." Her voice caught as she said his name.

I couldn't help the rushing sigh of relief that washed over me, or the guilt that followed. "What happened? Did the sentencing come through already?"

"No, Quinn, he—he died. They got the call about an hour ago. There was nothing they could do for him. He's gone."

I felt like the wind had been knocked out of me. "What happened?" I asked again in a whisper. "He wasn't sick? He's still in jail, right? Was there a fight?" Annie was staring at me, her eyes wide, her hand holding the pencil frozen in midair over her assignment.

"He hung himself. He wasn't on suicide watch." I gasped. It was like Lydia all over again. The thought of losing Annie or Nate, the pressure on my chest, the struggle to breathe. I could feel the tears behind my eyes, the sob at the back of my throat. This would kill Nick.

"Nick?" I repeated in a whisper, unable to ask more.

"He took it badly. Jack told him, and Jack's terrible at that kind of thing. They got into an argument. He hung up on his dad. He's alone at his apartment. Hannah's been calling nonstop since he got the news. He won't even answer for her." Marie was crying now, her voice wavering with every word.

"Should I?" I asked tentatively, my own voice choked with emotion.

"Try. It's worth a shot. I don't know what he'll do, Quinn," I could hear her uncertainty and fear. I didn't know either.

"I'll call you if I can get him," I replied. "Thanks, Marie. And," I added after a moment, "I'm sorry. I'm so, so sorry." I set the phone down on the table and looked back up at Annie.

She stared at me, her eyes wide. "Well?" she asked impatiently, her concern obvious. "Is it Nick? Is he okay?"

"It's Blake," I explained slowly, answering her question. "He—" I choked on the words, feeling that if I said them out loud it would make it true. I took a deep breath and swallowed hard. "He killed himself."

Her shoulders fell and she bit her lip. "Go," she said simply. I nodded in silent agreement.

It took one quick text to get his address from Hannah, and twenty minutes later, I stood at the door of Nick's apartment, gathering the courage to knock. I had called repeatedly on my way over, with no luck. He lived in a tiny little apartment complex near the train tracks. The parking lot was gravel and full of holes. It was a cold night, and the only light was a flickering porch light over my head, dimmed by years of dead insects trapped in the fixture. I still hadn't figured out what I was going to say to him, or what I was going to do, but I couldn't stand the thought of him being alone.

I rubbed my hands together briskly, trying to warm them, before reaching up to knock softly, with no answer. I pressed my ear up against the door. I wondered briefly if he had a roommate. He had never mentioned one. I could hear the TV blasting and I knocked again, hard. Still no answer. I hugged my shoulders and watched my breath curl up before me as I debated giving up, trying later, letting him mourn in peace, but I decided it was worth at least one last shot. I pounded on the door as hard as I could and shouted.

"Nick! It's Quinn. Open the door." I pounded again. "Marie called me. Please open the door. NICK!"

The door opened slowly a moment later. Nick stood there in jeans and a wrinkled button-down. He looked terrible, a gray tint to his face and dark circles under his red eyes.

"Hey," he said. His voice was rough and quiet.

"Hey," I replied softly. "Marie called me." He nodded silently. "She's worried about you," I continued. "So am I."

He opened the door wider and stepped out of the way. I slid past him before he could change his mind, basking in the warmth of the apartment as I entered. It was the consummate bachelor apartment, very possibly the smallest I had ever seen, dimly lit, with little on the walls but a world map. The only furniture was a loveseat, old, nice and leather, but worn. It took up most of the room. A blanket and a pair of jeans lay across one of the arms. The kitchenette was tiny, no table, just a counter with a couple of old stools and a sink full of dishes. His bed was in the far corner, rumpled and unmade. I turned back to watch him as he closed the door behind me. I still wasn't sure what to say to him. I had never lost a sibling. Aunt Lydia's death was hard, but it wasn't the same.

"Nick," I began hesitantly. "I don't know what to say," I admitted. I paused, watching his face for clues. His eyes were on his feet. "I'm so, so sorry." I stepped closer, reaching out with my fingers to hook his hand. He glanced up at me, his face blank.

"You want to know what my dad said?" he asked slowly. I grimaced in anticipation. He continued without encouragement. "He told me it was my fault. If I hadn't enabled him for so long, Blake never would have killed himself. He left a note, you know. It was on his bed. He said he couldn't live with himself for attacking his brother. Said that he didn't want to hurt anyone else and this was the only way he knew how to fix that." Nick's voice was hollow. There were no tears, no dramatics. Just a monotone recitation of the news.

"Nick," I whispered in shock. "Your dad is wrong. He's angry, and he's just taking it out on you. It wasn't your fault." I stepped closer to him and gripped his arm with my other hand. "Blake was your brother. You had to do everything you could for him. You can't blame yourself."

Nick narrowed his eyes at me. "But I didn't," he barked. "I should have left him alone. I shouldn't have helped him. I should have let him hit rock bottom. Maybe then he would have gotten help."

"Maybe." I replied softly, silently praying that the right words would come out of my mouth. "Or maybe he would have died on the street or maybe he would have starved to death. You have no idea what would have happened. Nick, you did what you had to do, you did what you thought was right."

I shrugged hopelessly. "It's all you could do. It's all anyone can ever do." I bit my lip, praying that anything that I said got through to him, calmed him, soothed him. I tried to read his face, but it was passive and undecipherable. I tightened my grip on his hand. "Hannah's been calling. She's worried about you." He nodded. "She needs you right now. She needs to know that she won't lose you too."

His stare was intense. "Why are you here?" he asked, not angrily or sarcastically. His voice was full of genuine curiosity. "I was so horrible to you. I've been avoiding you for weeks. I was a jerk, but you keep coming back."

My eyes locked on his. "You weren't a jerk," I disagreed. He raised his eyebrows. "Well," I amended, "You were. But you had a good reason." I bit my lip feeling the humiliation from earlier wash over me. "My mom," I hesitated, hating the words as they came out of my mouth, "my mom told me what she did. I didn't know. I'm so sorry." He nodded briefly and I continued. "I was worried about you." I took a step toward him. "Marie called me. She told me that you wouldn't answer your phone and that Hannah was frantic." He nodded slightly, again. "I wanted to be with you." I added softly, "I needed you to know that you're not alone."

His eyes intensified and he pulled me to him, enveloping me. He smelled like citrus and aftershave. I wrapped my arms around his neck and pulled him close. Nick rested his forehead against mine. "I'm glad you're here," he breathed.

"You want me to stay?" I murmured.

Nick pressed his lips against my forehead. One hand cupped my face, tracing the outline of my jaw with his thumb. He pulled me closer and kissed me gently. "Please," he murmured, his lips still on mine.

I stroked the back of his neck, and he kissed me again. His hand slid from my face, down my shoulder and around my waist. Slowly, we stumbled toward the couch, sinking into it together. His kisses were frantic now, his breathing uneven. I felt lightheaded and dizzy, unable to catch a sufficient breath.

"Nick," I breathed, as his lips found my jaw and then my neck. I wanted so badly to stay like this, with him. The world, the grief, was so far away and all that mattered was us. For a moment, I felt like anything could happen, that anything might happen, and as the realization hit, so did the reality of it. It was at that moment my phone, still tucked in my back pocket, began to ring.

"Nick," I gasped, fighting for breath. I shifted under his weight and pulled my phone out. It's Hannah," I announced, clearing my throat. "Do you mind if I talk to her?"

Nick shook his head. He watched as I put the phone to my ear and answered. He ran a hand through his hair and leaned back as I spoke to her.

"I'm here," I told her. "With him. I'll stay for a while. Let Marie know, will you?"

Hannah was almost indecipherable through her sobs. "I'll make him come see you tomorrow, okay? Call me in the morning?"

Hannah agreed and I slid the phone back into my pocket. I turned back to Nick.

"She okay?" he asked gruffly. I shrugged.

"Not really. You will go see her tomorrow, right?"

"Yeah."

Nick leaned forward, kissing me again, more urgently this time. After a moment I pulled away.

"Wait," I whispered. Nick wound his fingers through my hair, trying to pull me back. "Nick, stop, wait," my voice was breathless and low. "We can't." He leaned his forehead against mine. I could feel his breath on me, shallow and quick.

"You make it hurt less," he croaked. I bit back a sob and closed my eyes.

"Not like this," I whispered. He offered an almost imperceptible nod and buried his face in my hair. I felt his shoulders begin to shake with the beginnings of a sob. I wrapped my arms more tightly around him and held him as the grief overwhelmed him.

We held each other a long time, crying together. Slowly, gradually, his sobs died down. I stood and got some water for him and pulled a blanket off of his bed to cover us both. I nestled on the loveseat next to him and handed him the water.

"He wasn't always like this, you know," Nick began, his eyes on the ceiling, unfocused.

"Tell me about him," I requested softly. Nick began to speak, his voice calm, tears only occasionally spilling from his eyes. He told me stories of their childhood, great adventures through the alley behind their house. The embarrassments of junior high and the near misses of high school. After a long while, the stories began to wind down and I allowed my eyelids to close briefly. His voice was soothing, and I relaxed into him, his stories growing further and further away.

25

I awoke to the sound of breaking glass. Still exhausted, I nestled deeper into the blankets, my eyes closed, waiting for Mom to chew out the guilty party. The explosion never came and I peered out from under my eyelids and immediately realized I was not in my own bed. My eyes opened the rest of the way and I glanced around me, not immediately recognizing my surroundings. I blinked my eyes a few times, trying to clear the sleepy haze from my head. Slowly, memories began to reappear.

"Nick?" I called sleepily, events of the night before coming back to me. It occurred to me that I was in Nick's bed, rather than on the couch. I had slept here all night. I sat up slowly. Nick appeared from behind the kitchen counter, a sheepish grin on his face.

"Sorry," he said. He held a few pieces of what used to be a plate. He was wearing a T-shirt and basketball shorts. I squinted against the bright light streaming in from the window and sat up slowly.

"What time is it?" I asked groggily, running my hand through my sleep-tangled hair.

"9:30," Nick replied.

"Crap," I yelped, throwing the blankets off of me frantically. "I'm late!"

Nick dropped the broken plate in the trash and approached me, shaking his head. "I already called Marie to tell her we're taking the day off." He smiled at me, but it was hollow, the pain from the night before was still etched across his face.

"I gotta text my dad," I groaned, rubbing my eyes. I felt my pockets for my phone, but it wasn't there. I glanced over the bed looking for it and then back to Nick. He was holding it up.

"It fell out of your pocket when I moved you to the bed," he admitted, tossing it to me. I quickly sent a text to my dad, reassuring him that I was alive and had spent the night helping a friend. I would get into the details with him later.

"What time did you wake up?" I asked, sinking back to the bed.

"Around four. I thought you might be more comfortable lying down, so I moved you to my bed and I slept on the couch." A mischievous smile crossed his face and he sunk to the bed next to me. "You know you talk in your sleep?"

I winced. "What did I say?" This was not news. I had a reputation at home.

"It was something about how it's not their house, it's your house. You were pretty adamant. I think Marie's overworking you if you're showing houses in your sleep."

I could feel my cheeks burning, but I was relieved that it hadn't been more embarrassing than that.

"I should go," I began getting to my feet again. The smile vanished from Nick's face.

"Don't," he pleaded. He took my hand, pulling me back down next to him. I looked from him, down the front of me, and back to him. My clothes were wrinkled from sleeping in them, and I was self-conscious about going without a shower. But I didn't want to leave him alone.

"Come with me," I suggested. "I'll go home and shower and we'll get some lunch and I'll take you to see Hannah." He began to protest the last suggestion and I brushed it aside. "She needs you, Nick, and you know it."

Finally he nodded in agreement. "I made breakfast," he offered, a little awkwardly. I smiled at his shyness. "It's just toast, but . . ." he trailed off. "You hungry?"

"Starving." We ate our cold toast with chocolate milk, both of us quiet. He kept his eyes on me as if I might disappear at any moment. He took a quick shower while I cleaned up breakfast and then we headed home.

Nick glanced at me hesitantly as we pulled into the driveway. "Should I be worried?" he asked.

"About what?" I replied, releasing my seatbelt with a click.

"Your dad with a shotgun."

I laughed at the image that suggestion brought to mind. "He's at work. If we run into Nate, though," I grimaced. "Or my mom."

"Maybe I should wait in the car," Nick suggested hopefully.

"Don't be silly. Come on," I encouraged, pushing my door open. He followed reluctantly.

I should have taken Nick's suggestion and let him wait in the car. I should have felt the change in atmosphere as soon as I stepped through the door, but I was too preoccupied with Nick to notice anything unusual. And I should have texted my mom as well as my dad.

"Why don't you wait for me in my room?" I suggested as we walked through the kitchen. "No one will bother you in there." Before we could enter the hallway, we were stopped short by a shrill screech.

"Where have you been?"

I whirled at the sound and found my mother standing in the center of the living room. She looked as if she had spent the night there. A blanket was crumpled on the floor at the foot of the recliner and her hair and clothes were disheveled. Her focus shifted from me on to Nick, and her voice shot up an octave. "With him? You spent the night, with *him*?" Before I could protest, before I could do anything, she continued. "I can't believe you. The second you find out that I intervened on your behalf, you run right to him, proving me wrong. Apparently you're no better than he is," she spat.

"Hey," I could hear Nick protest indignantly behind me.

I took a step toward her, surprised and hurt and furious. "You really think so little of me?" I yelled. "That I would sleep with someone just to spite you?"

"Do you know what I have been through? Do you know what your brother put me through, Quinn?" Her face began to turn its customary shade of purple. "The humiliation of it has been unbearable, and you are bound and determined to do it again and kill me off once and for all. Well, guess what? I refuse to be there when you get pregnant!"

I took a deep breath, trying to recover from the sucker punch that she had dealt. I felt Nick's hand on the small of my back, buoying me up. "This has nothing to do with you!" I screamed. "I can't believe that you would just assume the worst. That you think that I am so weak! And Nathan did nothing to you. You did it to yourself." I took a deep breath and hurled the words at her. "If you weren't so terrified of imperfection, you might have asked why I was gone all night. If you weren't so desperate to cling to this façade that our family is perfect, you might already know that this," I gripped Nick's arm, "is one of the best and most honorable, most loyal men that you will ever meet. If you were not so petty, I might have told you last night that I was going to find him because his brother committed suicide."

I could hear the rush of air leave her body as I said it. Her face went slack, but I didn't have the patience to wait for her to overcome her shock. I grabbed Nick's hand and pulled him back out of the house. I wrenched the car door open and got inside. He sat down slowly next to me and rested his hand gently on my knee. The overwhelming emotion of the night before, coupled with the anathemas of my mother and my own rage, pushed me over the edge and I began to sob. I rested my arms against the steering wheel and nestled my face into them, embarrassed. Nick reached over and pulled me into him, holding me tightly against the wracking sobs. We sat there like that until the tears slowed and I was able to breathe again.

"I'm so sorry," I gasped hoarsely. Nick just shook his head. "I'm sorry you had to see that. I'm sorry for what I said. I just, I shouldn't have brought you here. I should have known better than that. I should have—" My voice caught in my throat and I couldn't continue.

Nick wiped my cheek with his thumb and laughed mirthlessly. "Well, you did spend the night at my apartment," he said softly. The image of my mother's mussed hair and rumpled blanket rose before my eyes. She must have been so worried.

"Still," I shot back, pushing back the guilt, unwilling to excuse her just yet. "She didn't even bother to ask. Nothing happened."

"But only just," he breathed. I caught my breath, the memory of the night before washing over me. "I'm sorry," he murmured. "Not helping." This time, I shook my head. "Well," he said slowly. "At least she didn't have a shotgun."

Caught off guard by his unexpected humor, I snorted and both of us began to laugh. I wiped my cheeks with the back of my hand. "I love you," I gasped through the giggles.

"Really?" he asked, his face serious again.

"I really, really do," I placed my hand on his and squeezed. I loved this man, completely loved him. His face split into a grin.

"You don't know how long I've waited to hear you say that," he leaned forward and brushed his lips against mine. "I love you, Quinn Matthews. I should have fought for you from the day that you walked into that office. I should have gotten down on one knee right then and there."

I laughed at his hyperbole. "You didn't even like me, Nick." I chuckled.

He shook his head. "You didn't like me," he amended. "I knew from the day that you transferred into my district that I was in trouble. You remember Okeechobee?"

I stiffened. Of course I remembered Okeechobee. I nodded impatiently, waiting for more.

"You know how I got transferred out so quickly?" I nodded again. "It was because of you, Quinn. You were this huge distraction. I went to Florida for one reason, and it wasn't to meet girls. I couldn't focus on the work that I was supposed to be doing, and so I told President Jacobs."

"You told him what?"

"I told him how I felt. So many people had worked so hard and sacrificed so much to get me there; I had to live up to that. I had to get away from you and stay away from you."

"Really?" I couldn't help myself.

"Really. The day that you walked in to Jonas Realty was one of the best days of my life. Before that, I just figured that you were another sacrifice that I had to make, something I had to learn. But seeing you there, it was incredible. You were, I don't know, my ram in the thicket."

My jaw dropped. "But you were always so, well, mean," I exclaimed.

He offered an apologetic smile. "I couldn't let my guard down around you. Not for a second." He paused. "You are the best thing to ever happen to me." He pulled me close and kissed me again. "Let's go see Hannah."

I turned on the car and just as we backed out of the driveway, I caught sight of my mother watching us sadly through the living room window.

26

After our run-in with my mother, I left Nick with Hannah and headed straight for Kristen's apartment, praying that she would be home in the middle of the day. My prayers were heard and answered; she opened the door almost immediately.

"Quinn! What are you doing here?" she asked in surprise.

"That room still available?" We had tentatively discussed living arrangements several times, but with the relationship between her and Nate so fragile, we hadn't settled on anything. But after the morning that I had, I knew I had to get out of my parents' house as quickly as possible.

"Um, yeah, it is. My roommate actually moves out tomorrow. You still want it?" I heard a waver of hesitation in her voice, but decided to ignore it.

"I really do. Can I . . . do you mind if I come in?"

"Of course," Kristen opened the door and stepped out of the way. "You okay, Quinn?" I shook my head and stared at her helplessly, wondering where to begin. "Sit," she pointed to the couch. "What's up?"

I took a deep breath and dove in. I told her everything, more than she needed to know, and it felt so good to get it all off my chest. "I have to get out of there, Kristen. I can't live in the same house with her anymore. I just can't." I shrugged helplessly.

"Day after tomorrow," she promised. "It's all yours."

"I hate to put you in that position. I know it will be kind of weird, what with the way things are between you and Nate. I just, I didn't know where else to go."

Kristen shook her head, a shy smile appearing on her face. "It might not be as weird as you think."

I raised my eyebrows at her. "Care to explain?" Kristen's smile widened.

"We ran into each other. Last night. I got behind him in line at Cafe Rio and it was either awkwardly pretend he didn't exist for twenty minutes, or talk." Her cheeks flushed slightly. "We ended up eating dinner together. And we're going out again tonight."

"What?" My mouth dropped open.

"Yeah. We talked for a long time. I apologized for overreacting, and he apologized for not telling me." Kristen wound her long hair into a bun and then released it. "It's not perfect, but it's a start."

I let out a sigh of relief. "I just want you to know that I have been nagging him for weeks to call you. Weeks."

Kristen laughed. "He told me. I'm glad you did. Even if it didn't totally work." She gave me a quick once over. "Hey, since we're basically roommates, if you want to shower, I can lend you some clean clothes." I surprised her, wrapping my arms around her in a grateful hug. She laughed and hugged me back. "Bathroom's over there. I'll grab you some clothes and a towel."

"I owe you one, Kristen."

"Nah," she replied, as she stood up.

I spent the least amount of time possible at home for the rest of the week, packing quickly in one- or two-hour increments when I knew Mom wasn't there and spending the rest of my time at work or with Nick. Nate helped me move out and Nick helped me move in. I struggled to admit that maybe some of the blame was mine. I couldn't deny that what she had done, however misguided, was done out of concern. The image of her rumpled and tired haunted me. I remembered when I was little, crawling on her lap and nestling my head against her while she played with my hair. I knew, with every bit of me, that she would never, ever let anything happen to me. She was my ally, my defense. When did that change? When did she become my enemy?

Dad sent me several texts and called daily, each time with a new reason, but ending each call or text with a request to call Mom, talk to Mom. I knew I should, but my wounded pride wasn't ready. Despite her best intentions, she had hurt me and she had hurt Nick. Forgiveness was harder than it should be. By the day of the funeral, I hadn't spent more than ten minutes in the same room with my mother since Blake's death.

On the morning of the funeral, Nick stopped by my apartment to pick me up for the services. The funeral was small, the chapel only about halfway full. As I scanned the room during the opening hymn, I caught sight of my entire family in the back row. Mom kept her head down, her eyes on the hymnbook, but Dad winked in my direction and Annie sent a little wave. I offered a watery smile in return.

Blake's funeral was short and simple. Nick's father had delivered a beautiful eulogy, Hannah spoke briefly, and Nick sang "How Great Thou Art." After his song, Nick resumed his seat next to me in the chapel and proceeded to sit stoically straight for the rest of the meeting. His voice hadn't wavered once while singing, nor had I seen him break down all day. His face was drawn and pale, his eyes red and bloodshot, highlighted by the dark circles under them. I wondered how much longer he could maintain this mask.

"I don't want to do this anymore," he whispered. I squeezed his leg and he glanced over at me.

"Just a little bit longer," I reassured, struggling to keep my voice steady. "That's all."

After the services, my family followed us out. Dad wrapped me in his arms and Nate officially introduced himself to Nick. Mom stood awkwardly off the side while Annie gave Nick a consoling hug. I caught Dad's eye and he glanced expectantly in Mom's direction.

"Mom," I murmured, "thanks for coming."

"You're welcome," she replied stiffly. "How is their family doing?" she asked politely.

"Um, as well as can be expected, I guess." I glanced down at my hands, gathering all of my humility. "Mom, I, um, I'm sorry about the other day."

"Me too," she replied softly. She rested her hand briefly on my forearm. "Will you introduce me, please?" Her eyes were on Nick. I took a deep breath and nodded.

"Nick," I called softly. He glanced in my direction. "I want you to meet my mom."

The muscles in his jaw immediately tightened, and I pleaded with him silently to give her a chance. He took half a step forward.

"Nick, this is my mom, Melanie Matthews. Mom, this is Nicholas Ryan." Mom held out her hand. Nick hesitated a moment before stretching out his own and shaking hers very briefly.

"It's nice to meet you, Nick. I wanted to say how sorry I am for your loss." She paused a moment. "I also want to apologize for the way I reacted both last week and last month. I was only concerned about my daughter's well-being and I overreacted. I'm sorry." I could tell how hard that speech was for her, and I glanced at my father, eyebrows raised, knowing that there must have been some coaching on his part. He returned a sad little smile and stepped forward, sliding an arm around Mom's waist. He held out his other hand to Nick.

"Nick, I'm Dan Matthews. It's good to finally meet you. Both of my daughters have a very high opinion of you." Nick shook my father's hand with a small smile.

"It's good to meet you too, sir. And," he glanced in my direction, "the feeling is mutual." I gave him a grateful smile and took his hand in mine.

"We should get going so we're on time for the graveside."

Nick nodded and looked back at my parents. "It was nice to meet you. Thank you for coming." As we walked to the car, Nick slid his arm silently around my waist and squeezed.

Nick pulled the car slowly into the cemetery. It was a cold and windy April day, but the sky was blue and the sun was shining. Nick parked the car off of the road and switched off the ignition. Rather than push the car door open and head to what would be Blake's gravesite, he stared blankly out the front window.

The cemetery was empty, save for a small white canopy, stark against the brilliant green grass. Blossom petals swirled in the wind before the cars, a sort of spring snowstorm of pink and white. The hearse was parked, large, dark, and looming, several cars ahead of us. As one of the pallbearers, Nick would help unload the casket and carry it to its final resting place.

He stared at the hearse a long while, took a deep breath, and nodded succinctly. Without a word, he opened his car door and stood. I hurried around the car to stand next to him, my heels catching in the muddy ground. We walked hand in hand to the hearse, where he let go and went to stand with cousins and uncles. I kept walking to where Hannah sat next to her father, waiting for the graveside services to begin. Her eyes lingered on Nick before turning to me.

"How is he?" she asked softly, her voice wavering with concern.

I shrugged. "Done," I replied. "How are you?"

Hannah shrugged. Her eyes matched Nick's and were full of tears. An icy breeze blew past, rustling through the flower arrangements tastefully displayed around the grave. The breeze played with my hair, sending a shiver coursing down my spine. Hannah noticed and took my hand in hers with a sad smile. I squeezed as we watched Nick and his cousins struggle to bear the coffin to the empty stand. Nick led the way, his face as stolid as ever. They gently rested it on the garish rails of the chrome stand and backed away slowly. Nick sat next to Hannah and I stood behind him, my hands resting on his shoulders.

The service was nice. Nick's uncle dedicated the grave. As the crowd behind us began to slowly disperse, Nick stayed where he was, stiff in his seat. Several relatives approached, shaking his hand and offering their condolences. Hannah approached the casket and ran her fingers gently over the edges, saying her own good-byes.

As Hannah finished and moved away, Nick finally stood and took her place. His eyes were downcast, both hands on the coffin, steadying him. From where I stood, I could see his shoulders begin to heave with sobs. I hesitated briefly, not wanting to interrupt this private moment of good-bye, and before I could move, Mr. Ryan appeared, wrapping an arm around Nick's shoulders. Nick glanced at his father and allowed himself to be further enveloped. He sobbed desperately into his father's chest, Mr. Ryan speaking softly into his ear.

I glanced over to find Hannah watching them, tears streaming down her face. I stayed where I was until they broke apart, both with tear-stained faces. Mr. Ryan headed directly for Hannah, and Nick glanced around looking for me. I approached with a sad smile on my face.

"Hey," I said softly.

"Hey," he replied.

"You okay?" I asked reaching out for his hand.

He studied me for a moment, thinking. "I will be," he said, pulling me into his arms. I nestled my head into his chest and wished desperately that I could carry him through this.

"I love you," I murmured gently, wondering if he could hear my muffled voice. He kissed the top of my head softly and held me tighter.

"Love you, too," he replied.

If you don't hurry, we won't make it in time for sunset," Nick called back impatiently.

"Sunset is just as great at the bottom," I muttered under my breath as I shot a fake smile at him. Nick, it turned out, felt about hiking the way that I felt about running. Sadly, as I had discovered over the past few months, the feeling was not mutual. I was perfectly willing to run thirteen miles on concrete, but walking up a mountain was pure drudgery. Don't get me wrong, the scenery was (usually) gorgeous, but it just wasn't my thing. We had, however, come to an agreement: for every hike I went on with him, he had to go on a run with me. It had dramatically cut down the amount of hiking we had done since the agreement had gone into effect. Nick was not a runner.

Tonight he had insisted we hike to the Y in time for sunset. It was late enough in the season that the sun's rays were still warm but not crippling. I spent most of the dusty ascent devising a particularly harsh route for our next run, but when we finally reached the white expanse of the Y, I turned around and forgot all about it. The view took my breath away. I could see across Utah Lake, I could see the entire valley. The trees had burst into color a few weeks ago, but now, highlighted by the last golden rays of the night, the whole valley was on fire.

"Wow," I breathed.

"I told you," Nick murmured behind me. I felt him slip his arm around my waist, but I couldn't pull my eyes away. "You want to go up? To the top of the Y?"

I snorted. "I'm good." I was willing to reluctantly admit that the climb had been worth the view, but going higher wouldn't improve it. We had made it in time for the sunset and watched silently as the sun fell farther and farther behind the mountains.

I searched the southern end of the valley, wondering if I could pick out my parents' house or the office. I wondered if Annie and Marie were still there. I was almost an official realtor now. The exam was the last thing on my list. I was still going to school part time, online, and in the mornings I took care of the secretarial duties until Annie arrived after school. Annie was loathe to quit and Marie didn't want her to. I wondered if even after I became a full-time real estate agent, Marie wouldn't find some reason to keep Annie on. Which was fine with me. I loved having Annie around, at least most of the time. Especially since we no longer lived under the same roof. Moving to an apartment was fantastic. I loved the freedom, I loved my roommates, I even loved my roommate's boyfriend, but I missed having Annie around all the time. Working with her was the perfect compromise.

I sat down and wished for a blanket to separate me and the dirt and bugs. Nick settled on the ground next to me, and I leaned my head against him. "So, how far am I going to have to run to pay for this hike?"

"Hmmm," I considered aloud, "I haven't decided yet."

"The view didn't do it for you?" I could hear the smile in his voice.

"Not quite. It definitely shaved off a mile or two, but not quite."

"What about the Creamery? Would that help?"

I smiled. "Getting closer."

"There anything that I can do to get out of this run?"

"Nope. But, for ice cream, I will make it as level as possible." I shot him a mischievous smile and planted a kiss on his cheek for good measure.

"I'll take what I can get," he muttered, but pulled me closer. It was nice to be alone with him for a little while. He had gone down to part time at the office and had gone back to school. I only got to see him a few days a week between all of his homework and his clients. His class had been canceled tonight, so I had taken advantage and left work a little early.

"How's school?" I asked, laying my hand over his.

"It's good. I told you about my psych teacher, right? He's a great teacher, but I swear, he's crazy." Nick went on to describe his day, and I let my eyes wander the valley some more. Blake had been gone almost six months now. Nick seemed fine most days now, but the first couple of months had been touch and go. Nick had lost a lot of weight, and for a while it seemed he couldn't find his purpose. It wasn't until he had decided to go back to school that he really found himself again. He was working toward becoming a counselor. He was taking psychology and sociology classes and it was obvious he had found his niche. Not a day went by that I didn't get a text or hear about some random fascinating fact he had learned that day in school. It was nice to see him happy again.

The sun was almost completely hidden behind the opposite peaks. "You brought a flashlight, right?" I asked a little hesitantly. Going down the mountain was usually my favorite part, but going down the mountain in the dark made me a little nervous.

"I brought a few. We should go before it gets too dark. But first—" he leaned down and kissed me deeply. I smiled as he pulled away. "I had to do that up here at least once."

"It would be okay if you wanted to do it again." He did. The trip down the mountain was mostly uneventful. I only tripped once and managed to catch myself before sliding the rest of the way down on my face. I was grateful when the flashlight beam landed on the car in the nearly empty parking lot at the bottom. I was even more grateful when I had a giant waffle cone of cookies and cream in my hand. We found a table in the corner of the Creamery and watched as the store emptied out for the night. Just minutes before closing, the door opened and in rushed a harried Sister Giles. She strode purposefully down an aisle, obviously in need of something before the Creamery closed. I waited for her to reemerge from her search before calling her over. Her face broke into a smile as she saw me, and in almost a repeat performance of our last encounter, she did a double take when she saw Nick next to me, this time much too close to be simply a colleague. I stood and hugged her, but she pushed back and shot a look between the two of us.

"Don't give me the whole 'we work together' bit this time. What is up with you two?" I shot a smile at Nick and slid back into the booth next to him.

"We do work together, though," I giggled at her obvious annoyance. "But you're right. We're together."

"Seriously? I need details."

I looked at Nick and back at Sister Giles. "Do you have a couple of hours?"

Nick laughed and nodded. "At least."

We were kicked out by Creamery employees shortly thereafter. Sister Giles had to get home, so I promised her a lengthy phone call the next day and got into the car with Nick.

On the drive back to Springville, he brought up the topic we had both been avoiding for weeks. "How do you want to handle it?" he asked.

"Handle what?" I asked, purposefully oblivious.

"Quinn." He glanced at me. "How are we going to do this?"

"You mean, do we go as a couple, or do we pretend we haven't seen each other since Okeechobee?"

Nick chuckled. "I guess that is indeed what I mean."

"You know, we don't have to go at all. We could just stay home. Or go hiking."

Nick laughed a little harder. "You would rather go hiking than to the mission reunion? You really think it's going to be that bad?"

I shrugged. "I don't know. I think it's going to be Sister Giles times a hundred. That's what I think."

"I gotta ask, Quinn, what exactly is wrong with that? I'm not embarrassed to be with you, so what's the problem?" He waited for a response, and when it didn't come, prompted, "This is the part where you reassure me that you're not embarrassed either." I laid my hand gently on his shoulder.

"Not even a little bit embarrassed. I love you, Nick." I paused, trying to find a way to say this without feeling stupid. "You know I don't like being the center of attention."

"Okay. So, let's go, we won't make a big deal of it, I will do everything in my power to keep you out of the spotlight, and we get to see President and Sister Jacobs and everyone else. Okay?"

"Fine," I agreed reluctantly. "But I'm throwing some hills into our next run." Nick made a face at me, but reached over and squeezed my hand.

The reunion was at a church building in Salt Lake. I was torn between arriving early and just hiding out in a corner while everyone else arrived, or arriving late and sneaking in with the crowd. Nick made the decision for me by picking me up half an hour late.

"I'm so sorry. I had three showings that took way longer than they were supposed to."

I nodded empathetically. I had been on several long and drawn out showings that never seemed to end. Some people just had to look at everything in a house, and I do mean everything.

"Well, I guess sneaking in is the way to go." I pulled the seatbelt across my chest and resigned myself to the evening ahead. Nick pulled out of the lot and headed north.

"So, I got a call yesterday." I waited impatiently for the story to continue, but it required a little nudging.

"And?"

"And, Sister Jacobs found out that I would be there and insisted on my providing a little entertainment for the evening."

"You have to sing?"

Nick nodded. "I promised her three songs. She told me that she can play anything as long as it's in the hymn book. Any suggestions?"

"Hmmm. You know I love 'Be Still, My Soul.'"

Nick nodded. "And I was thinking 'Called to Serve,' unless you think that's a little too on the nose."

"It's a hard call." We brainstormed for the rest of the drive and had an adequate set list by the time we pulled into the parking lot. The decision had distracted me from my nerves, but they came roaring back as I stepped out of the car.

"You okay?" Nick asked, as he held the church doors open for me.

"No. But I'll live." I tried to smile, and he took my hand and squeezed. The halls were quiet, with a low hum of conversation coming from the gym. The doors were opened and I could see the crowd, dotted with familiar faces. Sister Giles spotted me and I felt the butterflies ease up a little. Then Sister Birch came over and Nick left to say hello to Elder Torres and it suddenly felt like I was back in Florida at a zone conference. Even more so when Nick got up to sing.

"I still can't believe the two of you are together," Sister Giles leaned over and muttered softly during "Called to Serve."

"Me either," I giggled. "It's weird. It's like he's a different person."

"He'd have to be. You hated him." I nodded and smiled as Nick caught my eye. He smiled as he began to sing "Be Still, My Soul." Sister Giles noticed and leaned in again.

"You guys pretty serious?"

I nodded and felt a familiar jolt go down my spine. "Yeah," I said softly, keeping my eyes on him. "We're serious." She slid her arm through mine and squeezed. He finished the second hymn and moved on to the third. I was surprised when he didn't sing "High on the Mountain Top." Sister Jacobs played the first few bars and it took me a moment to recognize "Lead, Kindly Light." I heard his voice crack just the tiniest bit during the first verse. "The night is dark, and I am far from home." I thought about Blake and Hannah. I thought about the last year and everything that Nick had been through. I thought about my own family, and despite everything that had happened, everything we had been through, I was so grateful that I had them by my side on the dark nights. As he began to sing the last verse, his eyes found me again and held.

> *"So long thy power hath blest me, sure it still*
> *will lead me on*
> *o'er moor and fen, o'er crag and torrent, till*
> *the night is gone.*
> *And with the morn those angel faces smile,*
> *which I have loved long since, and lost awhile."*

There were so many things that I thought I knew when I left for my mission. I knew the church was true. I knew my family was normal. I knew I loved Josh. I knew what I wanted. And it's funny, it wasn't really the eighteen months that I spent on my own in Florida that changed all of that. I had to come home to really grow up. Now, there were very few things I knew. I knew that the gospel was true, but it wasn't a Band-Aid. It wasn't a magical wall that would keep me safe from the bad stuff. It's faith, and it's strength, and it's a little, tiny light in the darkness that keeps me going. I knew that my family was just as normally unhappy as anyone else's. What's that line? "Each unhappy family is unhappy in its own way." And we had our own challenges; I still struggled to have a conversation with my mother without some kind of disagreement. But it was slowly getting better. I knew that Josh made the best decision the day he sent me that email: without the blanket of darkness he threw over me, I would never have found Nick. I knew that I loved Nick. I felt my breath catch as he smiled at me again. We had been led "o'er crag and torrent" and I knew many, many more lay in our path, but with the light and with each other, we would make it through the gloom and all the way home.

The last few bars of music died and the hum of conversation began to grow again. Nick made his way through a crowd of admirers back to my side. "You ready to go?" he murmured in my ear. I looked at him in surprise, but nodded. We said our good-byes and I received a particularly long hug from President Jacobs. It seemed he couldn't stop smiling at me.

"I'm just so glad that you could make it, Sister Matthews." From the way he kept looking between Nick and me, I surmised that he was more pleased that we had made it to the reunion together.

Nick pulled out of the parking lot and glanced over at me. "Want to go for a drive?"

I raised my eyebrows. "A drive in the direction of Springville? You realize we do have a ways to go?"

He nodded. "I want to show you something first." He wouldn't give me further details, but I agreed, regardless. I didn't ask too many questions until we arrived at the mouth of Emigration Canyon.

"You know that I love you, but I am not about to go hiking in the dark," I announced.

Nick laughed. "No hiking required, I promise." We didn't

drive very far before he pulled off the road. “Come on.” He got out of the car and pulled a blanket out of the trunk. I looked at it suspiciously, but he just laughed again and threw it over the hood of the car. “It’s better than the ground.” He pulled me onto the car with him. We leaned back against the windshield and I realized what he wanted to show me. He had somehow found the perfect spot. Before us, the Salt Lake Valley, lit up to the foot of the Oquirrh Mountains. Above us, more gleaming stars than you could ever see in the city.

“Good job,” I murmured, sliding closer to him. I could see the lake, silver in the moonlight. Three temples dotted the valley, standing out brightly from the sparsely lit homes.

“You like it?”

“It’s beautiful. How did you find this spot?” I leaned my head against him and tried to find the North Star.

“A friend of mine told me about it. It’s actually a trailhead, but the view from here is perfect without the hike.”

I laughed. “You can say that again.” We drifted into silence, breathing the cool mountain air and reveling in starlight.

“Quinn?”

“Hmm?” My eyes were still heavenward.

“I just, I wanted to tell you,” Nick paused, and I could feel him tense slightly as he pulled me even closer, “the last year with . . . everything, thank you. I don’t know if I could have made it without you.”

I smiled and found his hand. I pulled it close and kissed the back of it. “I love you.”

“I know.” I felt him kiss the top of my head. He pulled his hand out of mine and shifted around until he was sitting up next to me. “Quinn,” he said again quietly. He moved into my line of vision and held up a closed fist. “I love you more than I have ever loved anything. Will you marry me?” He opened his palm and revealed a beautiful diamond ring.

I gasped, totally caught off guard. “Of course!” I threw

my arms around him, almost knocking him off the car, and knocking the ring out of his hand. After ten minutes of frantic searching, we found it lodged behind the license plate. I held it up with a sheepish expression and asked if he still wanted to marry me.

"Yes. But only because you found the ring."

I wrinkled my nose at him, but he just laughed and pulled me close. He took the ring out of my hand and slid it onto my finger. I admired it for a moment, sparkling in the moonlight, but Nick took my face in his hands and kissed my forehead softly. "I love you more than anything," I whispered. "Except for maybe this ring." I giggled for a moment at the look of exasperation on his face, but his mouth covered mine, and I shut up immediately.

We determined that we would make the formal announcement to our parents the next day, but I couldn't help calling Annie on the drive home.

"Guess what?" I asked as soon as she picked up the phone.

"What?" she asked in her standard, slightly annoyed voice.

"I'm engaged!!"

"Again?" She sounded bored and I made a noise of disgust.

"You're supposed to be excited for me. Also, surprised."

Nick made a funny sound, and I looked over at him. "Well, I kind of already knew," she announced.

Now I made a funny sound. "What? You knew?" I stared at Nick accusingly. "You told Annie?"

He shrugged. "I needed help to pick out the ring."

"No, Quinn," Annie said over the phone. "Be grateful. My taste is way better than his."

I gazed at the sparkling ring on my finger. "Well, I guess you did do a pretty good job. I suppose I can forgive you for conspiring against me." I paused. "Did you tell Dad?"

"Nope. Nick swore me to secrecy. Nobody knows but me. Well, and I guess Marie. Because we went while you were showing houses, and she knew where we were going, but that's it. Really." She sounded like she couldn't wait to get off the phone with me.

"Okay. But you still should be excited." I was not going to let her get away with attitude at a time like this.

"Quinn, I am excited. Nick is the only person you could marry that I would be excited about. Congratulations."

"Thank you. Was that so hard?"

Annie scoffed. "I have to go now. I'll see you tomorrow?"

"Yep." We hung up and I turned to Nick. "So," I asked. "When should we get married?"

"Tomorrow?" he replied hopefully.

I laughed. "Seriously."

Nick looked at me and smiled. "I would marry you in a second. So, don't ask me when I want to get married. I want to get married as soon as humanly possible. I would drive to the temple right now if it was still open."

I leaned over and kissed him on the cheek. "I am just so very glad that Marie liked me enough to hire me on the spot. And that you were willing to put up with the crazy that seems to follow me around."

"I am happy to take your crazy, as long as you come with it." He paused. "And I hope the same goes for me."

"For you, I will take it all. Every last drop."

Book Club Questions

1 Do you think Quinn's mother was justified in her actions? Should she have interceded to protect Quinn, or was she overstepping her bounds?

2 What kind of relationship do you think Quinn will be able to have with her mother while in a relationship with Nick?

3 How does the instinct to keep up appearances affect the characters in the novel? What kind of influence do you think the culture had on creating that instinct?

4 Do you think Quinn and Annie are too critical of their mother? Or does her behavior justify their attitudes?

5 How do you see Quinn and Olivia's friendship playing out? Do you think that it can survive Josh and Quinn's breakup again?

6 Do you relate more with Quinn or with her mother, Melanie?

7 What would your response have been to the revelation of Melanie's interference?

About the Author

Rachel grew up reading every book she could get her hands on and spending time with her cat.

At least, that was the report in every annual Christmas letter. The humiliation was enough to spur her into action, and she began writing. And she never stopped. Rachel studied English at Brigham Young University–Idaho and then wrote and blogged in between the births of her six children. She currently lives in West Jordan with her family, and while she no longer has a cat, she still reads every book she can get her hands on.

0 26575 18939 1